LEGACY OF TIME

Books in the *After Cilmeri* Series:

Daughter of Time
Footsteps in Time
Winds of Time
Prince of Time
Crossroads in Time
Children of Time
Exiles in Time
Castaways in Time
Ashes of Time
Warden of Time
Guardians of Time
Masters of Time
Outpost in Time
Shades of Time
Champions of Time
Refuge in Time
Unbroken in Time
Outcasts in Time
Hidden in Time
Legacy of Time
Renegades in Time

This Small Corner of Time:
The After Cilmeri Series Companion

THE AFTER CILMERI SERIES

LEGACY OF TIME

by

SARAH WOODBURY

To my Carew

Cast of Characters

In Avalon

George, a CIA agent tasked with abducting David's son, Arthur, and later an employee of **Chad Treadman**, upon whose plane he arrived in Earth Two (in *Shades of Time*). His associates are **Andre**, a pilot, and **Sophie**, both of whom have lived in Earth Two.

In Earth Two

David is the King of England, a time traveler, and married to **Lili**, who is also Ieuan's sister; They are parents of Arthur and Alexander.

Anna, along with David, her brother, first came to Earth Two in *Footsteps in Time*. She is married to **Math**, and they are parents of Cadell, Bran, and Rhiannon.

Meg married **Llywelyn, King of Wales** in *Daughter of Time*. They are parents of David, Anna, **Gwenllian**, Padrig, and Elisa.

Bronwen first appeared in *Prince of Time* as an archaeology graduate student. She is married to **Ieuan,** who started out as the captain of David's guard. They are parents to Catrin, Cadwaladr, and Gweneth.

Callum arrived in Earth Two on the heels (literally) of Meg, Llywelyn, and Goronwy in *Children of Time*. In *Exiles in Time*, he meets **Cassie**, another twenty-firster, who was stranded in the Middle Ages by Meg's plane in *Winds of Time*.

Rachel arrived initially with Anna and Meg on the Cardiff Bus in *Ashes of Time*. She is a physician and married to **Darren**, who is a former MI-5 agent. Parents of Esther.

Abraham is Rachel's father and a physician in David's court. He arrived in Earth Two in *Guardians of Time*.

Michael is David's bodyguard from *Champions of Time* and married to **Livia**, a former MI-5 agent. They arrived in Earth Two in *Refuge in Time* and are parents to Arya.

Christopher is David's cousin. He traveled to Earth Two in his car in *Masters of Time*, after which he became known as the Hero of Westminster. The rest of his family came to Earth Two in *Shades of Time*: and include **Ted, Elisa**, and **Elen**. He is married to **Isabelle**, daughter of Matthew Norris, the Master of the Paris Temple.

Huw is a Welsh companion we first meet in *Footsteps in Time* when David was abducted.

William de Bohun is heir to the Earldom of Hereford and has been part of David's court since *Crossroads in Time*. He is famous for saying *you've got to be kidding me!* He met his wife, Daisy, former Princess of England, in *Hidden in Time*.

Robbie in Avalon grows up to be Robert the Bruce, King of Scots. We first meet him in *Exiles in Time* as one of the Bruce men all named Robert. At the time, he is dubbed *Baby Bruce* by Bronwen.

Others

Venny - Captain of David's guard

Margaret "**Daisy**" – Daughter of King Edward and Queen Eleanor, married to William de Bohun

Mary "**Molly**" – Daughter of King Edward and Queen Eleanor

Elizabeth "**Lizzie**" – youngest daughter of King Edward and Queen Eleanor

Boniface – The Pope

Francesco – Pope Boniface's nephew

Iwan – Archbishop of St. David's

Gilbert de Clare – Earl of Gloucester (deceased)

Bogo de Clare – fugitive, brother of Gilbert, Thomas, and Maggie

Edmund of **Almain** – Uncle to Lizzie, Daisy, and Molly

Margaret "**Maggie**" de Clare – Almain's wife, sister of Bogo, Thomas, and Gilbert

Thomas de Clare – banished brother of Maggie, Bogo, and Gilbert

Philippe – King of France

John "Primus" - Duke of Brabant

John "Secundus" – Count of Zeeland and Holland

Isabel – Bogo's "niece" and former companion

A Quick Recap of the Previous Book...

As usual, I expect your recall of the past books is better than my own, but just in case you need some catching up to where we left things:

In *Hidden in Time*, the previous book in the *After Cilmeri* series, we are introduced to three of King Edward's surviving daughters: Daisy, Molly, and Lizzie. Years ago they were stashed away in a convent by none other than Gilbert de Clare, with the approval of their Uncle Almain, as part of Gilbert's bid to take the throne of England (*Masters of Time*). Gilbert died on the front of Christopher's car, and Almain left the girls in their convent to languish until such a time as he could find a use for them, putting out a false story about what had happened to them.

With David otherwise occupied in France, Bogo de Clare, Gilbert's younger brother, decides that the time is ripe for another attempt to take the throne, and he intends to use Daisy to do it. He abducts Daisy and Molly from the convent and brings them to Berkhamsted Castle, Almain's seat. Almain goes along with the plot because he genuinely hopes to put Daisy on the throne—and through her control England for himself. However, Lizzie escapes Bogo's clutches and, despite the fact that she has been raised to despise Meg and Llywelyn, rides to Kings Langley where they are keeping an eye on England while David is gone.

Bogo is a ne'er-do-well and a schemer, and he complicates the plan by abducting Meg, Gwenllian, and Elen, in an attempt to force Llywelyn to support his bid for the throne. Elen sacrifices her freedom for Lizzie's, allowing Lizzie to return to Kings Langley to raise an army against Berkhamsted. The book ends with the women escaping from the tower as David's forces assault the castle from the front. Almain is captured, but after the castle is taken, they discover that Bogo has already fled ...

1

Avalon

George

"I don't know what angel you have looking over your shoulder," the guard started speaking as he was pulling open the heavy metal door to George's cell, "but you're getting out of here, just like you said you would."

George was quite sure the creature riding him was a demon, not an angel. Even so, he wasn't going to argue with an open door, discuss fraught theology he didn't believe in anyway, nor tell the guard that he'd said he was getting out of his cell more to keep up his own spirits than because he thought it was the truth. He had been sitting cross-legged on the floor by the toilet, meditating, as he'd done every day at this hour for the last three years. Other than what went on in his own brain, which they couldn't take away from him or monitor, he'd been allowed pencil and paper, all the books he could read or listen to, two hours of exercise a day, and no visitors.

Not a one.

By CIA standards that meant he hadn't been tortured, not even with methods that left no physical damage. By this point, he might have welcomed any attention.

And still, even with all that, he could never regret shooting David.

Shooting *at* him, that is.

Once he'd sent David back to Earth Two, George had been bundled into a car, where he'd been immediately blindfolded and drugged. He hadn't been given a chance to talk to anyone, and when he'd asked for a phone call, Paige Blanchard had laughed.

Laughed.

Chad, *reliable Chad, good old Chad*, had run after them, protesting, but as far as George could tell in the few moments he'd had before that bag had come down over his head, the representatives from MI-5 had quietly faded away. With David gone, they didn't care one whit about the man who'd taken action, especially since George had been the schmuck who'd brought David to Avalon in the first place.

Besides, the people at MI-5—and certainly at their sister agency, MI-6—had to work with the CIA. International diplomacy took precedence over the welfare of one man, and the UK agencies were well aware which of them was the big brother and which the little sister, who did as she was told.

David, meanwhile, had disappeared, as George had meant him to. They never knew where David would end up when he time traveled, but wherever he'd gone, it was far away from that park in

Oregon. What George did regret were the words he'd said to Paige, right before his fellow agents had tackled him to the ground. A portion of his daily meditation addressed what had been a dangerous arrogance: *"Before you arrest me and toss me in a deep pit of despair, might I remind you that I know where your bodies are buried."*

What a laugh. Paige had surely had the last one.

"What day is it?" George shoved his feet into his lace-less sneakers. That was the sum total of what needed doing before he could leave.

"September 19th." Then the guard paused as if he had more to say.

George looked at him curiously. "And the year?"

He had been attempting to woo his guards the whole time he'd been incarcerated. He knew a great deal about many of them—their wives, their kids, and the fact that this particular guard had burned the hamburgers at the Fourth of July picnic. Every morning when one of them delivered George's breakfast, George had asked him the date, and he had never given it, always changing the subject. At long last, today was different.

Maybe for that reason, since this guard was one of the few who'd treated George like a human being, his expression turned rueful before he said, "2025."

George absorbed that news with something of an increased heart rate. His captors hadn't stolen three years from him as he'd thought. It had been hardly more than two years since he'd shot David. But even as the realization came as a relief, it was accompanied by a spurt of anger. They'd screwed up his biorhythms so profoundly he'd thought he'd been locked away one-third again as long as he actually had. They *had* tortured him. Who knew what horrible illness he was going to get as a result?

Even when his captors had given George the chance to exercise, they hadn't taken him outside but instead to an interior gym with fake sunlight. His captors even blindfolded him on the way so he couldn't see or speak to anyone.

It seemed like an awful lot of trouble to take for not much in the way of reward. He had been kept on ice all this time for a reason, but with no questions asked of him, nothing required, and nobody to talk to except for a few guards who'd been instructed to keep their interactions to a minimum, George still had no idea why that might have been.

At the guard's news, the old George would have cursed long and loud, maybe throwing in some of the more flowery profanity he'd learned while he was in Earth Two. The new George might have too, if it would have done any good. But if nothing else, he didn't want to give anybody watching the satisfaction of seeing him flip out.

In addition, if he allowed himself to truly give in to the rage that had been brewing inside him for the last three—strike that, *two*—years, it might consume him. This was the battle he'd fought every day in his little cell, and why he'd pushed himself for every second of those two hours they gave him to exercise.

So instead, he forced himself to breathe and, once again, to accept. He reminded himself that two years ago he had done what had been necessary at the time. Because of it, he could leave here with his head held high. He didn't know what he'd face when he stepped out the front doors of this facility, but he would put one foot in front of the other until he ran into a wall, which he would then find a way around, over, or through. That was how Paige (ironically) had trained him: to accept the process; to adapt; to reassess. One had to keep moving at all times.

Another breath and he was back to his serene self. He couldn't change what had been done to him, nor get back the time he'd lost in captivity. He would remember the feeling of that bag coming down over his head for the rest of his life.

But he didn't have to live inside it anymore.

2

Carew Castle – Earth Two

David

"I know you're right, *cariad*," Lili said, "but in this instance, being right isn't going to do you any good if the people aren't on your side. I'm with you on this. Your sister and Bronwen might be too. But we aren't the ones who matter."

David recognized the way his wife was using the endearment, *cariad*, which meant *my dearest* in Welsh, to mean something a bit different from common speech. He knew she loved him, but by employing the term the way she'd just done, it carried more than the usual weight. She was asking him to listen to her in a way that went beyond the times she simply called him *Dafydd*. She was appealing to the part of him that loved her.

And whether or not he wanted to listen, or would have preferred to march on as he had determined was necessary, she was making him stop and reconsider. Partly, it was because she was his wife. The other part was because this wouldn't be the first time he had been right and wrong at the same time.

"It isn't true. They know it isn't true." He refrained from using the word *lie*, even in a private discussion with his wife. "It's long past time everyone admitted it publicly. If we did that, we could start talking about what's really going on. At a minimum, how can I play the role when I know it isn't true?"

"By *playing* the role, Dafydd. Think of it as a pantomime. We are pretending. You are King Arthur; Ieuan is your brother, Cai; Michael is the valiant Lancelot. And so on. It's for *fun*. It isn't as if you are going to send them on real Arthurian missions, though come to think on it, that could be fun too." She beamed up at him. "I don't mind being your Gwenhwyfar."

His family had come to Carew Castle because Nicholas de Carew, the owner of the castle (naturally), was putting on a tournament in the spirit of King Arthur, with David playing the central role. *Everybody* was invited, commoner and nobleman alike.

When Carew had first proposed the event, David's mom had coughed and laughed at the same time, practically having to be revived from lack of air. Then she'd explained that King Edward, back in 1284 Avalon, had put on a similarly-styled tournament to celebrate his conquest of Wales. His purpose had been to place himself in the lineage of Arthur. That was, of course, Carew's intention too, except he wanted David to take on that role, admittedly one he had been playing from the moment his father had acknowledged him as his son.

David had been persuaded to go along with the tournament mostly because his father had been one of its biggest proponents. After all, Wales was still independent, and David was Welsh, genuinely descended from that great line of kings. Unlike Edward, David would not be remaking the story of Arthur into an English, rather than Welsh, legend. So why not throw a party? Why not admit what everyone else thought was true? Play the part. *For fun.*

Thankfully, unlike his role as King Arthur in this ongoing play/tournament, consultation with his wife wasn't performance art, even if they were up on the wall-walk of Carew Castle, grabbing a last moment alone before they headed to the feast being held in the central pavilion in a nearby field. A dozen people were within sight but nobody was within earshot.

"I'm just feeding the beast with this tournament. It's a celebration of the old order, Lili, even as I am trying to usher in the new."

She looked at him with a gentle expression. "That was, undoubtedly, Carew's point."

There was a finality in her voice that told him he'd lost the argument. Plucking the sweet she was about to eat from the dish in her hand, he popped it into his mouth. He didn't even know what it was. Something nutty. The point was to tease her and probably to distract himself from disagreeing with her again.

"Thief!" Lili wrinkled her nose at him.

Truth be told, he'd never much liked nuts, hated them, in fact, even peanut butter, which he couldn't get here anyway since peanuts were a New World food. He thought about spitting out the treat, but it was beneath his dignity to spit food he didn't like over the wall of the battlement, like he was a five-year-old forced to eat eggplant parmesan. Too many people were watching, even if none were within earshot. It was one thing to observe at a distance an intense discussion between Lili and him; it was quite another to witness the king spewing over the battlement. What he *said* could be kept private. What he *did* was always public. *Performance art,* when one was the King of England, was relative.

So he swallowed it down. That would teach him to tease his wife by stealing her food.

Watching the sour face he made, Lili laughed. "There are some things that have been so important you've had to put your foot down, Dafydd. But I don't think this is one of them, and I don't want to see you wasting your political capital arguing about whether you are or are not the return of Arthur, especially when things are going so well."

"That's *why* I should be doing it now." He couldn't help countering. "Do people care if I claim the mantle of Arthur or if the place we time travel to is Avalon or the future in an alternate universe?"

"Of course they care. You feel like you're lying to everyone every day. I saw the way you swallowed down the word earlier." She stepped closer to him. "But what about it is a lie, really?"

"Everything."

"Is it?" And then, when he didn't respond immediately, she added, "You can order anyone in the entire kingdom to do what you want. You can force change upon them, and you have done so, time and again. But every time you do, you find yourself dragging half the people along behind you, kicking and screaming. Most of them don't ever give up their old position. And your role as Arthur is something in which they take pride. It was one thing to force the guilds to admit women. It is quite another to take away an idea people *love*—particularly one that has no material cost."

"It feels like it does to me."

"I know it does. And I honor you for your integrity. I wish it could be the right time. Truly, I do. But the people aren't ready. Even your *friends* aren't ready. You can't make them be ready."

He was about to say "I think I can," but he was distracted by a strange discomfort in his mouth. He swallowed again. "I thought I could until I started talking to you. England is entering a new age. We have a functioning Parliament and a prime minister!"

Much of the last two years had been devoted to explaining to his people how their country and their lives could be better. David had wanted to convert England into a direct democracy with an elected president, but he'd been persuaded that the idea was unworkable—maybe in much the same way Lili was persuading him now. At a minimum, all the nobility, many of whom still had important positions in the government and at court, held their estates directly from him. If he wasn't king, if in fact there was no king, would they all lose their lands? And if so, to whom would they be given?

David honestly didn't doubt that a complete restructuring of land tenureship in England *was* in order, but open revolt and civil war would undermine all the other things they were trying to do. Thus, once again, theory had run head on into practice. They'd settled for a constitutional monarchy. A month ago, David had met with the newly elected Prime Minister of England, one Ralph Sandwich, and given him the authority to form a new government.

What would happen to David's personal power, and his role as England's king, given the obvious and continuing potential threats to pretty much everything, remained to be seen.

"That is exactly my point, my love."

My love. They'd been talking in Welsh, but by switching to English, Lili had pounded the final nail into his coffin. By now, he was arguing for argument's sake anyway. Lili was fluent in French too, but somehow her talking to him with the same American accent he still employed always made him smile.

She saw it, and it annoyed her. "Don't laugh at me." She shook her finger at him.

"I am not. I would never." He grabbed the offending finger, kissed it, and then pulled her close, unable to help himself. He didn't want to diminish her in any way, but he couldn't have her glowering at him without falling in love all over again. "Truly."

She pushed back slightly to look up at him, refusing to be distracted by the attention he was paying her. "Countries are built on myth and legend, which is why the story of Arthur has always been so powerful."

"I know that—" David broke off to clear his throat, trying to rid himself of the worsening tickle that had formed there.

Now she smiled. "Bad enough that England has a prime minister. They can't lose their king too. It means too much to them. Don't take away something that gives them such pride."

"The irony, of course, is that in pushing through the change in our government, I was trying to rid myself of some of this power—" He coughed into his fist and wondered if he was coming down with something. It would be just so typical if the exact moment he went on vacation with his family, for the first time since he had been crowned King of England almost ten years ago, he got sick.

Lili remained undeterred in her position. "Be that as it may. Everyone still looks to you for leadership, even if you've devolved much of your power to parliament and the prime minister. Change is hard. You know that. You don't have to rub their noses in what is right in front of them. They'll stumble through it themselves soon enough."

David was genuinely listening, even as he rubbed his eyes, finding them itching and watery. First he'd been thinking he was getting a cold; now he was wondering if a change in the weather was sparking his allergies. That would have made sense if he wasn't a bit flushed too. He sneezed three times, and then coughed. Once he started, he couldn't stop.

Lili frowned at him. "Are you okay, Dafydd?"

All of a sudden, David was finding it hard to pull air into his lungs. "I don't know." He put a hand to his throat. "I can't—" He stopped talking in his struggle to take a breath. It felt like he'd swallowed a golf ball. His head started to spin.

David never went anywhere without bodyguards so, by now, others had noticed his distress. As he'd told himself when he hadn't spit that treat out over the battlement, someone was always watching.

In this case, it was David's captain, Venny, who'd been standing a respectful distance away near one of the towers, not wanting to involve himself in their marital dispute. At some point, they'd conveyed to him a more complete story of his family's time traveling—or rather, world shifting—but even to him, their home world was still Avalon, and David was the return of Arthur. Full stop. Even in his distress, David could see Lili's point.

Venny took a hesitant step towards them. He was right to, since David was having trouble even staying on his feet. He would have been cursing himself for being such an idiot if he wasn't in such trouble.

"Dafydd! What is wrong?" Lili had her hands to either side of his face, looking up into his eyes.

"Can't breathe." Clamping one hand on Lili's shoulder, he put the other on the stones of the crenel beside him and hung on for dear life. "This happened once before, when I was little, though not as bad. I thought I didn't need to worry anymore."

Until David was fourteen, he'd been such a picky eater that avoiding nuts hadn't been a particular challenge, on top of all the other foods he didn't like. He'd always been a bread and meat kind of guy, with an occasional vegetable thrown in for nutrition. As a prince of Wales, and then the King of England, he never had to eat anything he didn't enjoy, and everyone who cooked for him knew not to serve him nuts. He didn't like them, so he didn't eat them. Until he stupidly tried to tease his wife. *Unintended consequences.*

"Dear God." That was David's mother's phrase. Coming from Lili it carried real weight, even more than when she'd called him *cariad*. She swung around to Venny, who was almost upon them. "He needs help!"

Venny slammed to a stop, took one look at David and started back the way he'd come. "I'll get Abraham!"

David had been too focused on drawing in air to tell him that finding Abraham wasn't going to help, because David himself knew what this was and what he needed. Fortunately, Ieuan had also seen that something was amiss and had run from the opposite direction along the wall-walk. Arriving on David's other side, he took in what was happening with a single glance, and asked, "What can I do?"

"Find Michael," David managed to say. "Tell him I need an EpiPen."

"I don't know what that is."

"He does."

Ieuan still hesitated, looking now at Lili. "Has he eaten anything since lunch?"

"He-he ate the sweet I brought from the kitchen. Honeycomb and walnuts."

"Did you have some of it too?"

"N-n-no. I didn't get a chance, since we were talking, I put the plate down over there in a crenel." She pointed down the wall-walk.

That got Ieuan moving when the request for an EpiPen hadn't.

Lili by now had David by both arms. "What did you ask for? Why do you need Michael?" She was back to Welsh instead of American English, which told him all he needed to know about how dire his situation was to her eyes.

If he had been thinking clearly, he would have kept Ieuan with him instead of sending him to find Michael, since David was now in such dire straits he didn't think they could make it back here in time to save him. The EpiPens were in a box in Abraham's stores somewhere, not to mention long since expired. Meanwhile, the lack of oxygen was literally killing David where he stood.

Venny was long gone too, since Abraham had been all the way over in the hospital tent at the tournament. That would teach David to ask for a few moments alone with his wife. At least he was smart enough to talk to her on the battlement. An old habit.

You need to go now!

For a moment, David heard his mother's voice, even though he knew she wasn't here. He was losing himself; he was certainly about to lose his life if he didn't do something drastic. He could feel his breathing getting more ragged, and by now his eyes were nearly swollen shut. Finding Lili's face amidst the chaos, he said with as much urgency as he could muster, "Remember to ask for an EpiPen."

Lili clutched him tightly, as if somehow she could breathe for him if only she were close enough. "Are we going to Avalon? What about Michael?" She glanced around desperately for their friends.

"No time." He sure hoped Chad had taken to heart some of what they'd talked about over the years. It might mean the difference between getting shot upon arrival and getting the help he needed. Given what David had experienced the last time he was in Avalon, however, maybe he should just be hoping it was still *there*.

With effort, he unbuckled his sword belt and dropped it to the stones at his feet.

All he could see through the slits that had become his eyes were Lili's beautiful gray ones inches from his own. They were the same color as Arthur's. The thought of Lili alone in Avalon if he himself didn't survive what was happening to him was terrifying, but the thought of her raising his boys without him here terrified him too. David pushed the fear away. He couldn't think about his sons right now. It wouldn't help his breathing. He knew what he had to do. He just wished he wasn't doing it with Lili. At the same time, he also knew he had to have someone with him. A vision of their first kiss flashed before his eyes, and he managed to fight his way to another breath.

"I can't lift you," Lili said.

David was on the verge of passing out. His hip hit the edge of the crenel, but then he had no power to get into it, not to mention drag both of them over it.

"Gotta find a way to go." He hadn't meant to say the words out loud, but maybe his mouth had moved anyway, in between his attempts to catch a breath.

"Not without me you don't!"

"Never." That single word came out clearly. He had no intention of leaving without her. It was just that he had no way to take her.

Lili flung her arms around his waist and held on, expecting him to throw them together over the battlement. But he couldn't move. He couldn't breathe. Panic rose within him. *He was dying!*

The certainty of it overwhelmed his mind, even as his arms tightened around Lili. If only he could—

One, two, three ...

3

September 19 -Earth Two

Anna

"He's late." Anna took a sip from her cup. "I knew he was going to have trouble with all this. You know how much he hates the King Arthur mantle."

"He'll come." Papa was serene. "And when he does, I will be happy to give up my seat for him."

When they'd arrived, Papa had taken one look at the way the high table was arranged, noted David's absence, and settled himself in the central seat, with Mom on one side and Nicholas de Carew on the other.

Carew had been one of David's, and thus Llywelyn's, loyal supporters almost from the moment of David and Anna's arrival in Earth Two, having gauged which way the wind was blowing and decided to move with it. In all the years since King Edward's death, he'd had no cause to regret his allegiance. David was a strong enough leader that he didn't feel the need to slap down anyone who had the nerve to stick his head up above the crowd.

The other members of David's family, plus nobles like Humphrey de Bohun and Edmund Mortimer, had dispersed themselves in the remaining seats. David's court was informal, but this was a ceremonial occasion and protocol was to be observed.

"If he doesn't come," Mom said, "with your father front and center, few will notice or care about David's absence."

"That's not entirely true," Anna murmured, her eyes on the next table over where John, the Duke of Brabant; and John, the Count of Holland and Zeeland, had taken seats.

With their arrival at the tournament, there'd been significant confusion amongst the twenty-firsters about whether *Zeeland* was even a real place, different from *New Zealand* (which didn't yet exist as a political entity) and *Zealand* (which was part of Denmark). Furthermore, in the hopes of keeping the two men straight, Bronwen had dubbed them John Primus and John Secundus, respectively, from the Latin.

In Avalon, John Primus had married Margaret, the daughter of King Edward, known to them as Daisy. Here in Earth Two, she had married William de Bohun instead. John Secundus, who at only thirteen was coming to act as John Primus's squire, should have married Daisy's sister, Elizabeth, known to them as Lizzie, earlier this year. Clearly that hadn't happened, and wasn't going to happen, at least not yet. This was just as well since the Avalonian version of Lizzie hadn't liked him anyway. After John Secundus's death in two years' time from dysentery, or possibly murder, she had married William de Bohun. *Their* William. To whom her sister Daisy was now married. The mixing up of their two universes wasn't without irony, and it was quite a job for the twenty-firsters to keep everything straight.

The Johns had come all this way because they genuinely believed David to be the return of Arthur and thought that if they fell at his feet, he would help them. This summer, the Johns' combined armies had lost a significant battle against French forces led by none other than Robert d'Artois, whom Callum had released two years ago as part of their negotiations with the King of France. In Avalon, the lowland province of Zeeland, in particular, had never recovered from that defeat. Over the centuries, it had been subsumed into one political entity after another, always fighting a losing battle for its own autonomy, much as had been the case with Wales, but with even less support from the rest of the world or its diaspora. Zeeland was ultimately incorporated into the modern Netherlands.

David had expressed his remorse about that, but he feared involving himself in war after war between aspiring nations and petty states. Not meddling wasn't without its advantages either. The Battle of Stirling Bridge, one of the major engagements in King Edward's war in Scotland, should have taken place nine days ago.

"More than just those two will notice," Math said darkly from his seat next to Anna. "Look who just arrived."

The pavilion was open on the sides, since it had been a nice day and so many people were crowded into it. There was no point in restricting their comings and goings, and the interior would become sweltering without fresh air. In addition, the most notable bards in Wales were having their own *eisteddfod*—a musical contest—this week, and each night a variety of contestants were performing on a stage set up on the opposite side of the pavilion.

Several musicians had been tuning their instruments, but all of a sudden, they stopped abruptly and rose to their feet.

Soon others in the pavilion began to rise as well, something they might not have done for anyone other than Llywelyn or David tonight. But religion was a way of life here, and even if the kings of Europe, David among them, distrusted the current pope, they showed deference to his representative, in this case Iwan, the Archbishop of St. David's, whom everyone recognized immediately. He had brought an extensive entourage of at least a dozen other men, none of whom Anna knew, but even she could spot a cardinal when she saw one.

They processed towards the high table, each portion of the pavilion quieting as they passed, until finally they stood before Llywelyn. Nobody could be sorry now that Papa had taken David's seat. He was the King of Wales, after all, and St. David's was within his purview. In Avalon, the seat had never been elevated to an archbishopric, and they'd dropped the apostrophe, making the place *St Davids*. But this was Earth Two, where things were still done the right way.

"King Llywelyn." The archbishop bent his head, as did Papa in return, though he didn't come around to kiss the archbishop's ring.

Even after all these years, Anna wasn't sure of the proper protocol in these situations.

"Archbishop. You honor us with your presence."

Archbishop Iwan made a general motion with his hand, which those within the pavilion took to mean they could return to what they had been doing. "This is a noble gathering, and I have brought you a noble visitor: Cardinal Francesco Caetano, Pope Boniface's nephew and guardian of Britain to the Curia, to speak to you and your son of France."

Llywelyn accepted this news with another respectful nod, but if he was suddenly glad not only to have taken David's seat but that David wasn't present, he wouldn't be the only one. Pope Boniface was currently embroiled in a long-running dispute with the King of France about temporal versus spiritual authority—meaning the Pope wanted everyone on the planet to be answerable to him on all things and King Philippe objected. To have the Pope speak to *David* about his current relationship went against everything David himself had been trying to change about the way this world worked. Certainly David wasn't any more interested than Philippe in being controlled by the Pope.

"He will be happy to hear you, I'm sure," Llywelyn said, lying through his teeth. "He should be arriving for the meal soon." Then he gestured graciously, and several of their closest friends and companions, including Nicholas de Carew himself, vacated their seats. Anna watched Carew step away from the table with a tinge of jealousy. It was just too bad it wasn't quite time to put her children to bed.

Thankfully, the exuberant trio of Gwenllian, Elen, and Lizzie had already gone off with their younger siblings and assorted friends, having had their fill of both the food and the adult conversation. Ever since the three girls had been imprisoned together in Berkhamsted Castle—and escaped in large part through the use of their own wits—they'd been inseparable.

Anna found herself approached by one of Francesco's companions, who bowed over her hand. But instead of speaking French with the Italian accent she'd expected, he said in perfect Norman French, "I was already grateful for the hospitality of Wales, but what a pleasure to be at the side of such a beautiful woman tonight."

Anna could feel her husband glowering from her other side. She herself had blinked at the compliment, which she wouldn't have expected from a churchman. "Are you saying you've been here long? I was under the impression you had just arrived."

"We have just arrived at Carew, of course, but we were all very ill during the crossing from France and have spent a week recovering at Lamphey." He was referring to a country residence of the Archbishop of St. David's. It had initially been built by the Normans when they'd ruled the area, but since then it had been taken over by the Welsh diocese.

Then Francesco waved a hand, having settled himself in what had been Carew's seat next to Llywelyn. "You, of course, wouldn't know yet, my lady, but we have some very good news. My esteemed colleague has been newly named cardinal by His Holiness Pope Boniface."

In the Middle Ages, cardinals were elevated by the pope himself, who could do it whenever and however and for whomever he pleased.

The man beside Anna smiled. "I received word of my elevation after we left Rome, and thus am not dressed appropriately for a cardinal. Truly, I find myself content in the simple attire of the priest I have always been."

Anna had already thought the man looked familiar, though she hadn't been sure exactly where she'd seen him before. Now a sinking feeling overtook her stomach—at the exact same moment Daisy, having just entered the pavilion, her husband at her side, gasped. She too had been a prisoner at Berkhamsted.

Cardinal Francesco continued smoothly, "May I introduce to you the newest member of the College of Cardinals, his eminence Bogo de Clare."

4

September 19 -Avalon

Lili

One moment they were surrounded by a darkness so oppressive Lili herself struggled to breathe, and the next they were through to a world of light and sound. David was unable to stay on his feet, and she went down with him to a polished floor so smooth it could have been ice, except it wasn't cold.

On her knees beside her husband, Lili shouted, "He needs an EpiPen!"

She knew how to say *EpiPen* only in English, but since they could be in France, she repeated what she could in French, then in Welsh, and then back to English.

Nobody had responded to her shout the first time, which she could understand, given the shock of their sudden arrival out of the void.

That they had made it to Avalon was obvious from the moment she blinked away the dark. If nothing else, she knew it from the lights above her head, which were so bright, coming in long rectangular shapes, she couldn't look directly at them.

On either side of where they'd come to rest on the floor were massive shelves filled with boxes and packages in multitudinous colors, sizes, and shapes, every one covered in words and pictures. Neither the pictures nor the words made sense to Lili, even though they appeared to be in English. "Nasal spray!" was touted by one, with a picture of a smiling woman wearing a white shirt and dark pants on a bright red box. "Night time cold relief!" said another, though how something in a box that small could alleviate the chill of night, Lili didn't know. It was hard to imagine anything better than a down blanket and a cup of warm mead.

In truth, she didn't care. As Dafydd drew in another ragged breath, but barely, she knew his breaths were coming too slowly to be doing much more than keeping him alive. His face was so swollen by now that his eyes wouldn't open. She still didn't know what an EpiPen was, but Dafydd had been clear about what he needed, in a moment when he could have said so many other things.

She trusted him, along with the God who'd brought him into her life and made her his wife, so she shouted the request one more time. "He needs an EpiPen!"

A number of people were in the vicinity, every one of them gaping open-mouthed at them. Behind a nearby bright blue counter, three women stared at them with equally stunned expressions. The general lack of response was the reason she'd thought to try one of the other languages she knew. Still, that same faith that had her calling for an EpiPen had her believing they had appeared in this building *for a reason*. Dafydd always went where he was supposed to go.

But given the lack of motion from anyone in front of her, she was worried now that she had misunderstood what Dafydd had wanted her to say, and the people here didn't understand her either.

Then, after what felt like an hour but might have been a matter of seconds that was the twenty-firster preferred unit of time, an older woman with short, gray, curly hair, who'd been standing at the counter as Lili and Dafydd had arrived, held out a white bag with writing on it.

"I-I-I have one." The bag said *Walmart* in big blue letters, followed by *pharmacy*.

Lili was so relieved she almost forgot to breathe herself. She knew both those words from all the times the twenty-firsters had come back from Avalon. "Please help him."

The woman was already moving forward, since anyone could see the kind of trouble Dafydd was in, and fell to her knees beside Lili. "I actually have two EpiPens, in case we need a second. I literally just got them from the pharmacist." Ripping open the bag, she pulled out a yellow box and then ripped that open too to reveal an elongated object, some six inches in length. "Have you ever used one?"

"No."

"Then I'll do it." As if Dafydd were an enemy she meant to stab with a knife, the woman pounded the point of the object through his trousers into the middle of his thigh and held it there for a count of five.

Lili let her do it. At this point, whatever that thing was—EpiPen or an instrument of torture—Dafydd was dying anyway. It seemed foolish not to let the woman try.

Then the gray-haired stranger sat back on her heels, rubbing the spot where she'd stabbed him and studying his face. Lili clasped her hands together and prayed. An even older woman, who sat hunched in a nearby chair, had her eyes closed and was going through a rosary in her hand, mouthing the words of her prayer. Lili took comfort in the familiarity of it and redoubled her efforts.

A man in a white coat came through a door next to the blue counter, carrying a—*something*—which he proceeded to put over Dafydd's face. It turned out to be a clear mask for his nose and mouth attached to a tube and then a *something else*. "We're on hold with 911."

The older woman stared at the newcomer. "I didn't think that was possible."

"It wasn't always like this, not even during Round-Up, but with the budget cuts, they're short-staffed, which is not a good thing to be with a hundred thousand extra people in town." After the man put the mask on Dafydd, he felt at his neck for a pulse.

"He's alive?" Lili's heart was in her mouth.

"Yes." He looked meaningfully at the older woman, implying to Lili that Dafydd was even worse off than she'd feared. "He might need the other."

"I've got it ready." A second device appeared in her hand.

The man nodded. "We need to give him another minute first. He's already breathing better."

Lili hadn't realized that was true until the man said it. Dafydd's breathing *was* coming more frequently and evenly, condensing inside the mask, like breathing on a mirror.

And then, at long last, he took a genuine deep breath, albeit one that was still rasping. And then another. Where a moment before his face had been puffed like a new feather pillow, it started shrinking back down before her eyes.

Lili grasped his hand. "Dafydd?"

"Yeah, I'm here." He spoke in American English and, in a manner of moments, had gone from half-dead to having the wherewithal to pull down the mask to talk to her.

The people around them had been watching intently, some with their hands to their mouths, others praying like Lili and the old woman, and others holding up what Lili knew to be cell phones, but for a reason she couldn't discern. They had also been tensely quiet, in a way she'd seen just that very day on the tournament field when William de Bohun had fallen from his horse.

But at the sound of Dafydd's voice, all of a sudden everyone in the shop broke into wild applause, even cheers. "He's alive!" "Thank God!" "Wait 'til I tell Mom about this!"

Dafydd had been lying on his back, but now he rolled more onto his side, curling up. "We made it, I see." This time his words were in Welsh, coming softly for Lili's ears alone.

"We did." Lili suppressed an impulse to laugh and ask, *So this is Avalon?*

She supposed she should have known from everyone's descriptions that the experience would involve an almost unbearable cascade of light, color, and sound.

And, to her amazement, extraordinarily kind people, if the few she'd encountered so far were anything to go on. That was something she hadn't been prepared for. The stories told by the twenty-firsters involved being chased from one end of the planet to the other over and over again. This chasing had happened pretty much every time they'd come here. It might still happen. But first impressions indicated that the people here were as human as she was, in all the best possible ways.

Now that Dafydd was breathing, she could take a deep breath too. It wasn't just that Avalon was open to them. It had reached out and taken them in. Dafydd hadn't even had to *act*. Lili's faith had been shown to be well-placed—as it had been every time up until now that Dafydd or a member of his family had *traveled*.

Her husband had needed an EpiPen, and they'd arrived in a place where one was not only to be found, but immediately available, in the hands of a woman who not only knew how to use it, but cared enough about helping a total stranger that she *would* use it. Lili couldn't pretend to understand how any of this world-shifting worked, but that it was still working for Dafydd was indisputable.

As to what Avalon was really about? Five minutes in, she hadn't a clue.

5

September 19 -Avalon

George

After a few more cleansing breaths, George's anger subsided. Since the guard was answering questions today, George decided to try another. "Do you know who, if anyone, is meeting me? Am I simply being let go on my own recognizance?"

"As far as I know."

While George believed the guard might not know, he didn't believe the CIA would genuinely just let him go. They'd follow him, for sure. Though, now that he was adjusting to his new reality, it occurred to him that even that wouldn't be necessary since they'd put a chip in his wrist. He'd woken up to it in his cell that very first day and had hated it every one of the days since. His skin twitched involuntarily just thinking about having it burrowed into his body. He somehow doubted they'd take it out if he asked them to, and he decided then and there he shouldn't ask. Better for them to think he was so excited about breathing free air again that he'd forgotten he had it in him.

"Do you know where Paige is?"

"Who?"

George managed to refrain from rolling his eyes. "Paige Blanchard. Your boss?"

"I'm sorry. I've never met anyone by that name." The guard seemed to be regretting his forthcomingness.

Now that he was in the corridor, George also knew where he was. If it had been physically possible, his head would have exploded. This was the very same installation from which he'd walked away two years ago. He would have recognized those same sterile white walls and ceiling, that particular pattern on the doors, and the way the buttons on the elevator at the end of the corridor lit up, with sub-basement three brighter than all the rest.

As it turned out, he'd been exercising in the very gym he could have gone to when he'd been here as a free man. He didn't know why he found it almost more horrifying to still be in Oregon than anything else they'd done to him.

He'd known ever since he'd sent David back to Earth Two that Paige Blanchard had been in charge of his branch of the CIA all this time, with the full support of his and her superiors. They had sent her to that park to meet with David with the expectation that he would take her back with him to Earth Two. That had been David's marvelous compromise: he would bring from each agency one woman for the purpose of allowing them the opportunity to create a kind of refuge for Avalonians in Earth Two.

If George hadn't shot David, she would be there now, wreaking who knew what kind of havoc.

That same latent rage rose in him again, and he swallowed it down. In the past, it had controlled him, and he was pleased to note that his hard-won serenity held firm.

As much as he hated Paige, he had to forget about her. From now on, his mission had to be as it always should have been: to keep the world safe, both this one and however many others there were. He'd done what he could for the planet when he'd sent David back to Earth Two. He would do it again if necessary and he would keep on doing it until the CIA ran out of black sites to keep him in.

As the elevator doors closed and they started rising through the floors, a lightness of being inside George rose with it. He'd told the truth; he'd done the right thing. Maybe there really was something about virtue being its own reward.

He might have added *who knew?* But the answer to that question was self-evident: David knew.

If George ever saw him again, he'd tell him.

6

September 19 -Avalon

Lili

The darkness of the void had been so absolute, Lili hadn't been able to think, much less move, even as she'd tried to keep her eyes open as if they were pinned. Oddly, now that Dafydd was breathing again, she felt exactly the same way. She didn't want to miss a single moment of what her senses were taking in. If she could have looked everywhere at once, she would have.

"It's a miracle I was standing right here when he needed these." The gray-haired woman, who'd introduced herself as Susan, remained on the floor beside Lili. She didn't seem as old as she had at first, sitting casually cross-legged, with an elbow on her knee and her chin in one hand, which was possible because she was wearing trousers. Lili could have sat like that too, since she wore her usual split skirt and leggings, as the twenty-firsters called them. It's what she always wore, even for a formal feast. Just because she could move her legs didn't mean her gown wasn't of the finest quality. But she chose to remain on her knees, with one hand on Dafydd's shoulder. "I literally had just gotten them from the checker."

Lili didn't know what a *checker* was, though, given the context, she could guess Susan meant one of the women behind the counter. Lili didn't know why that would be what they called her role, though. *Clerk, maybe? Or merchant? What could she be "checking"?*

The elderly woman who'd been sitting on a nearby chair, praying, rose to her feet, smiling and nodding at Lili, as if Dafydd's survival had been no more nor less than she'd expected. She said something to one of the women behind the counter in a language Lili didn't speak, and the other woman laughed. The relief in the air was palpable.

Although the applause had ceased, Lili continued to hear other people talking and laughing excitedly throughout the very large shop, of which the *pharmacy* was a small part. Even to call it a shop seemed a misnomer. Likely the Americans had a word for a shop the size of Westminster Hall, but off the top of her head Lili couldn't recall it.

She had seen places like this in some of the videos Mark had shown her on one of his devices. Dafydd himself had watched *movies* with her, most of which she hadn't been able to follow, and he had described both Walmart and Tesco to her. The fact that this was a *Walmart* implied they'd arrived in his own country, the United States. If they'd been in a Tesco, perhaps they could have been in Wales. She would have liked to see that.

Lili pressed her hand to her mouth, overcome for a moment by a cascade of emotion. Tears pricked her eyes, and she forced herself to swallow them away. She was six thousand miles and thirty lifetimes away from her boys. It felt for a moment like she would never see them again.

Somewhat hesitantly, Susan put a hand on her shoulder. "It looks like he's going to be okay."

Dafydd meanwhile reached up a hand and squeezed Lili's where it still rested on his shoulder. "I'm good, *cariad.*"

He'd reseated the mask, but that didn't stop her from leaning over to kiss him on the forehead. "I came so close to losing you."

He pulled the mask away from his face again and said, as clear as day, "I know. But you didn't. I'm still here. As I said on the battlement, I'm not going anywhere without you."

Then he tugged the mask all the way off his head and set it aside. The man in the white coat, who'd introduced himself as Josh, appeared to be about to protest, but then as Dafydd looked at him unspeaking, in that commanding way of his, he subsided and simply asked, "Do you know what caused this?"

"Honeyed walnuts."

Lili wrinkled her nose. "They were mine."

"Have you ever eaten them before?"

"I have," Lili said. "He hasn't."

"I've never liked nuts, and I haven't eaten any since I was little. I honestly didn't think I was allergic to them anymore or I wouldn't have eaten them today." Dafydd closed his eyes for a moment. "It was dumb to try them. I'm an idiot. This was all my fault."

Lili had been looking from Dafydd to Josh, her brow furrowed by their conversation. "I don't understand what he just said. I thought he'd been poisoned."

"He had an allergic reaction," Susan said. "That's why he needed the EpiPen."

Allergic reaction wasn't an entirely new concept for Lili, having spent the last ten years with twenty-firsters. She'd never seen anybody have one before, however, and the memory of how close Dafydd had come to dying had tears pricking at her eyes again, this time because she was feeling like all this was *her* fault and could have been avoided if only she hadn't brought the walnuts to the wall-walk. Dafydd had eaten of them because he'd wanted to tease her. She had been winning the argument, and he'd known it.

She wouldn't call it *winning* now.

"I should try to call for an ambulance again." Josh had been bending over, his hands on his knees as he'd looked at Dafydd, but now he straightened.

"Do I need one, really?" Though Dafydd's eyes were still puffy and his lips a bit swollen, his breathing was coming normally. He seemed more exhausted now than anything else.

"What exactly is an ambulance?" Lili asked Dafydd in Welsh, while sweeping a lock of his hair off his face to distract her other listeners from thinking too much about what she might have asked.

"A vehicle dedicated to taking sick or injured people to a hospital," Dafydd said, in the same language. They'd had hospitals in Wales before Dafydd's family had arrived, thanks to the Hospitallers, an order of knights and healers sworn to protect pilgrims. The Welsh word was *ysbyty*.

Meanwhile, Josh had reached across the counter for a black object. It had a cord coming out one end that attached it to another piece on the counter. With one finger, he punched what unmistakably, even to Lili's novice eyes, was a keyboard, and as he did so answered Dafydd's question, "Protocol says *yes*. I'll get you some Benadryl and a glass of water in a second, after I'm done talking. I've got samples I'm allowed to give out."

It was then that Lili realized from the way he had tucked the black object between his shoulder and his ear that this was another type of phone. The twenty-firsters all had *phones*, which Americans might call *cell phones* and those from Avalonian Wales or Britain *mobiles*. They didn't look like this, but the similar function was obvious.

Dafydd squeezed Lili's hand again, getting her to look down at him. He was back to Welsh. "The clock started ticking the second we arrived. I don't know how long it's been since then. Ten minutes? Regardless, we need to get out of here as quickly as possible."

"Why?" Lili's brow furrowed. As had become almost normal in those same ten minutes, very little about that sentence, even spoken in Welsh, would have made sense to her in any other context, any more than the English sentence spoken moments earlier by Josh.

Dafydd motioned to the number of people still standing around with phones in their hands. She had thought the crowd had started to thin out, but all of a sudden people seemed to be pressing closer on all sides. "Because I know where we are, Lili, which means so does everyone else. Mom wasn't allowed to stay when she briefly traveled here two years ago *for a reason.* If I don't get up off this floor very, very soon, we are going to discover exactly how unsafe for us Avalon really is."

7

September 19 -Earth Two

Michael

"This is my fault." Ieuan, typically, was taking full responsibility for David's disappearance, which was almost more frustrating to Michael than doing it himself. But by claiming it, he was also revealing all the ways neither of them were at fault, nor, in fact, had been given any say in the matter.

Michael wanted someone to blame too, but if what Ieuan had seen and relayed to them was correct, as well as what several witnesses in the bailey had reported: one moment David and Lili had been on the battlement, and the next, they were gone. That was nobody's fault but that of whatever power controlled his world-shifting. Michael couldn't even blame David for leaving without him, since he hadn't actually jumped off the battlement.

What's more, it was to *him* David had sent Ieuan. Not Callum. Not his mother. *Michael.*

"I should have—"

Michael cut Ieuan off before he went any further down that road. "Whatever you're kicking yourself about, we both could have done. Venny ran for Abraham, which was only sensible under the circumstances. You also saw he was in trouble, he sent you to me, and we went for the epinephrine. We need to stop talking about *fault* and start figuring out where to go from here."

He ran his hand through his hair, unable to completely suppress his own frustration. That David had gone with Lili to Avalon without another guard was intensely aggravating. Ieuan was blaming himself, but it was really Michael's fault. Rather than asking Ieuan to help find the EpiPen, Michael should have sent him straight back to the battlement. Or gone himself. Either one of them could have picked David up right there and then and jumped off the battlement with him in his arms. Or just wrapped his arms around David and waited.

Honestly, it had never occurred to him that David could just *leave*, even if he had known it was a theoretical possibility. In the heat of the moment, he'd been thinking like a medic rather than a bodyguard.

Nicholas de Carew, whose castle they were inhabiting, had just been entering through the main gate and had witnessed the moment David and Lili had vanished. He had already been bearing the very grave news that Bogo de Clare had been made a cardinal. Michael hadn't been raised Christian, and thus didn't pretend to fully understand the nature of the medieval Christian Church, but even he could see that for the pope to elevate a criminal banished by the English crown in such a fashion was practically a declaration of war.

Why Pope Boniface would declare war on David at the same moment he asked him to join him in his efforts against the King of France remained a mystery. Like most political acts, it was probably about determining the edges of his control.

Although Carew had still been shaking his head at the sight of the King of England and his wife disappearing from his battlement, since he had never seen it happen before, he had come to the rescue in terms of settling his people. In this castle, his word was not just law but unquestioned. Though the news had spread amongst the guards and workers like wildfire, a few calming words from Carew, explaining there was no need to worry since Avalon had reached out and taken David in, had gone a long way to assuring everyone that all was well.

Soon enough, the inhabitants might come to understand all the ways it wasn't. For now, David's departure hadn't put the tournament in jeopardy nor its participants in an uproar. Carew's first act had been to lock down his castle to prevent the news from spreading until they could figure out if any threat remained. At the moment, the guards were letting people *into* the castle, but not *out* again. That could last only so long, but because those on the outside were preoccupied with Bogo's arrival and elevation, those within had a few more minutes respite.

And while Michael hoped David's illness had been anaphylaxis (maybe *hoped* wasn't the right word), if he had been poisoned instead, that person was someone to be pursued with the full extent of their resources. The culprit might even have remained among them long enough to watch the results of his handiwork. Or even, with David's departure to Avalon, realized his work wasn't yet done.

Worst case, David's illness was just the beginning. It was Michael's job to plan for the worst case.

Michael and Ieuan had been waiting for Callum and Abraham, and once they arrived, the four of them retreated off a passage between the inner and outer baileys, not wanting to broadcast their conversation—or even have it witnessed—by anyone else. The whole point was to keep the story quiet and tamp down any concerns.

"Better he left us than died," Callum said flatly. As an opening line, it was a good one and served to settle Ieuan a bit more, if not Michael.

"That seems clear, if nothing else." Abraham bent over the bowl of candied walnuts, which Michael had brought down from the battlement from where Lili had set it in a crenel. They looked very similar to those his mother used to make. While the treat had never been his personal favorite, they had never been the hazard they appeared to be for David. "Your description of his face, Ieuan, and the fact that he asked for an EpiPen, imply he knew what was happening to him." He straightened, one of the sticky nuts between his thumb and forefinger, before popping the walnut into his mouth.

"What are you—" Michael surged towards him.

Abraham put up a hand. "I appreciate your concern, but you and I both know that this is the most direct way to discover at least one truth today." He spoke around chewing and swallowing. "The king was puffed up with his throat closing? That sounds as much like anaphylaxis to me as it does to you."

Callum had been standing with his arms folded across this chest, staring at the wall, which meant looking at nothing at all, since they were in a storage room with no windows. "We'll know in a moment if you're wrong."

Even among twenty-firsters, everyone understood that Callum was the highest-ranking adviser out of all of them, even outranking Carew, never mind that Wales wasn't Callum's country. Currently, he, like the king, was on holiday with his family. If he had not come with David, he might have been acting regent with the ability to rule England on Arthur's behalf.

For now, since David had absented himself entirely from England, that authority resided with Godfrid de Windsor, the Master of the London Temple, who happened also to be Nicholas de Carew's illegitimate half-brother. Fortunately, David had arranged for his leadership before he'd left London. For the time being, David's absence changed nothing politically. These days, most of the day-to-day running of the country was done out of the office of the Prime Minister anyway.

David and Lili's son, Arthur, meanwhile, had taken the fact of his parents' disappearance with a degree of equanimity Michael wished he could emulate. Arthur was almost eight years old now and had traveled to Avalon when he was three during an attempted coup by Gilbert de Clare. Michael suspected he still thought of it as the land of chocolate chip pancakes. When Michael had reassured him that his parents would be fine, the boy had replied, "I know they will. We should be happy he just *went*. He didn't even have to fall from a tower like Nain did."

He was referring to the fact that Meg, his grandmother (*nain* in Welsh), had traveled to Avalon two years ago, during the siege of Berkhamsted Castle, and been sent back so immediately there was some question as to whether she'd gone at all. David was convinced she had, and Michael thought it just as well Meg and Llywelyn were at the feast with Anna and Math, so they could remain ignorant of what had transpired for a little while longer. Bad enough Anna was now sitting next to Bogo de Clare.

At this tournament, since they were in Wales rather than England, King Llywelyn was the reigning power, not David, even in his guise as King Arthur. What's more, in this instance, Nicholas de Carew was *Llywelyn's* vassal, as Earl of Pembroke, rather than David's, as the Earl of Winchester.

Besides, it wasn't impossible that in another hour, David and Lili would be back. It could happen. It had happened before.

For now, David's family remained at the feast, which was in full swing in the pavilion in a nearby field. Earlier, they might have been wondering why David and Lili hadn't put in an appearance, but now they'd be pleased at his absence, else he'd have had to confront Bogo. It was only fitting that David didn't have to see this, and some tiny superstitious part of Michael thought maybe all these coincidences added up to a plan that had intended him not be here.

It was bad enough Llywelyn was facing the traitorous Norman lord, now cardinal, over his own table. That Llywelyn had offered him hospitality, even if unknowingly, coupled with the fact that Bogo had somehow persuaded Pope Boniface to make him a cardinal, meant he couldn't be ejected from the pavilion—nor even challenged.

Abraham, meanwhile, wore something of a smile and had started humming a tune Michael recognized as one about King Arthur that was usually applied to David (against his will). "I'm happy to report that I am well. It isn't the walnuts. Or rather, for David it was the walnuts, but nobody else is at risk from them unless they share his disposition."

"Maybe it takes longer than this to affect you as compared to him." Ieuan was looking at the physician dubiously.

"Then I'm wrong, and he was poisoned, and I'm about to die." Abraham took a big slug of wine, essentially rinsing out his mouth with it. "But I don't think I am. I feel fine. I'm not allergic to walnuts."

"We didn't know David was until today," Callum said wryly. "You feel nothing?"

"Nothing."

"That the walnuts are blameless doesn't mean the king *wasn't* poisoned," Ieuan was no less frustrated than when they'd started. "It just might have happened earlier, from something else he ate."

"Which is why we are being cautious about letting anyone know the walnuts may be to blame," Michael said. "We all agreed to play this down, even if every impulse is screaming at us to *do* something."

But then Livia arrived with a look on her face that boded poorly for their equilibrium.

Michael made a gesture towards his wife that was half rueful, half despairing. "Just tell us."

"The castle healer found one of the castle workers vomiting in the middle of the outer bailey. She got him into the laundry room, which at this hour was otherwise empty. Cassie is there with Aaron."

"This just happened?" Michael still hadn't entirely conditioned himself not to look at his wrist for his absent watch and the time.

"As he is unconscious now, we don't know how long he's been ill. Fortunately, the healer kept her head. She told only Cassie, who found Aaron and then me."

"Did he eat any of the walnuts?" Abraham's tone was urgent.

"We don't know." Livia's voice hitched. "Aaron won't commit to what he thinks the problem is, but you were also on my list of people to find."

Before she'd finished her sentence, they had all started moving towards the door.

8

September 19 -Avalon

Lili

Now didn't seem to be the time to worry about sorting out exactly what Lili did and did not understand. The part about running out of time was clear, and Lili knew exactly what Dafydd meant by it.

Thus, with Josh occupied, Lili turned to Susan. "You've already done so much, but may I use *your* phone?" Lili didn't question for a moment that Susan would have one. *Everybody* in the shop had one. Everyone in this entire world had one. It seemed to be a way of life, since every single person in the store within hailing distance had pulled out his or her phone at some point in the few minutes since they'd arrived. In retrospect, she'd realized many might have been using those phones to video Dafydd's rescue. It wasn't a concept that had meant anything to her before today.

Susan still held the second EpiPen, but with the other hand, she reached into her purse for her phone. *Purses* dated back to Lili's time period, and there was something comforting about the continuing concept, even if Susan's purse was of an unknown, shiny material.

At first glance, the phone's screen was entirely black but, before giving the phone to Lili, Susan poked at it and thus called up a similar screen to one Lili had seen on the phones of the twenty-firsters, most recently Elen's, who used hers to read books. "Just put in the numbers and press the green phone button."

Lili was grateful for the instruction, even as she was able to connect the picture of the *green phone button* to the shape of the object Josh was still holding to the side of his head. That one was black, not green. Green, as she recalled from many twenty-firster conversations, meant *go*. Sometimes she could appreciate the succinctness of English.

She tapped out the number Dafydd had made her memorize years ago and showed the screen to him. "Is this right?"

"It was at one point. Let's hope it still works." Dafydd paused. "Are you okay talking to him? I am probably well enough now to do it."

But the phone was already making a sound Lili recognized as *ringing,* something she knew from a movie she'd watched with Dafydd rather than from her own experience. She could have handed the phone to Dafydd at that point, but part of her wanted to experience fully every moment she was in Avalon, and that meant talking on a phone for the first time.

"Hello. Please hold for Mr. Treadman."

Lili took the phone away from her ear and looked at it. "The woman said to *please hold for Mr. Treadman*. Hold what? The phone?"

Dafydd gave her a little smile, the first one since they'd been on the battlement, a quarter of an hour and seven hundred and twenty-eight years ago. "Yes. *Hold the phone*. It means that the person on the other end of the line wants you to know you'll be speaking to Chad shortly, and you should wait."

Lili put the phone back to her ear and waited.

A matter of moments later, a male voice came to her from within the phone, a little breathless. "Who's this? Who's come through? Why wasn't there a flash?"

"You would know better than I," Lili said. "We are inside what I understand to be a Walmart."

"Who are you?"

"Lili."

She was about to add, "Dafydd's wife," when the man on the other *end* of the phone line cheered. "Is David with you?"

"Yes."

"Oh, thank God. We've had no idea what happened to him when he was sent back two years ago. He just disappeared—" His voice suddenly cut off in mid-sentence.

Lili pulled the phone away from her ear and frowned at it.

"What happened?" Dafydd said.

"I don't know. It suddenly stopped."

Susan leaned closer. "That's odd. Let me try to get him back for you." Without asking, she took the phone away from Lili and poked at it repeatedly.

Looking around the shop, Lili knew before Susan did that whatever she was trying wasn't going to work. Everyone else was mumbling to themselves and poking at their phones too with increasing desperation.

While Lili had been talking, Josh had returned, apparently still unable to summon an ambulance, and had given Dafydd two pills, which he swallowed down with a cup of water. Then Josh went back to his phone, on which he was now pounding with two fingers, seemingly in something of a fury.

Then he swung around and said more matter-of-factly. "The phones are down."

"That is something about which we should all be very concerned." A tall, slender woman, with streaks of gray in her shoulder length brown hair and dressed in dark blue trousers and jacket, arrived out of one of the aisles of items for sale to crouch beside Dafydd. "Sir, can you move? We need to get you out of here."

Dafydd looked up at her. "Who are you?"

"Deanna Hudson." She reached inside her jacket and pulled out a leather folder. Opening it, she showed its contents to Dafydd. "FBI."

Dafydd's expression was nothing if not wary. "Where do you want me to go?"

"Somewhere out of sight would be a good start."

"How did you know I was here—" Dafydd broke off at the sight of Susan pointing at him with her mouth open, as if seeing him for the first time. Maybe she was.

"Oh!" Her eyes were very wide. Her back had been turned when Lili and Dafydd had arrived. She could have thought everyone was just worked up about the fact that he was having an allergic reaction, not knowing that he'd also arrived out of nothing. With Dafydd's puffy face and longer hair than the last time he'd been to Avalon, he hadn't particularly looked like himself. And nobody had ever seen Lili before. "I can't believe you're here! And I saved your life—"

Deanna put out a hand to cut her off. "Don't give him away. We'll have a feeding frenzy if everyone else makes the same connection. It's a miracle they haven't already." She made a motion with her head. "Actually, some have, it's just that they would rather see him on their phones than in the flesh."

Josh was frowning as he looked from one person to the other, clearly not understanding, so Susan mouthed at him, "This is King David. You know—" She pointed upwards to the ceiling.

Josh's eyes grew as big as platters. Although he'd been helpful up until now, all of a sudden, he couldn't do enough. "This way." He pointed them towards a bright blue door located to the left of the similarly-colored counters, one which he'd come out initially. *Employees only* was written in English in red letters on an otherwise white sign. Even though they were definitely not employees, Josh opened the door for them and ushered them inside a little room, hardly more than four feet by six, with two chairs, a shelf, and a second blue door directly opposite the first.

With the sudden quiet, Lili found herself calmer than she might have thought herself capable. Dafydd was alive, they were in the custody of the FBI, which as far as she knew wasn't quite as bad as being with the CIA, and nobody was trying to harm them.

Maybe she should tack a *yet* onto that sentence, but she would take what she could get. She was finally in *Avalon!*

"What does he need most immediately?" Deanna asked Josh. She had her arm around Dafydd's waist to hold him up, even as Dafydd seemed to be coming more to himself. Hopefully that meant his face would soon be looking a lot more normal.

"More epinephrine, most likely. I'll probably be fired for helping him at all. I'm not a doctor!" But then he waved both hands quickly. "Then again, nobody is going to be fired because we saved King David's life. We all knew he might come here, but it's really different actually *having* him here."

Deanna didn't allow herself to be distracted. "You know how drugs work. How can I get him what he needs after we leave here?"

Josh gestured towards Susan, who'd followed them to the little room. "She has a second EpiPen if he needs it. Otherwise, keep the Benadryl handy. I just gave him two, as a precaution. I'd suggest you take him to the hospital, but I'm sure the emergency room is packed, and you might have to wait hours to see anyone. That's why an ambulance would be better."

"I have an EpiPen in my kit in the car." Deanna settled Dafydd in an orange chair and then turned to Susan, blocking her from coming fully inside the little room. "We can manage from here."

"Oh." Susan looked nonplussed. "Okay."

"Please tell me your name, so when we get him safe, we can thank you properly. Please believe we are incredibly grateful to you for saving his life."

"I'm Susan Jones."

"She's Welsh, or her family was at one time." Dafydd had overheard and murmured the words loud enough for Lili to hear. She wasn't sure about Deanna.

"Here's my card. Please reach out if you need anything, any time. I mean it. We'll also reimburse you for the EpiPen."

"Oh, it was no prob—"

"And don't tell anyone where he is!" Deanna practically shoved the woman back out of the doorway so she could close the door in her face. It was only then that she turned back to Dafydd and answered the question he had asked before Susan had realized who he was. "At least one person was livestreaming from the pharmacy as you arrived. My daughter sent me the link before the phones went down. I realized immediately who you were and that I had to get you out of sight."

"I still don't understand about the phones being down." Lili was proud of herself for using the proper terminology.

"I don't either, truth be told, but it can't be good. Getting you out of sight was step one. Next, we need to get you out of this Walmart. Preferably right now."

"But if the phones are down, we can't be tracked, right?" Dafydd said.

Deanna shook her head. "The video is online. Even if we were to get a court order to take it down, that takes time. Whoever it was who shut off the connectivity didn't do it in time."

"Apparently, there also wasn't a flash of our arrival, which seems impossible," Dafydd said. "There's always a *flash*."

"I have no idea about that either, but—" Deanna grimaced. "We've been picking up some worrisome traffic in the last few weeks indicating an unholy alliance between the Russians and at least one power in the Middle East." She paused. "Your name has been mentioned."

"My name? Why would there be any traffic about me?"

Deanna tsked. "You have no idea what's been happening in the world since you've been gone, do you?"

"No," Dafydd said.

It was that simple. They didn't.

"The political and social unrest in Avalon has increased tenfold in the last two years. Because of *you*, David. This isn't just a few people either. It's whole societies who know what you've done for Wales and want a better life as they see it for themselves. You have every rebel group in every country asking *what about* my *people? Why can't* we *be free too?*"

When Dafydd didn't reply right away, Lili said, somewhat uncertainly, "You sound like that's a bad thing."

"It's bad if you're part of a government that is still hoping to control how people think," Deanna said.

Dafydd gave a little sigh. "I'm not in favor of more control, that's for sure. But freedom can't be about every splinter group carving out a little piece of land for itself and excluding everyone else. People are too mixed up with each other, even in Earth Two. It needs to be about working together, as equals, moving towards a better world. Fighting against historical oppression takes you only so far. That's what I've been trying to get people to understand for years."

"Falling on deaf ears," Deanna said.

"It isn't as if we are there yet in Earth Two, that's for sure." He let out a grunt of disgust. "So you're saying that an unintended consequence of Wales's independence in Earth Two is a renewed emphasis on nationalism in Avalon?"

"I am saying exactly that." Deanna studied him thoughtfully. "There are opposition groups to the opposition groups."

Not unlike most of the conversations that had gone on around Lili since they'd arrived, Deanna and Dafydd might have been speaking in Greek for all that Lili understood—though admittedly, the *unholy alliance* part was more than a little familiar.

"What I don't understand," Lili said, "is how anyone can be reacting so fast? We didn't know we were coming until we did. Certainly nobody else could have known it. It's been *two years* since Dafydd was here."

Deanna gave a little scoff. "That's two years for every spy agency on the planet to figure out how to have a presence in this town. You can't walk ten feet without tripping over one. Not to mention the fact that Pendleton has become the new Roswell, New Mexico."

Dafydd eyed her. "I don't know what that means, but it doesn't sound like I want to."

"Roswell, New Mexico has a reputation similar to Area 51." Deanna laughed briefly. "Even if Chad hadn't commissioned a mini-series on your life last year, the entire world knew you arrived and departed from Pendleton a half-dozen times two years ago. You disappeared from a public park! And, of course, your mom and Anna came here before that. Did you notice the artwork across the ceiling out there depicting planets and solar systems? This store has two entire aisles devoted to tourist knick-knacks having to do with time travel. These days people in Pendleton buy more tinfoil hats than cowboy ones."

Lili rarely had seen Dafydd so thunderstruck. "I don't know whether to cry or laugh!"

"At least learning Welsh has become cool. There could be a dozen people in this store who understand what you're saying."

Lili could admire Deanna's straightforward and to-the-point manner, even if virtually everything out of her mouth was madness.

"How is it you're here alone?" Dafydd rested the back of his head against the wall.

"Chance." Deanna looked down at him. "As you said, it isn't as if you gave us fair warning."

"Why are you here instead of someone from the CIA? If I'm truly all over the internet, shouldn't they be here too?" He sounded resigned to this fact. "I am intimately familiar with their installation up by the airport."

"Langley West, they call it." Deanna made a motion with her head. "I don't answer to them."

"Who do you answer to?"

"My boss, his boss, and the president." She put out a hand. "I know just telling you to trust me isn't going to be enough, but you really can."

"Where can we be safe if all that you're saying is true?"

"I honestly don't know for sure. If I could get you to the reservation, we'd at least cut down on surveillance." She paused. "I know about Cassie and her grandfather, but I don't know exactly where Art's house is." She made a rueful face. "I'm not sure he'll be real happy to see me anyway. I had to arrest one of his relatives a few months ago."

Throughout his conversation with Deanna, Dafydd's expression had remained tight, distrustful even, but now it softened. "I know where he lives."

Deanna let out a sharp breath that might have been of relief and turned to Josh, who'd been listening to this conversation with rapt attention. "How do I get them out of here once I get my car? The front entrance would be a last resort."

"We have a back one, right out of the pharmacy."

"Give me five minutes. Three, if I can manage it, though it was a zoo out there even before you arrived." Deanna bit her lower lip as she surveyed Lili and Dafydd one more time. "Word will have spread by now that you're here."

As the FBI agent departed out the rear door, Lili settled herself beside Dafydd in one of the chairs. "Can we trust her?"

"I have no idea, but the FBI was good to Christopher back when he was taking care of Gwenllian and Arthur. As always, we have to rely on the kindness of strangers and hope we fall in with the right ones. She lives in this community. She knows people; she may be telling the truth."

"What about the other people Deanna mentioned? Russians, I think she said?" It seemed important not to unquestioningly accept what she didn't know, and they didn't appear to be immediately leaving this little room. She thought that was just as well, since her husband's face was still not entirely right.

At least he was breathing.

Dafydd grimaced. "You would know them as the *Rus*, Vikings again, naturally, just like the Normans. Though, as always, seven centuries have passed. The Middle East is what we call Persia at home."

"The Mongols rule Persia. And Russia." The only thing that had stopped the Mongols from taking over all of Europe fifty years earlier was an unusually wet spring. Things were starting to make sense—or so she thought until she saw the look that crossed Dafydd's face at her reply. It wasn't one of exasperation so much as an indication he wanted to explain but knew it was too complicated to bother with right now.

In the end, he settled for, "Not anymore."

9

September 19 -Avalon

Sophie

Sophie was accustomed to Chad Treadman's foibles. He always wanted everything done immediately, if not five minutes ago, and he usually didn't pause to ask if what he wanted interrupted her plans or even if she had plans. Since she'd come back from Earth Two, she mostly didn't. For all of her best intentions about what she was going to do when she got back to Avalon, and all the things she'd missed, she didn't even have a cat for whose care she had to arrange while she was gone. That had been fortunate yesterday when he'd put her on a private plane to Oregon.

Being back in Avalon, where she still felt she truly belonged, had nonetheless been *an adjustment* to say the least, as she'd told her therapist. Dr. Martin hadn't understood what was going on with Sophie, of course. Nobody but another time traveling twenty-firster could. She thought she should receive full marks for trying to talk about it, however. If nothing else, speaking of her experiences out loud had given her the ability to make herself functional. Some of the survivors of the Cardiff bus had started an annual reunion too, which had helped her healing process. Otherwise, she had Andre.

Dr. Martin had tried to encourage her to look at going to Earth Two along the same lines as living in a foreign, albeit very different, country or culture. But while some of the specifics might end up being similar, the issues were so much broader than that. It had taken Sophie a full year *after* she'd come back to come to terms with the fact that everything she and everyone else had ever thought about the physical world or the way the universe worked was wrong. Or at least not what they had assumed. Before David, before *Meg*, the universe had been so much more staid. Safe. Predictable.

Sophie had liked predictable. She had started rock climbing specifically to shake herself out of her own comfort zone. That had turned out well in the end, though she hadn't done any training since she'd come back.

That another universe existed alongside their own was a fact now—not a dream or a fantasy or speculative fiction. If nothing else, she could be grateful to David for entering and exiting this universe so publicly. It allowed the rest of the world to move past the point of admitting her to an asylum for believing something that wasn't real. It wasn't as if she was talking about alien abduction, though that was the closest she could find to a reasonable comparison.

Truthfully, these days, she was perfectly willing to believe aliens were real too.

"You!" George came to a full stop in the entrance to the airplane hangar that was the cover for Langley West. He found himself unable to process the sight of Sophie leaned up against the side of the big, black SUV favored by government agencies and corporate moguls alike. The airport runway was behind her, and she was glad now that Chad had the foresight to direct their flight yesterday to a small, privately owned airstrip rather than this particular airport, which appeared to have doubled in size since she was last here. Otherwise, their plane could have been held hostage by the CIA.

Andre poked his head out the driver's side window and gave George a wicked grin. "Us."

"What are you doing here?"

"Picking you up, evidently." Sophie said. "Andre says he has forgiven you for drugging and abducting him, by the way. I can't say I have, but he has convinced me to give you another chance."

The George she'd known from two years ago might have glared or laughed or made some sarcastic comment, any of which would have been in character for the man he'd been as an undercover CIA operative. This new George walked straight up to Sophie, looked her in the eye for a moment, and then wrapped his arms around her in a huge hug. "It is so good to see you. Thank you for coming to get me."

"Welcome back." She gave him a few pats. The hug wasn't creepy or anything, just unexpected, and surprisingly emotional. Before this moment, she would not have said *emotion* and *George* went hand-in-hand.

He released her with an honest-to-God rueful look in order to reach for Andre's hand, which he shook heartily. "You are the first two people I've talked to in two years, other than my guards, and even that wasn't much."

Sophie had been opening the rear door of the SUV for him, but she stopped with the door partly open to see that George had tears in the corners of his eyes. "You mean that, don't you?"

"And now you're here," Andre said in a tone that wasn't necessarily unsympathetic, just matter-of-fact. "Get inside before they change their minds."

"But why am I free?" he asked Sophie as she ushered him into the back seat. The tears, if they'd been real and not imagined by her, had abated as quickly as they'd come. Then he exclaimed joyfully at the sight of the McDonald's bag and large drink in the back seat's central console.

Honestly, George and David should have rubbed along better together than they had, given their similar food preferences. Of course, as had been the case for Sophie, the dishonesty, not to mention the fact that George had threatened Arthur and abducted David in his stead, was a little hard to get past.

"They didn't tell you?" Sophie said.

"They never even asked me any questions. Until this moment, I'd concluded the whole point of keeping me imprisoned had nothing to do with *me*. It must have been for Paige's benefit, or for deniability, or because I was a scapegoat to be trotted out when the time was right. Or maybe it was simply out of pique."

"Or because you know how to think—and even more, how to think like Paige," Sophie said. That answer was obvious to her, but it caused George to blink in surprise. In a way, what she'd just said was a compliment, probably the first she'd ever given him. She came around the other side of the vehicle to get into the front passenger seat. "What you wouldn't know is that, while your imprisonment was implemented with the full power and support of the CIA and the US government, the new administration isn't as sympathetic. Nor is the Senate Intelligence Committee. We don't know for sure if the findings of the SIC were the instigating event, but two days ago, an investigation into various CIA operations was announced, and almost immediately afterwards we got a call that you would be released at five pm Oregon time today. Andre and I got on a plane an hour later."

"You mean Chad—"

"—didn't forget about you, old boy," Andre said. "He testified before the SIC on your behalf. He told the truth! And it set you free."

George looked like he was having trouble swallowing. "He did all that ... for me?"

"For you, and for David, and for anyone else who might be in a similar position," Sophie said.

"You are still an employee, you know," Andre said. "Chad's been paying you a salary the whole time you've been in prison and has inquired after you personally every week since we last saw you in the park after you shot David."

"Shot *at* David," George corrected, seemingly recovering from his bout of emotion.

Andre snorted.

Within a matter of minutes, they were back to the old repartee as if the two years (and the aforementioned deceit, treachery, and abduction) hadn't happened.

Shaking her head at them, Sophie said, "At first, we had no communication from the CIA, other than the requisite run-around. They weren't even willing to admit they had you. MI-5 ghosted us too. We didn't know where you were. These days, planes come and go all the time from this airport, so we assumed they'd put you on one of them, and you were at a black site somewhere very far away."

"I had assumed that too," George said, "until about twenty minutes ago."

"Chad spent hundreds of hours over the last two years lobbying members of congress in his quest to find you and to expose the overreach of the CIA. Until recently, he didn't feel as if he was making any headway at all. But now, with new legislation that could be the first step in dismantling the surveillance state—" Sophie broke off as her phone rang.

Seeing that it was Chad, she put up a hand to stop anyone else from talking. They had already driven away from the airport, having opted to take the dirt roads through the fields around the town to reach Chad's estate rather than driving directly to it on regular surface roads. She didn't answer with *hello*, which she knew from long experience Chad thought was a waste of time, but simply put the phone on speaker, so the two men could hear as well. "We've got George—"

Chad cut her off. "Lili called the hotline."

"Lili!" The name exploded out of Andre's mouth.

"She's here with David." Chad acted like he hadn't heard. "We managed hardly more than a single sentence before the phone cut out. I spent thirty seconds trying to get her back on the same number, but the phone wouldn't connect. My people are trying to ping every phone in the vicinity, but they're getting nothing either. You need to get to them now."

"Where?" Sophie spoke automatically, her mind racing through the possibilities.

"At the local Walmart. It's about six miles from where your phone is showing you right now. I see you were taking the back, back way."

"It made sense at the time."

The moment Chad had called, Andre had pulled into a layby, so he could focus on the conversation, but now he stepped on the gas and drove onto the road again.

Sophie began programming the location of the Walmart into the GPS. "How long have they been here? Why didn't you call as soon as you saw the flash?" Normally she was a little more polite with her questions to her boss.

"The satellite system was down. It was only for three minutes, but it was the right three minutes. They didn't catch it."

"All of them? How is that possible?" George asked from the back seat.

"The system is coordinated now," Chad said, "at least in the US and in association with our allies. I can't speak to the rest."

Sophie put out a hand to George, which of course Chad couldn't see. "Until two years ago, the satellites for each country, including those run by the intelligence agencies, were siloed. However, even before you shot David, there had been movement towards an unprecedented coordination across the globe, albeit with some typical exceptions."

"The Russians. The Chinese. Iran. North Korea," Andre said. "Those systems may have been online and caught it.

"We can hope their people have farther to go than we do," Sophie said.

"In this town?" Andre said. "I wouldn't bet on it."

"So how did we not catch it?" George asked, likely not having understood Andre's comment.

"Routine maintenance, planned for months," Chad said. "They were uploading new software."

"At five pm Pacific time." Andre added this with a bit of awe in his voice. "Precisely."

"They come through when and where they're supposed to." George settled back in his seat, as if made content by this news.

Chad didn't reply, as he seemed to have become distracted for a moment, because there was silence on the line. After George's comment, Sophie and Andre went quiet too. The only sounds came from George continuing to eat and drink. Sophie didn't know how he could, since her stomach was tied in knots, but then, she hadn't been locked up in a CIA black site for the last two years. And she knew, from her time in Earth Two, that a good soldier ate, drank, and slept when and where he could.

Then Chad was back. "I was pulled away just now by a video that's been uploaded. You can see them arrive out of thin air. David slumps to the floor of the Walmart pharmacy. The video already has a million views." As always, Chad was talking so fast his words were tripping over each other.

"What was wrong with him?" George asked.

"My experts say it looks like he was suffering from anaphylaxis. He responded to an EpiPen. Also caught on video."

"Do we know what he's allergic to?" Sophie said. "I don't remember him saying anything about that or any mention of an allergy in his file. They've done enough blood work on him that surely they could have checked that."

"My brother's allergic to peanuts." George said.

Sophie managed not to swing around and stare at him. He had never talked to her, or to anyone else, as far as she knew, about any member of his family. She hadn't even known he had a brother, and he hadn't made any attempt since he got in the car to reach out to his family to tell them he was alive. Maybe that was because they thought he was dead. If she had been locked up for the last two years with no contact with anyone, the first thing she would have asked to do was telephone her parents, David or no David.

"It was a severe response," Chad said. "My experts say another minute and he could have died. He had to come."

"Could he have been poisoned instead?" George was intent, focused on the phone Sophie had set on the console between her and Andre and looking like he cared. If the circumstances weren't all of a sudden so dire, she might have been enjoying this new George.

"I didn't get that far with Lili. This is what my people think. Your job is to get to them, and we'll evaluate from there."

They swung around a corner, the wheels slipping a bit on the gravel road as Andre put his training to good use. "We got this, boss."

"I know you do." There was another pause, shorter this time, and then Chad said, "And George? Nice to hear your voice. Welcome back."

10

September 19 -Avalon

George

George took a last bite of his cheeseburger, closing his eyes as he did so. It tasted *so good*. He didn't care if Sophie shot him a look of disdain at his food choices. She'd brought him the meal after all. For someone who'd spent most of his adult life in other countries, McDonald's *was* America.

He'd tried to get himself to slow down, but time was of the essence, and he'd basically inhaled his food. Before Chad's call, he had been trying to eat the fries more leisurely. Now he took a sip of his diet Coke, which Sophie had so kindly remembered was his preference, rather than the sugared version. He needed the caffeine. The day outside indicated it was heading towards evening, but his body had just woken up from a night of sleep.

It occurred to him that his captors may have carefully managed his intake of food and drink, including possibly caffeine, to regulate his sleep cycle. In retrospect, they could have dosed his food as well, including giving him sleeping pills. He honestly had never considered going on a hunger strike. If they were drugging him, it wasn't in such a way that he'd noticed. But maybe he wouldn't have.

And now that he had a little perspective on the situation, he wondered if his notion that they'd never asked him any questions was entirely misguided. He could have been interrogated while drugged and have no memory of it. He, of all people, should know that the science of interrogation had advanced far beyond the ethics that should be regulating it. It might be another good explanation as to why they let him out: they'd drained him dry.

At another time, he might have been terrified. Or angry. As it was, he, Andre, and Sophie were together again, on a mission, just like old times. How great was it to be able to think about them as a team after everything that had happened—and everything George himself had done.

Unless ... George leaned forward to poke Andre in the shoulder. "Am I dreaming? Is this real? Are *you* real? Am I really free?"

"You have to ask?" Sophie turned in her seat to look at him.

He knew he had mistreated her in the past, betraying her trust and all that, and he was sorry he'd done so. It had been necessary for the life he'd led. Or so he'd thought at the time. His mandate had not included honesty, to say the least, and over time he'd become entirely cavalier with the truth.

And still, he couldn't help but give her a sardonic look. "Did you or did you not just pick me up from a CIA black site in the middle-of-nowhere Oregon? Of course, I have to ask."

"This is real." Sophie surprised him by grasping his hand and squeezing hard.

"Of course, that's what you would say if I were hallucinating this." The more he thought about the events of the last two years, and where he thought he was now, the more likely it seemed that he'd fallen down a genuine rabbit hole. Given that his captors had deceived him about the time that had passed, it was perfectly possible he was dreaming Andre's and Sophie's presence now. He certainly wanted out of prison badly enough.

"We have had this conversation many times before, if you recall, even if under different circumstances." Andre had been driving with intent, the dust from the dirt road obscuring the view behind them, and they were almost back into the residential area of the town. "We were all worried the whole world-shifting thing was a product of our imaginations. Or a hallucination. The fact that we were all experiencing it at the same time in the same way was what convinced us otherwise."

George remembered. It still didn't make what he was experiencing now *real*.

Sophie had kept hold of his hand. "If we are in the Matrix, I guess that would be one thing, but can you see that if Earth Two is a real place, and we genuinely lived there, this is happening too?"

George took in a steadying breath, knowing he was all over the place emotionally and mentally and trying to find his bearings. To be fair, he had woken up this morning in a cell he'd occupied for two years, which he thought was three, and a half-hour later, just the amount of time it took to process him out, he was with the two people he trusted most in the world, never mind that they might not trust him.

He *had* shot at David. He *had* spent two years in prison.

He allowed himself another five seconds of sensory overload, and then he forced himself to focus again on the business at hand. It helped that he had a bunch of fries left. She'd bought him a large. "I have a chip in me. Maybe more than one. We have to get it out. I should have said something about it right at the start."

"We should have thought of it too." Sophie remained remarkably forgiving. It did nothing to convince George he wasn't dreaming. "Where is the one you know about?"

George turned his wrist over to show Sophie his forearm. The chip was clearly visible in the tissue next to his tendon. As far as he knew, it was the only chip in his body, and he had looked, but he had no way to be sure about the places he couldn't see. Thus, the urgency.

Andre, meanwhile, had pulled off to the side of the road again, in a proper lay-by, as the English called them. They were quite close to the scene of one of David's landings after the CIA had forced him to time travel. That time, if George remembered correctly, he'd nearly been beheaded.

"Get in the back, George." Andre put the SUV in park. "Sophie, you drive. If there was no flash, then maybe the CIA hasn't heard the news of David's arrival yet. We don't want to lead them straight to him, but we also have to get to him. And if we are going to do that, we have to do this first."

"Can you take out a chip while we're moving?" Even as Sophie asked the question, she was scooting across the middle console. He hoped she knew what she was doing, since for her and Andre as English people, they were driving on the wrong side of the road. Meanwhile, Andre opened his door and came around to the back, rather than stuffing his large body through the space between the two front seats. George had already crawled over the back of the second row of seats into the trunk. It was full of gear.

"Are you expecting World War III?" George spoke without thought, and then mocked himself for asking, since *of course* they were.

"When we left Chad's compound this afternoon to collect you, we thought we would be bringing you straight back, but it seemed prudent that we gather anything we thought we might need, just in case." Andre eyed him with a wry smile. "As you well know, the world can change in the blink of an eye. We knew about the chipping already, since two years ago you yourself told us they wanted to chip you on your way out the door. My apologies for not thinking of removing it immediately."

"We've both been busy." George could be forgiving too. He found it remarkably easy.

Andre's mouth twitched. "That said, the vehicle comes with a jammer. As long as you're within it, nobody can track you."

"I should have guessed." He didn't add, *are you sure?* It was in his mind that the CIA would be prepared to deal with jammers. Though, again, Chad's people would know that too, and thus the leapfrogging advance of technology as each side attempted to stay ahead of the other.

"I brought you a change of clothes. We'll bin what you're wearing." Andre motioned with his head towards the darkened windows. "You don't need to worry about anyone looking in."

George was already pulling off his shirt. "Someone has been watching my every move for the last two years. I'm not worried about stripping down in front of you." Andre started going over George's clothes with what had to be a scanner, though not of a kind George had ever seen before. For starters, it was the size of a matchbox. "Things have progressed."

"Always. Members of my security staff have spent the last two years waiting for something to happen, which meant they had time to field test every piece of equipment here." He eyed George. "Turns out this *is* the center of the universe."

"Two universes," Sophie said from the front seat. They were stopped at a light, with twenty vehicles in front of them.

"Sophie and I received a crash course today in how everything works." He had started running the scanner over George's now naked body. "This baby has just deactivated all transmissions coming from you." As his eyes met George's, they were laughing. "Just in case we miss one."

"Please don't." George meant to snort, but his reply ended up coming out more like the plea it was.

"When we get back to the compound, we can put you through the full body scanner," Sophie said, "but for now, we don't want to keep David waiting any longer than we have to. Traffic is difficult enough as it is."

George didn't question the need for every precaution. He knew what was necessary as fully as either of them. It had taken most of these last two years to forgive himself for forgetting the first rule of secret agenting, one he'd learned from Paige the day they'd met: *human beings are capable of anything.*

And some of those terrible things had been perpetrated by *him.*

"What's going on that there's so many cars? Pendleton is the closest thing to a one-horse town I've ever been in."

"This is *the Friday of Round-Up* as the locals say." Andre grunted as he pulled out another device from its case and took George's wrist in his other hand. "A hundred thousand extra people have come into the town for the weekend. In short, it's a big rodeo."

"The number of horses alone would put David's stables to shame." Sophie laughed as she sped through the intersection after the car in front of her with more gusto than was probably safe. George felt another spurt of emotion, less of anger than of protection. These people were his friends, and by the very act of aiding him, they were putting themselves in danger. "In years past, *only* fifty thousand people would come, but the town has grown since you last saw it. Half the people came this year because of David. Just think if they knew he was here!"

"Horses aside, I have never seen so many caravans in my life. This is going to hurt." Andre spoke the last words in a run-on sentence, as if it fit with the rest of what he'd just said.

George had never been so ready for pain. "At your leisure."

Andre attached the device to George's wrist. George believed Andre when he'd said the chip was already deactivated, but none of them were willing to take the chance of keeping it in his body, and George couldn't wait to get it out. It had itched at him from the day it went in, even though he wasn't supposed to be able to feel it.

He felt a sharp stab, and then Andre released the machine and handed him a band aid.

"We should keep that, so Chad's people can analyze it." George slapped the bandage on his wrist. It was as if his whole body had suddenly aligned properly. For the first time in two years, he could breathe again.

It was probably all in his head, but that didn't mean it wasn't real.

"Oh, we're keeping it." Andre dropped the offending chip into a portable Faraday cage, a device which blocked electrical signals. In the old days they'd used tin foil, which admittedly was a bit hit and miss in its efficacy.

George then started tugging on his new clothes. What he'd worn out of the prison would have to go in the nearest dumpster ASAP, just like Andre had said.

They reached a long sweeping overpass, the Walmart finally in sight, though the multiple parking lots and vacant yards around it had been transformed into a small city of horse trailers, RVs, and pavilions. George tried not to stare. "How are we going to find him in all that?"

"We know where he was, so that's where we'll start," Andre said. "In a way, being surrounded by this many people is good, because he can get lost in the crowd. We're lucky it's late afternoon. The roads were closed off this morning for a parade."

"*Lucky*? What are the odds of any of this?" George said. "How does one calculate odds when we're talking about universe shifting?"

Sophie spun the wheel and headed down one of the long rows of cars in the Walmart parking lot. "I wouldn't have said the odds were worth calculating anymore."

While it still niggled at George that Andre had found only one tracker, he didn't have the ability to do anything about finding any more right now. Instead, he clambered back over the seat into the second row. The fact that a six-foot grown man could do exactly that was why government agencies and Chad drove giant SUVs in the first place.

Still in the trunk, Andre had started packing away the equipment. "You spend the last two years in custody, and then the very day—nay, the very moment—you step out the door of your prison, King David shows up again, and it's Sophie and I who have come to collect you."

George swallowed down another snort. If he thought too hard about it, he might have to start believing in some kind of higher power. But even after two years in prison, he hadn't sunk that low. He'd much rather go on hating Paige and the CIA and trusting his own instincts.

And his friends.

Suddenly, as Andre might say, it was more than enough to be going on with.

11

September 19 -Earth Two

Ieuan

While Ieuan was worried about his sister's husband, the man who was at one and the same time his brother-in-law, his lord, and his best friend, he was even more worried about his sister. Dafydd in Avalon alone was a terrifying thought, but so was having his sister there, potentially all alone and with a possibly dying husband.

Ieuan himself was one of the few—and the first—from Earth Two who'd gone with Dafydd to Avalon, so he knew something of what it was about. All those years ago, Dafydd had brought Ieuan there to save his life, which had subsequently taken an entirely unexpected path, since that trip had resulted in Ieuan's marriage to Bronwen, a twenty-firster. Because of their adventures, he'd introduced his own sister to Dafydd, who at the time had been only a prince of Wales.

All in all, it was just as well Ieuan had a job to do to distract him from these thoughts that tripped over themselves in his mind, each one shouting more urgently than the next for attention.

Ieuan's immediate task was to take the first steps to uncover what might be cooking at Carew Castle, if anything. With the feast in full swing, the entire kitchen was in the throes of a grim determination to keep going despite Dafydd's absence. It was clear to Ieuan that the people here genuinely loved Dafydd and feared for his life. They also knew that if he needed to go to Avalon in the middle of this tournament, even though it was an event being put on in his name, then it was for a good reason.

The fact that a member of the castle staff, one Corwen, the castle woodsman, was lying on the verge of death in the laundry room was something about which none of the workers currently knew. He was keeping this secret from them with the same lack of qualms he felt at not yet telling Dafydd's family that Dafydd and Lili were gone. Their son Arthur knew about it only because he had been inside the castle when it happened.

First thing upon entering the kitchen, Ieuan had noted the relatively small dish containing the offending concoction resting on a sideboard.

"May I ask who made the walnut treat that Queen Lili was eating?" He spoke in Welsh because Nicholas de Carew had a strong commitment to his Welsh identity while in his lands in Wales. His Norman castles in England would find English staff speaking English and French instead of Welsh and French.

Enith, the cook, glanced up from where she was looking over the shoulder of a girl kneading dough. "That's my specialty. They're a favorite of Earl Bohun. Those are just what's left. My apologies, my lord. If I had known you liked them I would have made more!"

Ieuan smiled, trying to hide the fact that he was having difficulty swallowing. Never mind that Abraham was well, Dafydd wasn't. Maybe Humphrey de Bohun wasn't either. "Have you already sent them to his table in the pavilion?"

"Ages ago." Enith had moved on to the man ladling stew from a cauldron into large bowls.

"You tasted from the bowl?" As he asked this, Ieuan resisted the temptation to run from the room that instant to find Humphrey and anyone else sitting at the high table with him, including the rest of Dafydd's family. He told himself the dish had been sent long ago, and the fact that Nicholas de Carew had been at that table too and seen nothing amiss should be enough to quell his concerns.

"Of course." She shot him a quizzical look. "We taste everything."

"Who is *we*?"

"Me and the undercook. We ate from the bowl, as we always do and are obligated to do." She patted her somewhat rotund belly. "You see how this happens."

Both of them were clearly well too.

On impulse, Ieuan plucked a walnut from the bowl and put it in his own mouth, telling himself that if all these people, including the Earl of Hereford, had eaten of them, then he would be safe too.

He chewed, appreciating why Humphrey liked the treat so much and might have requested that the cook make it for him especially. Then he swallowed and waited.

When he didn't drop dead on the spot, he figured he ought to cruise around the kitchen being useful while waiting to expire. "Did anyone else besides you eat of the walnuts before they were sent out?"

Enith had a look in her eye that indicated she was beginning to catch on to the idea that he thought something might be awry with the dish she'd made. Her hackles went up, in her tone if not literally. "I suppose someone might have snuck his hand into the bowl. Some of the younger ones are always taking a bit of food when they think nobody is looking. They haven't yet learned they'll get regular meals here and can eat what they like."

"You don't seem concerned about that fact."

"We are well fed. Earl Carew doesn't begrudge us what we need. Any of them could have had a taste if they'd asked."

"I didn't see anyone take a piece ... except Lord Ieuan." That came from one of the vegetable girls, Sara, who was less than half his age. Her words were cheeky, and flirting, and Ieuan knew better than to respond.

Instead, he decided it was time to speak more broadly. "Could anyone tamper with one of the dishes between the time it's placed on a platter and when it is served?"

Enith finally left off supervising and approached, her hands on her hips and her eyes narrowed. "What is this about, my lord? Has someone complained about my food? Is someone ill?"

Ieuan made a motion with his hand by way of apology. Enith was very good at her job, and he truly didn't want to upset her. If Dafydd or Corwen had been poisoned, he needed to walk a fine line between investigating how that happened and not alerting the poisoner that they were on to him. At the moment, Ieuan had no notion at all of who that might be, if he existed at all.

So he backed off. "I am just confirming procedure. Don't mind me at all."

Enith harrumphed. Fortunately, there was so much going on in the kitchen that needed her attention she couldn't give Ieuan more than another glance or two before she went back to her work.

Before he'd visited the kitchen, Ieuan had spoken to the castle steward, a man named Elis, who had defended his people with admirable passion. "My lord, none here have any desire to harm the king. By my life! We have had many years of practice caring for lords and kings. We have procedures in place specifically to prevent what you describe from happening. I am sure you will find that King Dafydd's ailment had nothing to do with the food that came from our kitchen."

Ieuan had let the man go with an understanding nod, albeit with a warning not to speak to anyone else about their conversation. Elis had agreed, since it was hardly the first secret he'd kept in his sojourn as castle steward. Keeping secrets was practically his *job*. In this instance, he had been defending his staff, which Ieuan could respect. Dafydd was gone, however, and another man was ill. Even the possibility of poison in the castle should be roiling his innards. It was certainly roiling Ieuan's.

Thankfully, the walnut Ieuan had eaten had gone down without a hitch, and he let out a sigh of relief at the knowledge he wasn't going to die just yet. He'd eaten a sample on a whim because he trusted Michael and Abraham. Whatever had sent Dafydd to Avalon, Elis was correct that it didn't appear to be a deliberate event. Whether or not Corwen had eaten tainted food remained to be seen. The possibility wasn't worth upsetting the kitchen staff over just yet.

Having come to the end of his questions for now, Ieuan was about to leave in order to pursue the investigation elsewhere when Sara, the vegetable girl, added, "Didn't I see a handsome stranger leaving the kitchen the other morning, Cook Enith? He was almost as attractive as you, Lord Ieuan, for all that he was quite a bit younger."

She was deliberately flirting with him again, trying to get his attention, but her words were (to take something Bronwen would say) *electrifying*. "Who was this?"

Cook Enith shot Sara an annoyed look. "I don't know what you're talking about."

"Don't you remember?" Now that she was being challenged, the girl dug in, though not before shooting another pleased glance in Ieuan's direction. "He was someone I'd never seen before. His smile was ever so charming."

Enith's annoyance turned to exasperation. "Oh, *him*? I don't know why you bother to mention him. He didn't give me his name, just poked his head into the kitchen to ask where our steward might be, and when I said he could find him in the chambers above the gatehouse, he left."

"He *was* very handsome though, wasn't he?" Sara simpered.

Ieuan settled back against the frame of the pantry door, trying to appear uninterested in Sara as well as unconcerned about what she was saying, even as his curiosity was definitely piqued. He didn't know what a handsome stranger had to do with any of this, but he knew enough about solving puzzles to keep asking questions as long as someone was willing to answer them. "What does very handsome mean to you?"

"He looked like you, but different somehow. I would not have said he was Welsh, for all that he was tall and dark, with incredible blue eyes and oh-so-long lashes." Sara seemed to hug herself at the memory. "I had only one good look, albeit accompanied by a smile, so I couldn't say more than that."

"Did he speak Welsh?"

Sara looked at Enith for the answer. The cook blinked. "No, my lord. He spoke French."

"So he was Norman," Ieuan said. "And a nobleman?"

Enith blinked again, and the pause before she spoke was slightly longer this time. "Yes, my lord. He was clearly a Norman nobleman."

"But one you didn't know."

"No, my lord." This answer came more quickly, indicating she was no longer startled by the direction of his questions. "I saw him for a matter of moments. Honestly, I couldn't even tell you what he looked like. I hadn't thought of him again until Sara mentioned him. We have had so many visitors to the kitchen this week that once he left I never gave him a second thought."

Sara gave Enith an incredulous look, which Ieuan thought was deserved, given her description of him. Ieuan had been a leader of men long enough, and a father long enough, to recognize a lie when he heard one.

"Do you remember the exact day?"

Again it was Sara who answered. "Yesterday morning, wasn't it?"

"Are you sure you didn't see me? I have been in and out of the kitchen many times since we arrived." It was true, though Ieuan couldn't recall a specific instance on any of the mornings. Mostly he had been acquiring extra food for his children or his wife.

Sara's eyes widened. "Of course not! I would know you anywhere! Besides, you have a touch of gray at the temples, don't you? This man didn't."

Several other of the female kitchen workers, who of course had been listening intently even as they went about their work, nodded appreciatively at him. He tried not to roll his eyes.

"I don't know what all the fuss is about. As I said, all he did was poke in his head," Enith said, in something of an undertone.

Despite Enith's protestations, the description of a nobleman with incredible blue eyes and long lashes was very specific. This was especially true if one narrowed the field to Norman noblemen, who tended towards the blond or the red-headed. Even more difficult would be to find one who fit Sara's description and might be wandering about Carew Castle in the days before the tournament.

"Could the man have been Bogo de Clare?" If not for her assessment of this stranger's age, Bogo fit Sara's description perfectly. When Bogo had been at Berkhamsted Castle, he'd been sure Dafydd would be poisoned at any moment. His quest for the throne had been predicated on it. What's more, Bogo knew this area, having grown up as the son of the Earl of Gloucester. While under the best of circumstances it would be quite a risk for him to enter Carew Castle on his own, few might recognize him instantly since it had been many years since his family had lost their lands in Wales.

However, according to Nicholas de Carew, he had just arrived in the pavilion, having made the journey from Lamphey once he'd recovered from a sickness developed during the journey from France. According to Cardinal Francesco, Bogo had been as ill as any of them.

"Certainly not, my lord!" Enith looked startled that Ieuan had suggested it.

"You're sure?" After all, the man was physically *here*.

"I never met him myself, but I was told by those who should know that his image on the posters put up after his offenses against our brave princesses was a good likeness. The man we saw was much too young." She was certain, and thus Ieuan was unsurprised to find Sara nodding as well.

Bogo lied and deceived as easily as he breathed. No amount of treachery was beyond him. But as far as Ieuan knew, he hadn't yet fallen under the spell of a sorcerer who could make a fifty-year-old man look thirty.

With great reluctance, Ieuan had to give way.

12

September 19 -Avalon

George

After George had thrown himself into the clothes Andre had brought for him, he also received an earpiece, a weapon, and a cell phone. It felt good to be an agent again—not to mention the fact that they'd entrusted him with a firearm. Back at the park two years ago, he'd had to appropriate a gun from another agent in order to shoot at David. George gave credit to Chad that he had absorbed him so immediately back into his organization. Though according to Andre, he'd never been jettisoned and had been paid a salary all this time.

It felt good to be ... wanted? Respected? It was testament to how badly things had ended with the CIA that George expected to be treated poorly and was surprised when he wasn't.

As he ate one last fry, Sophie pulled up in front of the main doors of the Walmart. Then she and George got out of the vehicle, while Andre settled himself in the driver's seat once again.

"I'll circle the building." He made a twirling motion with one finger. "If I can."

He was right to be concerned about his ability to do so, given the hundreds of people moving about. It was just as well he had no intention of parking because the vast lot was packed with vehicles, all the way to the last slots.

Once inside the store, the aisles were no less full. George honestly couldn't understand why a bunch of rodeo attendees would be buying home goods, but he supposed all those RVs had to be filled somehow. Plus, Walmart also sold food. And, apparently, time-travel knick-knacks.

At the pharmacy, the line of people waiting was ten deep. After a brief inspection of his options, George stepped in front of a rightfully outraged elderly man, who looked on the verge of whacking him with his cane, in order to ask where they'd find the man who'd almost died on their floor. The checker's eyes widened, indicating she knew exactly what he was talking about. She didn't make any reply, however, instead turning away to speak to one of the male, very busy, pharmacists.

At first, he merely glanced up from his work, but then at the woman's urgent words, looked hard at George, and then past him to Sophie. Since they both wore dark suits, they were out of place amongst the t-shirts and jeans of his usual clientele. The checker returned to George and asked that he wait by a blue door beyond the counter.

While the pharmacist took longer to get back to them than George had the patience for, eventually he came out.

"What can I do for you?" His nametag read, "Josh."

"I'm George. This is Sophie. We are here for David."

At least the man didn't ask, "Who?" or pretend not to know what George was talking about.

"Just a sec." He reentered the pharmacy through the door, returning a moment later with a scrap of paper in his hand. He didn't show it to them, but instead said, "Who sent you?"

"Chad Treadman," Sophie said.

"What's his phone number?"

That was a stumper for George, but Sophie immediately rattled off a number, prompting Josh to nod, since it appeared to match what was written on his little paper. George was impressed that David had not only assumed someone would ask for him but had come up with a measure of security all on his own. Then Josh held the blue door open and gestured them inside.

George had come to this very Walmart for hair dye in his initial quest to disguise himself two years ago. Those years of absence hadn't made the Walmart pharmacy area any less utilitarian, though it was located in the back of the store now instead of right up front. Undoubtedly this was the result of a corporate remodel for no good reason and merely served to prevent shoppers from finding what they wanted. For George's purposes, the pharmacy had retained its delightfully generic anonymity.

They entered a private room for giving immunizations, something he hadn't realized the pharmacy did before this moment. George had honestly expected David to be sitting in one of the seats, but they were empty. "Where is he?"

Josh put up both hands defensively at George's abrupt question. "He left with a woman from the FBI, one—" he looked at the paper again, "—Deanna Hudson."

This wasn't going to be as easy as he'd hoped. George felt a wave of despair wash over him. "Where did they go?"

"I don't know. I asked them, and they said they didn't know yet."

George—or at least the old George—wouldn't have been above threatening the man to get a different answer. He supposed the new George wasn't either because he might have done exactly that if he hadn't believed him.

"Did David go willingly?" Sophie asked.

Josh nodded vigorously. "He hoped you'd come. Or someone like you. That's why he came up with this test."

"Why did he go with her? Why didn't he wait?" George was trying hard not to keep the whine out of his voice.

"The phones had gone down, and the FBI lady said the Russians were coming after him. I think he felt like he didn't have a choice." Josh was proving to be gratifyingly talkative.

"Did he say what the anaphylaxis was about?" Sophie asked.

It wasn't relevant, but George could agree that the pharmacist was the one to ask. "Sugared walnuts. Or honeyed? He'd reacted to walnuts as a kid, but not this badly. He hadn't had them again until today."

George could see Sophie filing away that bit of information for future use. At least they knew what not to feed him, if they found him. He hoped this Deanna was legit and not from the Russians herself. People in the US *did* still have straightforward English names, but Deanna's was exactly the kind of name he himself would have used as a cover identity, except, of course, he would have been *Dean*. As it was, *George Hanson* was a pseudonym too.

"Did he indicate he had a plan?" George said.

"He was going to call that number again as soon as he could, if he could," Josh said. "Our phones are *still* down, so—"

The checker to whom George had initially spoken opened the inner door to the pharmacy. Her eyes were even wider than before. "Someone else is here." The words came out a whisper. "They don't look right."

"Give me your coat." George snapped his fingers at Josh, which was rude, but he was feeling an overwhelming urgency.

Josh's brow furrowed, but he obeyed, if a little slowly. "What are you going to do?"

"I'm going to impersonate you. I need to see for myself what we're facing, and I don't want them to know Sophie and I got here first."

"That's smart." Josh adjusted his nametag on George's chest.

George took the checker's elbow and ushered her in front of him into the working innards of the pharmacy. He'd never been on this side of the counter before, and he would have looked around curiously if not for his laser focus on the two men who'd jumped the queue, just as he had. The coat and nametag would work as a disguise only if these men didn't recognize him as former CIA. He should have had Sophie do this, despite her English accent. *Too late.*

"May I help you?" George decided to mimic Josh in more ways than just by wearing his white coat.

The man flashed a badge. "FBI. We are here for the man who was ill in the aisle a few minutes ago."

It was more than a few minutes ago by now, but George was hardly going to argue a minor point. He had been late, but these men were further behind. It wouldn't do to crow, since George had lost David too.

Instead, George held out his hand for the badge. "May I see that again?"

The man handed it over instantly, as if confident in its genuineness.

"What's your name?" George inspected the badge. It did look real, but then, if these men were CIA, they would have acquired the badges directly from their fellow agency. If they were Russians, their forgeries could be the best in the world. Nobody did sleeper agents better. They'd certainly known not to send someone with a Russian accent to this little town in Oregon.

"Robert Steele." He tipped his head to his partner. "Dean Hudson."

George managed to stop his head from coming up at the second name. He looked hard at the badge one more time, and then at the one "Dean Hudson" held out. "I'm sorry to tell you that the man left."

Robert's eyes narrowed. "He *left*? Where did he go?"

George thought he affected a properly casual shrug. "He didn't say. He didn't want to stay here, not with the phones down. I think he saw someone he knew who said they had a camper van he could rest in."

The last bit was inspired, and George's words certainly caught Robert's attention. He looked at his partner, who nodded and said, "Thank you for your time."

"Sure. Glad to help."

The men walked away.

George watched them until they were out of sight. While he certainly was worried about where the earlier Deanna Hudson, if that was her real name, had taken David and Lili, the checker was right that this "Dean" and his partner "Robert" had given off a bad vibe. George might not have David and Lili in hand right now, but he could be glad those two didn't either.

13

September 19 -Earth Two

Callum

Callum wanted to curse at the way the afternoon had imploded, but he restrained himself. His son, Gareth, had just turned four and repeated everything his father said. Even if he wasn't currently present, Callum needed to break himself of the habit. As he crouched beside the unconscious man, who lay on a pallet in, of all places, the laundry room, covered to his chin by a blanket, he also had to keep reminding himself that Avalon had reached out and snatched David from Earth Two. He hadn't even had to risk his life by jumping. By those lights, his life was still worth saving.

Furthermore, if the past informed the present, he'd been taken in because he had something important to do there. Callum didn't have the simple faith of those who had been born in Earth Two, but that didn't mean he couldn't see the truth right in front of him. "There are more things in heaven and earth, Horatio, / Than are dreamt of in your philosophy," said Hamlet in a time and place less far removed from this one than when he'd taken his Shakespeare class at university.

At least Corwen didn't feel cold to the touch, what with the fire blazing under the water pot, one that so resembled a witch's cauldron that Callum was reminded of Shakespeare again, though this time of the play, *Macbeth*. He hoped the current adventure wouldn't end as badly. For now, the healer had lit the fire under the cauldron, which was serving to heat the whole of the room, not only from the flames beneath it but from the steam coming off the water in the pot.

The washing had already been done for the day. If someone missed Corwen, Callum hoped the general excitement—not only of David's disappearance but the arrival of newly designated Cardinal Bogo de Clare—would distract them until he could figure out if they even *had* a situation. They could see well enough, thanks to the fire and the light from outside coming to them from where the roof of the building had been raised above the walls to allow the free flow of air for drying laundry, even when it rained outside.

It was too bad the healer couldn't have encouraged Corwen all the way to her hut within the kitchen garden, but as he was a large man and she a small woman, she'd done well to get him this far.

Corwen wasn't in a position to object to his location. Besides, where they nursed him wouldn't change anything about his future, which at the moment appeared singularly dire. Both Aaron and Abraham, as well as Gwladys, the healer who'd found him, had given him a thorough going over. He might live, but he also might have a matter of moments left. And they didn't know why.

"What do we know?" Callum straightened, perceiving that if he crouched any longer, his knees would not forgive him.

"Hardly more than I'm sure Livia already told you." Cassie had set herself up in the doorway, which was Callum's usual position, or Michael's, keeping an eye out for any curious passers-by. Out of the corner of his eye, right before they'd entered the outer bailey, he'd caught sight of Elen, Gwenllian, and Lizzie, their royal girl version of the Three Musketeers (as Bronwen called them), never mind that muskets didn't exist in this world yet. But they were no longer in evidence. "Gwladys can tell you more."

The healer was standing at Corwen's feet, looking down at him with her arms folded across her chest. "Corwen vomited at least twice, which was why I didn't administer an emetic. Besides, by the time I got him inside the laundry, he was no longer able to swallow."

"If he was vomiting on his own, it was too late for the emetic to do any good anyway." Abraham had settled next to Aaron, near the man's head.

Callum was confident that, with Michael included too, the four of them contained as vast a body of knowledge of healing as was possible to find in Earth Two. While Gwladys was a lay healer, the two physicians were not prejudiced, and Abraham had already said they could use all the help they could get. Many modern medicines had started out as natural remedies, and he was never one to lord it over someone with less formal education than he, especially if her practical experience was great.

"Who is this man, anyway?" Michael asked.

"He is the castle woodsman," Gwladys said. "Think of him as a liaison between the forest and the castle."

"None of which tells us if we should worry about why he is ill," Callum said.

"He must have been worried about it himself or else why come to the castle at all? I'm thinking he came looking for me," Gwladys said.

Callum accepted that explanation with a nod. "If David hadn't just been taken to Avalon, we probably would have dismissed Corwen's illness as exactly that. But David was taken, so we must ask if Corwen's illness and the king's could be related?"

They hadn't bothered to keep from Gwladys the fact that David had been suffering when he'd left, out of the same spirit of putting the best minds available together to solve whatever problems they faced.

Abraham shook his head. "We do not believe so. We here—" he gestured to Michael, who nodded his agreement, "—have seen what David was experiencing before. He did not vomit, for starters."

Aaron's lips had been pursed as he listened, but now he too nodded. "Even if you're wrong about what happened with the king, I know of few herbs which could have had the specific effect you witnessed."

"I ate of the walnuts," Abraham said. "I am well. They weren't poisoned."

"This man, however, is dying," Callum said flatly. They'd all been speaking in Welsh, for Gwladys's benefit primarily, but he'd switched momentarily to English, in case Corwen was awake enough to hear him. It wouldn't do for him to learn the truth about his condition in such a fashion. "If this isn't a regular illness, what poison could he have ingested to cause his symptoms?"

"Strychnos, perhaps, from India, or arsenic," Aaron said. "My first choice, however, would be *digitalis*."

Michael frowned. "That's Avalonian medicine, isn't it, for heart disease?"

"Yes and no," Abraham had been working with Aaron within the royal court—and around the entire country—since Abraham had come to Earth Two five years before. "Our modern digitalis is derived from the herb *foxglove*. When those leaves are dried and ground, the resulting powder can be helpful for managing heart conditions, but obviously only in very small quantities. Too much results in nausea, vomiting, trouble with vision, a very slow and irregular heartbeat, and then, of course, convulsions and death."

"Of course." Cassie wasn't above a wry tone, even—or especially—in these circumstances. "Hence Corwen's unconscious state."

"Indeed," Abraham said.

"But not David's," Livia said.

"I would hear more of this anaphylaxis of which you speak," Aaron said. "I am aware of the word's Greek and Latin roots, but even if the king's symptoms were entirely different from Corwen's, if not for you, I would have assumed the king had been poisoned and these two events were related. It is only because my friend Abraham here has informed me otherwise that I have been considering another option in Corwen's case as well."

"They still may be related," said Cassie, speaking of what nobody wanted to be true. "This could be something we haven't seen before."

Absent from the conversation at the moment were both Bronwen, who suddenly found herself parenting five children instead of the usual three, and her husband Ieuan, who was still in the kitchen. While the twenty-firsters knew what anaphylaxis was, even if some hadn't seen it before personally, and Michael and Abraham were as sure as they could be that David had been reacting to something he'd eaten, it wouldn't do to get complacent. And if poor Corwen had ingested something poisonous, the kitchen was the first place to look for clues. Quietly.

At the moment, they were caught between an overriding interest in not alerting the staff at the castle that something might be amiss, and figuring out if something actually *was* amiss. They couldn't hide the fact that the king was gone, and dealing with David's absence would have to become a priority shortly. For now, Callum needed to find the edges of whatever was going on here, *if anything*.

Their usual cohort should also have included two more couples: Bridget and Peter; and Darren and Rachel. Both couples were parents of infants, however, and had opted not to travel, as much as they would have loved the family reunion, not to mention the spectacle on the tournament field. Both Ieuan and Math were entered in the archery contest, along with every red-blooded Welshman with aspirations for the golden arrow that was the prize. David had managed to evade participating in any of the contests by the fact that King Arthur wouldn't have done so either. Anna's son Cadell had been sorely disappointed when he'd been told eleven was too young to joust. He was taking part in several youth contests, nonetheless.

For Callum, a younger version of himself might have been tempted to examine Corwen's supine body in some fashion, since he wasn't without investigative abilities, but he was keeping his hands clasped behind his back, something he did often now to hide his tremor. So far, it was the only indication of an underlying disease.

That said, the tremor was worse than it had been a year ago. The irony of this situation was that only last week David had offered to take Callum back to Avalon. It was the most recent instance out of a dozen other times, with the idea of getting Callum properly diagnosed, whether with Parkinson's, MS, overactive thyroid, or an essential tremor, which Abraham said usually developed in men between the ages of forty and fifty.

That would be the best-case scenario, and also one for which there was little to be done but live with it, as he was already doing.

Callum had refused to go, unwilling to put David's life at risk.

He hadn't seen David teary-eyed very often, but he had been so then. For now, Abraham was keeping an eye on Callum, watching for the progress of a disease. All the medicines brought years ago on Chad Treadman's plane were expired long since, including the Ep-iPen Callum knew for a fact still resided in Michael's pocket and would probably remain there until David returned with a replace-ment. It had simply taken Michael too long to run to where it was stored and get back to the battlement.

Then Cassie moved out of the doorway to allow Ieuan to en-ter.

"I found something I need more experienced eyes to see." In one hand, he carried a small bowl, which he proceeded to set on one of the tables used for folding laundry. In his other hand, he held a clay vial with a stopper, which he removed. After showing them that the vial was full to the brim with small, brown seeds, each a few mil-limeters long, he proceeded to pour the seeds into the bowl. "Can an-yone tell me what these are?"

14

September 19 -Avalon

Chad

One of Chad's administrative assistants stepped into the room. "Sir, your sister is on the line."

Chad's residences were also home offices, which meant he could work at all hours of the day and night, from wherever he happened to be. His people were working late tonight because Chad was working late. It was appropriate, since New York was known as *the city that never sleeps.*

Chad accepted the phone from his staffer and put it to his ear. "Hey, Den-den."

"Just because you called me that when you were in diapers doesn't mean you have to call me that now. Denise is fine."

"I'll try to remember." Chad put up a hand to his employee, telling him all was well and dismissing him at the same time. All of a sudden he was finding he didn't trust anyone in his organization but Andre and Sophie—and George, God help him—all three of whom were three thousand miles away. Before yesterday, it hadn't mattered quite as much.

He also trusted his sister. She had married well, as their grandmother might have said, and was a leading Washington D.C. insider, in all the best possible ways. She would not be calling at this hour if it wasn't important.

After losing his connection to Lili, Chad had paced around his office, imagining her hovering over David, who was dying on the tiles of that Walmart in Oregon. Thankfully, Chad knew where they'd come in because his people tracked the location of every call, as a matter of course, and the hotline in particular. Television programs implied that tracing a call took time, but that was old news and for dramatic effect. These days, if your GPS was on (and whose wasn't?) your phone was a beacon to anyone with the technology to receive it.

Chad himself hadn't been to Oregon since David had left it. After the CIA operatives had tackled George, the representatives from MI-5 had slithered away, leaving Chad's people to stand on their own. Chad had wanted to intervene, but his hands had been as tied as George's, even if only figuratively. He couldn't ask his people to shoot members of the CIA, never mind that they were operating illegally on US soil. Even after everything that had happened, Chad had been naïve, and he'd trusted where he should not have.

Having kicked himself for not making sure another US agency was present, like the FBI, he had remedied that lapse in the intervening two years by reaching out and making friends. The FBI had agreed to joint classes with his own security people, and they were even training together on Chad's planes and helicopters, since his company had won the FBI's latest contract. The CIA might capture David, but if any other US law enforcement agency became involved, they would be bound to abide by the actual laws of the land.

The worst thing now was that he couldn't *do* anything concrete for David and Lili other than work from the rearguard. Chad was used to constant communication—as well as the immediate satisfaction of every whim. For once, he was stymied in his attempts to get either. Maybe he needed some chocolate to take the edge off his temper and stress. That last cup of coffee he'd had probably hadn't been helpful.

He had a call into MI-5, but, inconveniently, it was two in the morning there, five hours ahead of Chad and eight hours ahead of what was happening in Oregon. David had UK citizenship too, which gave MI-5 and MI-6 reason to care about him, if they didn't have plenty of reasons already. Having been gone for two years, however, priorities changed. Personnel changed.

The US government had changed too, which was how Chad had been able to testify before the Senate Intelligence Committee in the first place. Five years ago, he never would have thought he could have had that kind of impact, but meeting David had changed him and given him new purpose on the planet. He'd had the privilege of picking David's brains for a number of years now, during which time they'd had many conversations, beginning with that walk along the farm track in Wales. The events of two years ago had been a further galvanizing force, at which point Chad had finally understood David's vision of how Earth Two was going to help Avalon.

It was a vision Chad was uniquely placed to implement, beginning with establishing an institute associated with the University of Bangor in North Wales, as a means to coordinate and connect researchers and scientists across many fields and from around the globe. Anyone who wanted to learn from David's time traveling could participate. The variety of species, cultures, and languages that access to Earth Two would allow to be studied was mind-blowing. One particularly creative dissertation proposal Chad had read recently was from someone who proposed there was a measurable swapping of medieval air for Avalonian air every time David traveled, and he wanted to measure it if he could. The scholar might get that chance now if he, along with everyone else, hustled to the Walmart.

Rather than being about making Earth Two a safe haven for Avalonians, confirming Avalon's superiority, or allowing Earth Two to become a playground for intelligence agencies, the Bangor Institute's mission was predicated on David's political philosophy. They had physicists, biologists, historians, linguists, chemists and many more, all working together, much like they might in Antarctica or the international space station, all ready to get on a plane to wherever David was the moment they knew it.

"I have some news for you." That was what his sister said when she was underplaying something momentous, both good and bad. It was what she'd said when she'd called him at boarding school at fifteen to say that their mutual father had had a heart attack. It was how she'd announced the birth of her children. More recently, it was what she'd said when she warned him about some upcoming political disaster.

"I think I better call you back." Chad's palm was suddenly sweaty as he held the warm phone to his ear.

"Maybe you'd better. Just because we're paranoid doesn't mean someone isn't trying to kill us." It was their inside joke, that didn't feel much like a joke in this moment, even though Denise had laughed when she'd said it. "I'm on a burner, like you suggested." She rattled off the number.

"Five minutes." He hung up and was at his office door a moment later. He had a half-dozen employees, all from the night shift (for which they were well-compensated) and all currently gathered around a computer screen.

At the sight of him, his lead assistant when Sophie was gone, Jasmine, looked up. "You need to see this. It's breaking the internet."

He didn't want to take the time, but he didn't want his employees to realize how urgent he was feeling either, so he came closer, and those present made room for him. He didn't recognize anything in the image at first, but the headline was enough to send up every alarm bell. *The King is in the House!*

Jasmine restarted the video at the beginning. The first shot was of a girl posing with different hair accoutrements, asking, "Which one do you think is best?" And then, right behind her, two people appeared out of nowhere. Chad had seen footage of these appearances before, but he was as riveted as everyone else. The video then replayed the shot three times, the second time in slow motion with the addition of text helpfully telling the watcher, *this is real!*

Then came Lili shouting for help, as David was in obvious distress, his face puffed up like a marshmallow and his raspy breathing loud enough to be picked up on the phone's microphone. This was followed by the arrival of the patron with an EpiPen and David's subsequent survival. Fortunately, the person doing the filming thought the drama was over once David started breathing normally.

This video wasn't the first to be posted, but it was definitely the most watchable compared to others Chad had seen, which had picked up David and Lili's arrival much more peripherally. Some had been livestreamed, so had gone out before the connectivity at the Walmart had gone down. This one was more polished, thus the delay.

The views were in the tens of millions already. It really might break the internet.

Chad didn't watch it again, as tempting as that might be, instead thanking his staff for the information and departing the room. He nodded at his security people by the front door of the apartment to indicate all was well, and then strolled towards his bedroom. There were no cameras in here, nor any personnel, though one of them would very reasonably take up a stance by his bedroom door. He paid them well to be thorough.

No matter, he wasn't leaving the building. Ever since David's adventures in Paris, Chad had become increasingly sure he needed his own, private, escape route. Fortunately, he had the resources to shape things the way he liked. He entered his walk-in closet and opened one of the dressers like it was a door—the whole thing, not just a drawer—to reveal a secret passageway.

He ducked his head to enter and hurried down the carpeted stairs.

15

September 19 -Earth Two

Cassie

With Ieuan's arrival, everyone moved to surround the table, except for Cassie, who replaced Gwladys near Corwen's head and took his hand. It looked to Cassie as if Corwen's journey towards death had already begun, but if he was going to fight his way out of the depths, he didn't have to do it entirely on his own. Holding his hand might make no difference in the end, but she would lead him back, if she could. Carew Castle didn't have a designated infirmary, so she supposed the laundry room was as good a place as any to tend to him, at least for now.

Besides, one glance at the seeds Ieuan had brought in that vial was enough for her to know she wasn't going to contribute much to the conversation.

Abraham stood at Aaron's left shoulder, studying the seeds. "I hate to guess what those are without running a test. I would have said crab apple seeds if not for the look on your face."

"Those are poisonous too," Aaron said. "They contain cyanide. These are worse."

"We are so glad to know that," Livia said. "Don't keep us waiting. To you, the problem here is obvious and dire, but the rest of us are in the dark."

Abraham was the modern doctor, and Aaron deferred to him about many ailments, but Cassie had observed that patients asked for Aaron more than Abraham. Jewish doctors were known to be the very best, and while Abraham was Jewish too, he was also a twenty-firster. Whatever the veneration for Avalonians that many twenty-firsters experienced, the common folk knew instinctively they couldn't talk to Abraham in quite the same way. It was an instance where Avalonians were just too different. But in this case, it was also Aaron who knew about herbal remedies.

"These are seeds from a yew tree." Aaron let out a puff of air, implying frustration or even exasperation. Not with Livia, but with the circumstances. "Ieuan knows what they are and asked if we knew out of courtesy." He turned to Gwladys. "You needed a single glance too."

By way of an answer, Gwladys said to Callum, "Do you not have yews in Avalon, my lord?"

"We do, but not so many that I would have recognized these seeds."

"Yews grow in the mountains of Oregon," Cassie said. "Aren't they the source of that cancer drug, Taxol?"

"They are," Abraham said.

"So why is everyone worried? Don't we make bow staves out of yew wood?" Cassie herself was an accomplished archer, though she had declined to participate in the tournament. When she was younger, she might have enjoyed the test. These days she preferred not to be part of a spectacle.

"We do at times," Ieuan said. "For our purposes today, yews are also highly poisonous to humans and animals."

Cassie wrinkled her nose. "I suppose I could have guessed that."

"What's more, the seeds of the tree are the most toxic." Aaron beckoned Gwladys closer. "As far as I know, their poison has no remedy."

"None that I know of either, more's the pity," Gwladys said. "Long ago, we built walls around our churchyards to protect the graves from desecration by animals but also to protect animals from the yews planted within the walls, not the other way around."

"We don't have a cure in Avalon either," Abraham said.

"Still?" Aaron turned to him, surprised.

"Still."

Aaron was one of the few people native to Earth Two, not part of David's immediate family, who knew that Avalon was not only another world, but a future one as well.

"Are Corwen's symptoms consistent with yew poisoning?" Michael asked. "I mean, exactly like it?"

"I would say so, such as we can see of them. Nausea, vomiting, pain, convulsions," Gwladys said with a confidence in her voice that hadn't been there earlier. "And then death."

Callum lifted a hand, one that Cassie noted in this moment didn't shake. *Interesting.* "Would yew seeds have a purpose in the kitchen, culinary or otherwise?"

"No." All three healers were emphatic on that point.

"Can the poison be ingested by a means other than eating them?" Michael asked. "Like through the skin?"

Cassie knew nothing about yew poisoning, but she understood people better, and she saw that Michael's question had touched a nerve with those native to Earth Two. Poisoning was a known thing, and much feared. Every court had food tasters, specifically to protect noblemen, lords, and kings.

Allergic reactions like David appeared to have experienced, on the other hand, were extremely rare in this world. Cassie herself had heard of a couple of instances of severe seafood allergies. Walnuts, if they were, in fact, the culprit in David's case, were not a significant allergen among the populace, at least not that she'd heard. And peanuts, which caused such problems for children back in Avalon, were a New World food. They'd brought chocolate, tomatoes, and potatoes home to Earth Two, but not peanuts. It occurred to Cassie that might have been deliberate on David's part.

After a pause, Aaron said, "Yes, but not in this form, not just touching the seed itself. Even if Corwen had eaten them whole, they might have passed right through him without harm. The poison is released if the seeds are crushed, chewed, made into a paste, or employed in a tea."

Gwladys's expression was pensive. "A few years ago, an idiot of a man was working with yew wood, sanding and what have you, and poisoned himself by inhaling the dust. I couldn't save him. I would have said Corwen would have known better than to do that."

Cassie realized she did have something to add: "Agatha Christie killed someone with yew in one of her novels. The killer put it in marmalade to mask the bitter taste."

They all looked at Corwen and, with pity in her face, Gwladys returned to his side.

That left Cassie free to move closer to Callum. "I have been angry with you for not going with David when he asked, Callum; maybe I still am. But even I can see that you were meant to be here now."

Callum's eyes were still on Corwen, whose belly moved up and down with every breath, though the movement appeared even less robust than before. "What do you mean?"

"What needs to happen next is much more in keeping with the kind of thing you were trained to do at MI-5."

"I wasn't exactly a detective."

"No, but you are good at ferreting out intrigue and treason. And that's what we're facing here. We've already made a start." She gestured to encompass everyone present. "And you have better people to work with than you've ever had before."

While her friends had been talking, Cassie had been thinking that she and Callum had worked with smart people back in Avalon, but there had been excessive jockeying for power and one-upmanship at MI-5, a behavior that was entirely lacking in David's court. If people acted that way, they were no longer *in* his court.

Looking around at the men and women with them, Cassie knew she could trust each and every one of them with her life. She didn't have to fear any were involved in treachery, and every task they set themselves would be carried out to the best of each person's abilities—or they would ask for help. They were a remarkable group by any standard, and if something untoward *was* happening here, she had complete faith that they would discover it.

"Taking a step back," Cassie raised her voice so she was speaking to everyone, not just Callum, "two years ago, almost to the day, Almain, the Earl of Cornwall, believed David had been poisoned—or would be soon—by someone within his retinue. It came to nothing, but—"

"—but I've spoken with Princess Molly, who heard it directly from Almain, and he was sure of his information." Livia motioned towards her husband. "We spent months following up on this issue once we returned from France. I have always thought that just because we couldn't find a traitor at that time didn't mean there wasn't one. Almain and Bogo were too confident about their plan for taking the English throne for their attempt to have been based on a misperception."

"And now Bogo is here, David is gone, Corwen is ill, and Ieuan found yew seeds in the pantry," Callum said.

"There's more." Ieuan then told them about the handsome man who'd visited the kitchen. "I can't link him to the yew seeds or to Corwen, and the cook was certain he wasn't Bogo."

Livia's lip curled. "We need to determine Bogo's whereabouts from the moment he set foot in Wales, for our own sanity, if nothing else. This could be nothing more than a series of coincidences, but I don't like to see them pile up like this."

"According to Cardinal Francesco, Bogo was made very ill during the sea voyage," Ieuan said. "Was that poison too?"

"I refuse to see Bogo as a victim," Cassie said flatly.

"Regardless, the fact that the vial is full should be a huge relief." As everyone looked at him, Callum spread his hands wide, again showing they were steady. The human mind was a funny thing, and it would be ironic if a poisoning was the necessary distraction to reduce his tremor, if only temporarily. One would have thought he would have had plenty of equally significant diversions and responsibilities over the last few years. "It suggests to me that the contents of this vial have not been used, otherwise it wouldn't still be there."

"If that's the case, why is Corwen dying?" Livia said.

Abraham had been frowning as he thought. "Our focus has been on the parts of the yew tree that are poisonous, but yew pollen is highly allergenic too. Gwladys's case with the sawdust has reminded me of a similar instance I encountered. A patient trimmed his yew hedge during pollination season and was bedridden the next day. He recovered and finished the job the next week, at which point he was very ill again. My working theory was his illness came from breathing in the pollen."

"Seeds are not the same as pollen," Livia said. "Poison behaves differently from allergens, and besides, yews pollinate in the spring."

"True," Abraham said, "but David did have an allergic reaction."

16

September 19 -Avalon

Chad

Thick carpeting and sound proofed-walls—another lesson learned from King Philippe's secret passageways in Paris—muffled Chad's steps down to an apartment two levels below his penthouse. Since he owned the whole building, it had been easy to acquire another space for himself.

Compared to the penthouse above, this was a very modest space: one bedroom, one bathroom, with the kitchen and living room combined. It had no front door at all and thus was a black hole in the center of his building. The only way out was either back up to the penthouse, or down many more flights of stairs to a steel door which opened on one side into the laundry room through a vent shaft and to the outside world through a one-way maintenance door. It was his own, personal, postern gate.

Chad opened one of the kitchen drawers and surveyed his collection of burner phones. He chose one at random to use to call Denise back.

She answered on the first ring, "I gather you are alone now in your cave?"

"I am."

"I have news about your boy."

"I can't decide if I should be happy or afraid," Chad said. "You'd better just tell me."

"Everybody is looking for him. Half think he's a security threat. Some want to collect him like he's a classic car. The rest view him more like a nuke."

"None of that sounds positive."

"It shouldn't. I assume you've seen the video."

"Videos."

"Do you know where he is?" And then she made a disgusted sound he knew well. "Look at me, caught up in the excitement too. Better I don't know even if you do. I have more too. Worse, even. You have a mole."

This wasn't a video call, so she couldn't see how he'd swallowed hard, but she might have heard it, because her voice became a bit gentler. "The CIA implanted George and left him. You didn't seriously think he was the only one?"

"No, that would have been foolish and naïve."

"Neither of which you are." She was back to being no-nonsense, which was in general how he liked her.

Denise had been born first to a shared father. Her mother had divorced their father when she was a baby due to irreconcilable differences resulting from a workaholic lifestyle. Clearly, the apple hadn't fallen far from the tree, either in Denise's case or in Chad's. Denise had then spent most of her initial years involuntarily estranged from him until, at the age of fifteen, her mother had thrown up her hands at what she'd called Denise's *rebellious nature*. At that point, she had come to live with her father and his new wife, Chad's mother. Chad had been born a few months later.

Strangely, the age difference had not ended up being a barrier to their friendship. At the very least, there'd never been an ounce of sibling rivalry. Denise did still sometimes treat him like he was eight years old. By this time, at nearly forty, he found it endearing.

"Do you have a name?"

She gave him one, an administrative assistant placed just high enough to be one tier away from direct contact with him.

"Dare I ask how you know this?"

"You shouldn't. My only concern is that the answer came fairly quickly without much prying on my part. The man was maybe too talkative and unguarded, which makes me wonder if that employee isn't the only spy, just the most expendable."

"Did you get the sense he wanted something from you in return?"

"They always want something; they don't always get it. But we don't need informants to know what the CIA wants: a face-to-face meeting with your boy."

"That will not happen."

"My informant seemed to think the CIA had David's best interests at heart. I did not express my skepticism."

Chad snorted. "I wonder where throwing him out of an airplane fits into this picture?"

"You'll get no argument from me." She paused. "Don't think for a second David can't be found, however. Data is being analyzed in real time."

"As I would expect. George thought Paige was the worst person in the world."

"Sadly untrue."

"As always, you know more about these things than you should."

"You think so? I wouldn't say that. I know what I need to. It would be better if more people knew what I know." The pause was a little longer this time. "You might also be interested in my further news in that regard. I have become aware that your Paige is about to be hung out to dry. They are pruning the tree, as our father was known to say, with really big shears."

"Not *my* Paige. George's." All of a sudden, things were starting to make a little more sense. "They want her to fall on her sword."

"So it seems. My contact implied her bosses were unlikely to get their wish. It has occurred to me, Chad dear, that a growing number of powerful people within our government want to lock David up and throw away the key. He is a problem they can't solve, and that frightens them. The surveillance system you're battling against was designed to capture him. You've been attacking the watchers, Chad, but it sounds to me like the enemies you face are far more highly placed. The CIA has been at war with itself since your testimony. You don't want to be caught in the crossfire."

"I don't mean to."

"Can you protect yourself and *him* at the same time?" By *him,* of course she meant David.

This was more impassioned than was usual for Denise. It wasn't just Chad's life David had changed. "Such is my intent."

He sensed Denise shaking her head. "You don't know what it's like here. DC is on fire. While things became serious the day David disappeared right in front of everyone in that interview a few years ago, it got a lot worse after the docudrama you commissioned about him aired last year. My contacts say the threats against him are from all directions and so numerous they don't know who's coming after him. Everyone wants him; everyone wants to control him; some of them are even more up your alley."

"Business people?"

"More like oligarchs, but yes. Your Bangor Institute isn't going to be able to stop them."

Chad did, in fact, already know that. "If change was to happen, we had to start somewhere."

"You don't have to tell me that. I'll let you know what else I find out."

"Thank you, Denise. You're the best."

"Of course, I am." Normally she might have ended with that, but this time she paused and added, "You're a good man, Chadlie Brown. Stay the course."

As she hung up, Chad swallowed down a sudden lump in his throat. At times over the years as he'd supported David, he had felt like he was hanging out on an edge all by himself. The vitriol that had poured down on him during those Senate hearings had been hard to weather.

But Lili had called him; he had companions he trusted with his life; and his sister had told him he was a good man.

It was a relief to not be alone in this anymore.

17

September 19 -Avalon

Lili

Dafydd had already explained (in Welsh) to Lili what he was going to ask next, and she could see him brace himself for a crucial test. "Can I borrow your phone?"

Deanna gave a shake of her head. "I ditched mine in the Walmart parking lot before I came back for you. Phones can be tracked, even when they're off. I also disabled the GPS on this vehicle, although once my agency discovers they can't find me, they can turn it back on remotely. We're going to have to destroy it outright, probably with a hammer, if we keep driving in this car."

Lili wasn't at all sure what Deanna was talking about, but she could tell from how tightly Dafydd was holding her hand that it hadn't been the answer he'd wanted. She asked him in Welsh, "Pass or fail?"

"Undetermined." She knew he wanted to be certain for her, but since she could see right through him anyway, he then added, "I genuinely don't know. I may have to talk a lot in English, and we may have to run at a moment's notice. Are you good with that?"

Lili looked at him somewhat sardonically. "When have I not been?"

He grinned and kissed her. He'd already told her there would be cameras everywhere that could preserve their image if their faces showed in the windows of the vehicle. Fortunately, these rear windows were darkened. Only the front window, what David called a *windshield,* for reasons that were delightfully obvious, even to Lili, was entirely transparent.

Their time at the Walmart had made it abundantly clear to her that they needed to be careful about who photographed them. Bad enough that they'd been documented so robustly from the moment they'd arrived. What mattered now was having nobody know where they went next. Then, up ahead, one of the most awful sounds Lili had ever heard filled her ears, followed by bells and red lights. They had come to a stop behind a line of other vehicles. The roaring continued ahead of them.

Dafydd leaned closer to her, and though her hands were over her ears, she could still hear him. "It's a train, and it's almost done. See." He pointed beyond the vehicle to the monster disappearing into the distance. At that point, the gates came up all on their own, the blinking red lights went out, and the vehicles ahead of them started moving. Then he switched back to English to speak to Deanna. "The smart thing to do, obviously, is to boot you from the car and drive it straight into a tree. Even without ever properly learning to drive, I can handle that much."

"Please don't!" Deanna glanced behind her to meet Dafydd's eyes. "You're not serious."

A smile hovered on Dafydd's lips. "We have to get back somehow and some time. How else are we going to do it? Regardless, it's going to involve putting our lives in danger. This way you can be rid of us, and nobody needs to worry about us anymore."

"You need to be monitored for a little longer." Deanna's tone was firm. "You're not out of the woods yet."

Lili could have argued that they had Abraham at home, and Dafydd seemed himself to her. Tired, but essentially himself. Nonetheless, she had never seen anyone experience anaphylaxis before today. "She could be right, Dafydd. I would be willing to keep going, provided we can do so safely."

Dafydd made a motion with his head. "Safely? I wouldn't count on it. Honestly, going home immediately isn't my first choice either. It just might be the smart one."

"Not if you're not well." Then to Deanna, Lili added, "Dafydd is right that it would be better to return immediately than to end up in prison, like the last time."

"What exactly do you mean by that?" Deanna glanced up into a little mirror at the top of the windshield. "Prison?"

"You know about me but not about that?" Dafydd asked.

"I don't know what I don't know until you tell me."

"The CIA embedded an operative in Chad Treadman's organization, in hopes that I would eventually take him to Earth Two. Which I did. Two years ago, he abducted me, and I ended up in CIA custody." Dafydd pointed towards the north. "Up there."

"They threw him out of an airplane," Lili said flatly. "They shot him."

"Yes. I did know about that. I was thinking of an actual *prison*. There's a big one just to the west of town. They always build them in isolated areas." Deanna spoke with a narrowing of the eyes. "I also know what you didn't say: that his first plan was to abduct your son."

Dafydd sat up straighter. "Is that why you found me so quickly? Did the FBI post you here for *me*?"

"No." Deanna tossed her head a bit. "The FBI has had a permanent office here for decades to conduct federal investigations and to liaison with the Tribes. Today I was just at the right place at the right time."

Dafydd's hand moved towards the latch for the door, but Deanna spoke before he pulled it. "Please don't do that. I know you don't know me, nor do you know if you can trust me. You've had a bad time of it here for a long time, and I'm sorry about that. The FBI wasn't involved in any of what happened to you before. Honestly, I genuinely was shopping after work like a regular person—foolishly forgetting what day it was and how crowded the store would be—when my daughter texted me the video of you two arriving. I knew what it was about immediately, and also that things were going to get crazy. Then, when the phones cut out, I was sure of it. You needed help. So I helped."

"And the Russians?"

"They're real, believe me. I may not have been posted here for you, per se, but I have been briefed about you, since this is one of your known locations. We have had an active task force about you and a strong presence in Eastern Oregon for years. Everything crosses my desk."

"The CIA has a presence too," Dafydd said. "A big one."

"They can't work within the borders of the United States."

Dafydd laughed mockingly. "Did anyone tell them? Not that I'm bitter or anything."

Deanna's head was turning this way and that, looking out the side windows of the car. "I don't like this."

"Well, exactly," Dafydd said. "Such is my concern."

They were stopped again, behind another long line of cars, though not for any reason Lili could discern. There wasn't a train this time but there were still *so many* cars on the road. It was overwhelming.

"I don't mean you being here," Deanna said. "I mean that we are too exposed. If I am to keep you safe, we have to get away from the crowds. I can't take you to my home. Not only would it put my family in danger, but if anyone knows I'm with you, it would be the first place they would look. Every hotel within a hundred miles is booked up, even the run-down and anonymous."

"Are we still talking about the Russians?"

"We are talking about everyone who might want to harm you or control you." Deanna turned in her seat to look directly at Dafydd. "My agency is none-too-fond of the CIA either, by way of habit, not to mention what they did to you. If they know you're here, they'll have this vehicle soon enough."

"So we drive," Dafydd said. "Fast."

Deanna shook her head. "We are surrounded by fields and open land. Anyone on a highway in any direction is exposed."

"So then our best option really might be to drive to Art's house, even though he too is a known associate," Dafydd said. "Were you serious about there being less surveillance on the reservation?"

Even before replying, Deanna had swung out of the lane she was in, down a side street, and then turned again. "The Confederated Tribes have blocked government surveillance systems from operating within the reservation."

Lili knew what surveillance was, if only because Dafydd had discussed it so often—and because they were fleeing the Walmart before it caught up with them. A significant portion of the rest of what Deanna and Dafydd had been talking about wasn't clear to her. They could have been back to Greek.

"Why is that?" Dafydd asked, and then after a pause, added, "Can they really do that?"

"The reservation is sovereign territory. I am allowed entry in an official capacity since the FBI still has jurisdiction as a federal agency. But it's touch-and-go even for me at times." She grimaced.

"Maybe especially for me. I'm also serious about Cassie's family not liking me."

Just as had been the case in the store, this last comment caused Dafydd to settle more comfortably in his seat, and he said in a low tone to Lili, "The full name of the place we're going is the Confederated Tribes of the Umatilla Indian Reservation, shortened down to CTUIR, the Confederated Tribes, or even, the Tribes."

Deanna glanced at them again through the windshield mirror. The road was clearer of cars than it had been since they'd left the Walmart. "They're so serious about it, they've even blurred out Google maps."

18

September 19 -Earth Two

Meg

The remaining members of David's family, consisting of Anna, Math, Llywelyn, and Meg, clustered at one end of the high table to speak with Carew. Few others were paying attention to its occupants anymore, as the feast in general had broken up from its initial formal setting to small groups and a lot of inter- and intra-table interaction. They would notice if the group left entirely, but for now, they were not the center of attention, especially with the bards preparing to begin another session on the opposite end of the pavilion. It was the perfect cover for conversation.

Llywelyn had a tight grip on Meg's hand, and he bent close to whisper in her ear, "Dafydd is nearly twenty-nine now, not fourteen. He is a competent man. We have to trust that he knows what he is doing. Avalon took him in for a reason."

She looked into his eyes. "The rational part of me agrees, but then there's the mother in me."

He kissed her temple. "He will always be our son, no matter how old he is, but there's nothing we can do for him right now but pray."

Meg found herself flashing back to all those years ago when her sister had called to tell her David and Anna were missing. The police had assumed they'd run away, which had concerned them less than the fact that they'd done it in Meg's sister's minivan. For that reason, they had put out an APB (All Points Bulletin) on Elisa's vehicle. When she and Anna had *traveled* together years ago, the FBI had issued a warrant for Anna's arrest. It might be that in some quarters Anna and David were still considered fugitives from the law. That would also put in jeopardy anyone who helped them, though that fact hadn't ever seemed to bother Chad Treadman.

Had some part of Meg known in that first instant, and then in the days, weeks, and months of absence that followed, that they'd gone to Llywelyn in Earth Two? All these years later, she still didn't know for sure. But she remembered the punch to the gut the news had been and the long year and a half afterwards without them. She was feeling that punch again, never mind that David had traveled the other way—into Avalon instead of out of it—and Llywelyn was sitting right beside her. She and her son were still separated by the void and seven hundred and twenty-eight years. And dear God she worried.

David believed that Meg herself had traveled to Avalon two years ago and been sent back. He felt it had been for her own good because whatever was happening in Avalon was worse than what was happening to them here. Since she and Daisy had been climbing down from their room at the top of Berkhamsted's keep, and one of Almain's men had cut the rope hoping they'd fall to their death, that was saying something.

Meg could only be glad now that she and Llywelyn had taken the central seats from the start of the meal, even before the papal delegation had arrived and Carew had left for the castle. She had known from the moment he'd appeared in the entrance to the pavilion a quarter of an hour ago that something wasn't right, just from the way the various guards had suddenly become more alert. It had taken Carew a while to work his way around to them, and then another delay to find the right moment to tell them.

It was certainly taking *her* a bit of time to absorb his news.

By now, the papal entourage had taken themselves off, which appeared to be the event for which Carew had been waiting. Truly, Meg thought her family had done a credible job of disguising their horror—Daisy's gasp aside—to see Bogo de Clare in their pavilion, not to mention the fact that the pope had made him a cardinal. And if Cardinal Francesco had been surprised to find his news not well-received, he might now be wondering how extensively he, and the pope, had been lied to. Meg was all for sowing distrust when it put Bogo in disfavor.

More than anything, Bogo appeared frustrated by David's absence, and while she didn't think David would actually have run him through, he definitely wouldn't have taken kindly to his father being forced to keep to the laws of hospitality in the face of a known criminal, someone who'd not only conspired to take David's crown, but to murder him. That he'd imprisoned King Edward's daughters, as well as Elen, Gwenllian, and Meg herself, simply added to the injury.

Meg pushed away her plate. She didn't want to take even another sip of wine. Carew had assured them that Callum had a plan for determining the nature of the threat, *if any*. Yes, David was gone. Yes, Corwen was ill. Yes, yew seeds had been found in the pantry. Yes, Bogo was *here*. But anything that tied these events together was speculation.

Llywelyn very gently pulled Meg's plate back towards her. As always, he knew full well what was in her mind. "You still have to eat."

Meg stabbed at the bit of onion left on her plate and took a small bite. Vegetables were safe. The meat honestly ought to be safe too. Crushed yew seeds would be best hidden in something like a pie, although she would think the pieces would have to be very small. Truthfully, she'd never given a single moment's thought before now as to how one might introduce yew into a meal. Animals ate the needle-like leaves, but a human wouldn't do that, unless they were put into marmalade. The berries themselves were the only part of the tree that wasn't poisonous.

"How much would a person need to ingest before he became ill or died, and how long would it take?" Math asked.

Abraham had accompanied Carew, and it was he who answered. "Up to a full day."

"Which means the effects aren't immediate." Anna was tapping a finger on the table as she thought.

"Certainly in smaller doses," Abraham said. "In quantity, it would work faster. It's painful and ugly, regardless."

Now Meg really didn't want to eat. A few days of feeling this way might mean she could fit into the dress she wanted to wear on the tournament's final day instead of looking at it longingly. At a few years from fifty, and although her husband had no patience with any complaints about her expanding figure, she was not the lithe twenty-year-old, or even forty-year-old, she had once been. She could agree, however, that not eating because of fear of poison was probably not the best way to go about fitting into the dress. Better to pass it on to someone who might truly wear it.

"Was the outside of the vial dusty when you found it?" Math asked. "Perhaps the vial was left years ago. The seeds are perennial. They could have been there forever."

"Ieuan reports that the kitchen is immaculate," Carew said, "as I would expect it to be. Even more, the man in charge of the buttery told him that the stores of cheese were laid down in the last week, in preparation for the tournament. The shelf was half-full before then."

"I accept that there were yew seeds left in the kitchen, and that they were put there in the last few days," Meg said. "What I don't understand is why anyone would leave them there so openly. If someone was going to poison one of us, would they really just leave the vial there for us to find?"

"He may have feared being caught with it on his person, or even might not be the same person who was meant to use it," Carew said.

Anna nodded. "Person A could have left it for person B."

"Since you are implying at least one of the people involved works in the kitchen," Math said, "how many people are we talking about?"

"Dozens," Carew said. "We had to bring on additional staff for the tournament. Most are working in the outdoor facilities, but those in the castle kitchen are being pushed hard too."

Anna scoffed. "Great. So this could be a real conspiracy."

Carew shook his head. "At the moment, this is nothing. I am telling you now out of an abundance of caution."

Math let out a puff of air. "Be that as it may, a vial of yew seeds *was* found in the kitchen. It could have been left there an hour ago, intended for this very meal, or three days ago, intended for some time in the future. I agree that the poisoner wouldn't want to keep it on him, but he would also want to be prepared for the right moment and the right dish to ensure the right person was poisoned."

"Whoever that might be," Anna said. "David, Papa, even you, Nicholas."

"This could be the start of a true insurrection," Llywelyn said.

"So we concluded." Carew bent his head. "Any and all of what you say is possible. Or none of it, and this is the people who love you fussing about nothing."

"We appreciate the fuss," Meg said, "and if it is nothing, we will be content in your care."

"Did you speak to the kitchen staff about the vial?" Llywelyn said.

"No," Carew said. "Deliberately so. They are busy with the tournament, and if we aren't telling them about Corwen, then all the more reason to confer with all of you first about whether or not we even should."

"Why shouldn't we?" Anna said.

"Because we want to catch the culprit, not scare him off," Carew said. "Many of our staff have worked at this castle their entire lives. Hundreds of people have trusted them, including me and all of you."

Anna looked at Meg. "It isn't as if we can dust the vial for fingerprints."

"Sadly, no," Meg said.

"I assume Callum has a plan?" So far Llywelyn had absorbed Carew's news, David's illness and disappearance included, with remarkable aplomb.

"We are investigating, of course, and we are counting on all of you—" Carew gestured to the four of them, "—to show by your behavior that we are not concerned about David's disappearance either."

"I need to find the children." Meg prepared to rise to her feet. "Undoubtedly they have already learned about Lili and David, but the older ones have to know to be careful about what they eat."

"Bran is the weak link." Anna sent Meg a rueful look. "We all know it."

Bran was eight years old and had never met a secret he could keep. Meg's heart melted every time she looked at him. "He is as sweet as the day is long, though. And fortunately one of the pickiest eaters the planet has ever seen, barring David himself. They are royal children. They can keep a secret."

"Wait a moment, *cariad*." Llywelyn had stayed seated, and Meg recognized by the thoughtful look on his face that he was considering all the angles. That intelligence and wisdom were what had enabled him to guide his country for fifty years. She lowered herself back down to listen to what he had to say. "It is in my head that we should put the vial back where Ieuan found it. If the kitchen staff are still unaware of its existence, then they won't notice either its absence or its return. We *have* to know for whom it was intended and the only way to do that is to clear the field for the poisoner. He needs to feel safe. If we are going to get to the bottom of this, we need to let him use it."

19

Llywelyn

The uproar at his assessment of the situation was a bit louder and more immediate than Llywelyn had expected. In response, he raised a hand, waving them all to silence. "It makes sense. Surely you must see it. Ieuan must have been thinking of this when he decided not to question the kitchen workers more thoroughly or even disclose that we were concerned about Corwen's illness."

"There's a vast difference between thinking we should do everything in our power to make sure the culprit doesn't know we know about him and ensuring it." Carew's tone was forceful, for which Llywelyn couldn't blame him. It was his kitchen, after all.

"Be that as it may, right now we are in control of the situation as best we can be, and I would very much like it to stay that way. We can thank poor Corwen for that. But I didn't mean we should put the yew seeds themselves back. Can we substitute something that looks similar?"

Abraham nodded. "I thought they were crab apple seeds at first, which Gwladys has in her stores. In small quantities, they are an excellent aid for stomach disorders." His eyes narrowed. "When one baits a trap, one must be ready for whatever one catches."

"I do know that, Abraham." Llywelyn was used to the informality of the twenty-firsters by now, and his voice didn't contain anything in the way of censure.

"Of course, you do, my lord." The doctor seemed to shake himself. "I'll go find some seeds, shall I?"

Since the rest of the family was still looking at Llywelyn with something akin to horror, he decided he'd better explain. "If Corwen had anything to do with his own illness, hopefully he will wake and tell us about it. Until then, thanks to Ieuan, nobody needs to know anything is amiss, beyond Dafydd's disappearance. In fact, his disappearance is an excellent cover for our real investigation. It may be that once whoever was meant to use these seeds tries to poison someone, he'll notice we've swapped them out, but by then, he will have moved the vial. We can rotate guards through the kitchen until we learn his identity."

Math's expression turned rueful. "If only we had a better way to watch without anyone knowing. Guards are a little obvious."

Meg raised her eyebrows. "Well, we might."

Beside her, Anna gave a little laugh. "You mean a camera? What about one of those little ones Mark is always playing with? He may have chosen to stay in London, but he consented to ration a few of his toys out. I'll see if Livia can hunt one up." She stood and then bent to kiss Llywelyn's cheek. "I'm okay with this new plan. For now."

Llywelyn patted her hand where it rested on his shoulder. "Give the children a hug for me."

Anna walked away, greeting various members of the court on her way. Llywelyn was glad to see two designated guardsmen fall in around her. Nobody went anywhere without a guard under normal circumstances, much less this week.

Meg had been following their daughter with her eyes too but now she looked at him. "What if someone unrelated notices the vial behind the cheeses first?"

"It's the same risk the person who left the seeds behind the cheeses was taking in the first place," Llywelyn said.

"For that reason, I suspect they were intended to be used sooner rather than later," Carew put in.

"But on whom?" Although Math's words were intense, his manner was casual, with one arm draped across the back of the chair his wife had just vacated. To anyone watching, it looked as if he didn't have a care in the world.

"That is the question, isn't it?" Llywelyn said. "With Dafydd gone, our poisoner might well walk away."

"Or he'll pivot to someone else, an easier target." Meg straightened in her chair. "It goes without saying, although I will say it anyway, that Dafydd's guard needs to transfer its attention to Arthur."

"It was done from the moment his father disappeared from that battlement," Carew said.

"Which brings me to ask if you are going to let Arthur do something about it." Christopher had arrived at the table, having come in from a side entrance, and took the seat vacated by Anna. For once, he was not backed by representatives of his multi-national friend group. Usually that included William de Bohun, Huw ap Aeddan, and Robbie Bruce. Even the fact that both Christopher and William were married appeared to have made little difference in their bond.

"Who? Arthur? What do you mean by that?" Meg looked sharply at her nephew. "I can see in your eyes that you have an idea I am not going to like."

"Probably not, Aunt Meg." He turned his attention to Llywelyn himself. "We could go get him."

The family had responded with uproar when Llywelyn had talked about putting the yew seeds back in the kitchen. Christopher's far more outrageous proposal was met, by contrast, with silence.

Llywelyn respected the offer, even as he said, "We have to give Dafydd time. We wouldn't want to arrive in Avalon only to find he and Lili have already come home."

"I wasn't suggesting going right this instant. But I am worried, as you must be, that David did not survive—" he put out a hand to his aunt when she opened her mouth to protest, "—and if he didn't, right now Lili is alone in Avalon with no way to come home."

The fact that neither Christopher's friends nor his very perspicacious wife were with him made his suggestion that much more compelling.

With a glance at his mother-in-law, who was looking mutinous, Math countered, "Dafydd would have landed where he was meant to. After that, Chad Treadman is there. He will find them."

"Even so," Christopher refused to be put off, "if Aunt Meg really was sent back to us two years ago, even in the midst of battle and while falling from a tower, you know whatever is going on there has to be bad."

"I admit the thought has occurred to me too." Against all expectation, Llywelyn found himself in accord with his nephew.

"Exactly!" Christopher practically leapt at him to find him an ally. "It has never been more annoying that cell phone signals can't traverse the void from one universe to another."

"Well, they can't. Them's the rules." Meg's tone implied the need to put a stop to the conversation. "I don't want to lose any more family members to that same void."

"All the more reason to start thinking about alternatives," Christopher said with a finality, as if Meg had supported him instead of disagreed.

"And that alternative is sending someone after Dafydd and Lili?" Math's arm was still across the back of the chair, but there was more tension in his body than before. He knew what Christopher was asking as much as any of them, since he'd been to Avalon too.

"It is." Christopher soldiered on. "My point in speaking of Lili a moment ago was to suggest that we should put a time limit on how long we leave them there. I'm not saying to go now, tonight, but if they don't come back by the end of the tournament, we have to consider the worst: David is dead and Lili is there alone, or they have been captured and are incapacitated."

Math leaned forward. "Are you proposing that you yourself be the one to go?" There was a dangerous tone in his voice Llywelyn hadn't often heard.

Christopher either didn't hear it or persevered despite it. "Yes, of course. I'd rather not die in the attempt, however."

"So it's Anna you need." Math's tone darkened further. "Or Meg? Or maybe you do mean to ask Arthur."

Christopher raised one shoulder in a half-shrug. "I have never wished I had the gift more than I do now."

"Arthur is a child." Carew had been keeping silent in this family conversation, but he couldn't mask his aghast tone. "Would you ask this of your own child when you have one?"

"Not as an infant. Of course not." Christopher said. "But Arthur is eight years old. We know he can travel because he's done it before. Twice, obviously." He sounded remarkably like Dafydd. Llywelyn wasn't entirely sure when his nephew had grown up, but somehow it had happened when he wasn't looking. Christopher, in addition to being David's cousin and the Hero of Westminster, was a member of Earth Two's version of MI-5, known here as *Y Ddraig Goch*. Livia, in fact, was his boss. There wasn't much point in placing him in the post if they didn't appreciate his worth and use him.

"With David gone, my lord, Arthur is King of England. It isn't possible." The fact that Carew had suddenly become formal in his speech indicated how important he viewed his conclusion.

"Cadell could," Meg said softly, her eyes on Math's face. "He has done it before too."

Math's expression was remarkable for its lack of emotion. "If he knew what Christopher was asking, he would want to."

"Besides," Christopher attempted a grin, "with this whole poisoning issue, can you really say it's any safer to stay here?"

20

September 19 -Avalon

David

All those years ago, Cassie's grandfather had accepted her relationship with Callum, as well as the craziness of her time traveling, with hardly more than a blink. It had been his truck that Cassie had driven west with Callum, Mom, and Anna. At one point, they'd ended up at another Walmart in western Oregon, before taking the bus to California. There, they'd been "rescued" by MI-5, who hadn't turned out to be as completely an ally as they'd hoped.

They'd been saner than the CIA, however. David still didn't trust them, but he didn't despise them the way he did the CIA. Chad, on the other hand, so far had proved himself to be reliably in their court. Still, as Chad himself had said, his power was limited, even in a world run by oligarchs.

Here on the reservation, the Tribes seemed to be doing a respectable job of keeping the outside world at arm's length, and their priorities were much more in line with what David was used to in Earth Two. For starters, the political landscape here was very personal. Maybe that was one reason Cassie had been able to survive so well on her own for the five years she'd lived in Scotland before she'd found Callum.

As Deanna had driven them along smaller and smaller roads, the last one not even paved, Lili had begun to relax beside David. The trees and the quiet comforted her, just as they did him, even as Deanna grumbled, "Are you sure we're going the right way?"

She was definitely growing on David. "Are you wondering if the epinephrine—or the walnuts before them—addled my brain?"

At first Deanna didn't realize David was teasing her, and she whipped her head around to see him grinning. She swung back to face front. "I don't think that. I wouldn't."

"I'm exhausted and I feel like crap, but I like maps. I studied this whole area after Mom and Anna came here. Callum pointed out Art's house to me, and I remembered. It's just as well you had a paper map, because it made it easier to find it again." David leaned forward so he could see through the windshield. "This is your right turn."

Given that Deanna worked in this area, David would have thought she'd know how to get around better than he did. She could have studied the maps too. It only went to show how dependent on technology everyone in Avalon had become. You didn't need to memorize phone numbers because they were programmed into your phone. You didn't need to learn the way to a place because all you had to do was ask your phone to guide you. All of a sudden, those admittedly fantastic tools had become crutches.

They drove up the long driveway to Art's house. The sun had been setting as they'd left Mission, and they'd driven most of the way in the dark, which had made it harder to navigate and made them more visible from the air. Nonetheless, they hadn't heard any helicopters, nor detected any pursuit at all.

David was already opening the car door as they braked to a stop. "Let me do the talking, at least at first."

He walked towards the front porch, happy to find he wasn't unsteady on his feet. He felt like a mountain had been dropped on him, but he knew he had to keep going. The house had a handmade look to it, not unlike one of his father's hunting lodges in Eryri, though with several cable and satellite dishes poking up from the roof. *Someone* had internet and television. The front porch ran the full length of the house, and as David reached the steps, the door opened to reveal a young man in jeans, t-shirt, cowboy boots and hat, with a shotgun held down at his side.

"Hello." David was suddenly far more alert. He knew better than to step onto the porch, and the man didn't rack the gun. Before he could speak, David continued, figuring he was the supplicant here, and it was important to avoid misunderstandings. "I'm Dafydd ap Llywelyn." He went for the Welsh, hoping that would mean something to the man. "One of Cassie's friends."

"I know who you are." One might have thought this was a good thing. He could even have been happy and excited, but his face when he spoke was entirely without expression. Although possibly younger than David, he had the demeanor of a man who'd seen the worst and expected it to return at any moment, probably in the form of a bunch of yahoos in a black SUV. "Thought you were government people."

"We do have one government person with us." David tipped his head to where his companions waited. "Her name is Deanna."

Deanna had opened the car door and was standing behind it, like it was a shield. As the man looked at her, she raised a hand.

"I know her." His tone implied that wasn't a good thing either, but then he said, in Deanna's direction, "My little sister Paisley is on the soccer team with your daughter."

"I know Paisley! She's been a good friend to my Chloe."

Earlier in the Walmart, David had been relieved that Deanna was part of the community. Now he relaxed even more. This man genuinely knew her. Until now, they'd had only Deanna's word that she was who she said she was. Just because she worked for the FBI, rather than the CIA, didn't mean she was on their side, but that she'd told the truth put her one step closer to it. Last time he'd come to Avalon, he'd thought he could control the situation. He'd been arrogant to think he understood or could account for every possible level of complication, and he was working very hard not to make that mistake again.

The man still didn't let them in the house. "Art never got that truck back."

"I will apologize to him as soon as I see him." David had already said he was sorry to Art over the phone, and Callum had compensated him years ago. The point stood, however. Art never had gotten the truck back. David paused, thinking that if he was to be worthy of this man's trust, the only way to achieve it was through full disclosure. "Other government people may be on their way here, maybe some of the same ones who pursued my mom and sister back then. Maybe Russians too."

That prompted the man to finally purse his lips. He turned his head slightly to the left in order to call through the open door behind him. "Art! Someone's here to see you. It's that disappearing king from TV."

David supposed this description was as accurate as any other. He turned towards the car and made a motion to summon the others. Lili hopped out, and she was at his side by the time Art appeared on the porch. His hair was almost entirely gray, but his back was straight and his eyes clear.

At the sight of the three of them arrayed before him, Deanna a step or two behind David and looking wary, he nudged his companion. "What are you doing showing them your gun?"

"Sorry, Uncle. I thought I was protecting you."

"I know, Chuck." Art patted the young man on the shoulder, while at the same time urging him back inside the house with some words David either didn't hear properly or were in another language. They exchanged something of an intense look before Art added, "You are always looking out for me, and I appreciate it, but they're family. Close enough, anyway."

"Cassie sends her love," Lili said in her perfect American English. "They are all doing well. Gareth too."

"I'm glad to hear it." Art's heavily lined face split into a smile. He knew about Cassie and Callum's son, Gareth, and everyone else besides, because David had spent some time on the phone with him two years ago from Chad's house after his multi-death experience at the hands of the CIA. He hadn't been able to see Art then. He was glad he was getting the chance now, even if under adverse circumstances.

"My apologies that we are in need again," David said.

"When you told me last time about what they'd done to you, I was worried for you. I told you that your outside could look all right, even when you aren't so well on the inside." Art peered at him. "I'm thinking it's the other way around today. Your face doesn't look too good, but you seem okay to me. What did they do to you this time?"

David put his hands to his cheeks. It wasn't that he'd forgotten about the anaphylaxis, or wasn't completely exhausted in the aftermath of it, but they'd been busy.

"This isn't anyone's else's fault," Lili said, "except maybe mine. Dafydd and I were standing on the battlement at Carew Castle eating walnuts. They didn't agree with him."

"I have a cousin who can't eat tree nuts, just like you, and a nephew who almost died from his first peanut butter sandwich. I don't like nuts much myself, so you'll have no trouble here." The whole time Art had been talking, he'd been looking each of them up and down in turn. His eyes lingered a little longer on Deanna's face.

She made a motion with one hand. "I'm sorry about what happened with your great-niece."

"She has always had a talent for trouble." A gleam of amusement lit his eyes. "Let's get you inside. You're just in time for dinner."

"Thank you." Lili didn't hesitate.

Art tucked her hand in the crook of his arm in order to properly escort her. She didn't need it, but both of them seemed to like it. "Now, I want to hear all about Cassie and her little boy."

21

September 19 -Earth Two

Michael

"This still isn't my thing, you know," Livia said. "Investigating."

"You're the head of *Y Ddraig Goch*," Michael said. "Of course, it's your thing."

"The head of *Y Ddraig Goch*, as glamorous as that job is," Livia rolled her eyes, "means organizing people and letting *them* do their jobs. We didn't find a spy two years ago when we looked. Maybe that was a failure on our part rather than because there was nobody to find."

"In our former life, I was a soldier and a medic. Once I met David, I became his bodyguard, which I'm pretty sure doesn't qualify me as a detective either. Learning on the job is what we do here. Anyway, determining any individual's comings and goings over the last few days wouldn't be easy even if we were trained investigators."

Livia laughed. "I suppose I am the boss. What's the point of being one if not to run things as I see fit. If nothing else, we are good at keeping secrets."

Michael and Livia weren't much for public displays of affection, but he put his arm around his wife's shoulders nonetheless and squeezed once. They weren't even technically married, though he thought he might be the only one in Earth Two who remembered that. Now that their daughter Arya was a year old, maybe it was time they formalized things. It had never seemed important. Besides, if they ever got back to Avalon they'd have to do it again anyway, because they wouldn't have a marriage certificate. Just this week, Michael had been meaning to talk to David about it, but as with every week prior to now, it had never seemed to be the right time. He supposed he ought to start with a ring.

"We figured things out in Wales. We can figure them out here." She shot a grin at him. "So we do what we always do: we make it up as we go along."

The Wales investigation to which Livia was referring had occurred several years ago in Avalon, after David had been shot during an interview, which sent him back to Earth Two. Michael and Livia had gone after the shooter, an investigation which had ultimately brought them to Earth Two as well.

Michael pulled out the expired EpiPen he'd been carrying around in his pocket, almost like a talisman. "I should have managed things differently."

"David was dying, and Avalon reached out and plucked him like a flower. You need to stop feeling like it's your fault." Livia was matter-of-fact, but then she bumped her shoulder into his. "See, I can do pep talks too."

Michael wasn't sure that what she'd said qualified, but he could agree that her perspective was a good way to look at things, and they arrived a little more contentedly at the main gatehouse to the castle. They had already talked to those on duty at the inner gatehouse, who had seen nothing amiss that afternoon. While people of all types had been in and out of the castle, no complete strangers had been admitted to the inner bailey.

That wasn't a surprise, but it did reveal the most disconcerting thing about finding the yew seeds in the kitchen: the person who left them, and the person who intended to use them (if they weren't the same person), had access to the castle.

Once the vial had been returned to the kitchen and the camera placed in a spot nobody would notice, those that remained in consultation were just the former MI-5 officers, Cassie, Callum, and Livia, plus Michael. As the founding members of *Y Ddraig Goch*, and with no real duties at the tournament, nor a desire to participate in it, the bulk of this investigation, if that's even what this was, needed to fall to them.

Michael momentarily put away his phone, which was connected to the camera in the pantry. It gave him a notification when someone went in or out. Even this late in the evening, the stream was fairly constant.

The guard on duty at the entrance to the gatehouse straightened to attention. "My lord. My lady."

Like all the twenty-firsters, David had bestowed noble status on Michael and Livia to facilitate their progress through medieval society. In Paris, they'd been pretending to be visiting nobility from Sicily, but since their return, they had been given the Earldom of Lancaster, left vacant all this time since the death of Edmund Crouchback, King Edward's younger brother.

"I assume it isn't news to you that the king has gone to Avalon?" Michael didn't see any point in beating about the bush.

The guard's eyes lit. "I saw it happen! One moment King David and Queen Lili were on the battlement, and the next they were gone. I confess I ran around the outside of the curtain wall, so afraid of what I might find ..." His voice trailed off, as it would.

"My wife and I have been charged with speaking to you tonight about exactly what you saw, and if you noticed anything unusual up until that moment. Have you seen anyone you didn't know moving about the castle? Is there anything that gave you even a moment of concern?"

The guard, whose name was Adam, narrowed his eyes as he thought. He was working hard at it, but Michael could see he wasn't coming up with anything he wanted to say. A good thirty seconds passed. Livia shifted beside him, but she didn't speak, giving the man the time he needed.

As it turned out, he hadn't been racking his brain for memories but rather preparing to answer as fully as he could. For people who had nothing to hide, cooperation wasn't a problem. "My shift began at Nones, so I wasn't on duty before that. I can't speak to anything that happened this morning."

The liturgy of the hours was something Michael had known nothing about before coming to the Middle Ages. Because Christian religious time was the only time kept in this era, he'd learned the eight *hours* of the day: *Matins, Lauds, Prime, Terce, Sext, Nones, Compline,* and *Vespers.* The first four holy offices took place before noon, which was *Sext,* or *sixth* hour. The modern word for *noon* came from *Nones,* which meant ninth hour. In the Middle Ages, that was actually three o'clock. At some point a century or so from now (according to Meg), *Nones* came to mean the sixth hour instead of the ninth, and thus the modern *noon.* Go figure.

"When I came on duty, the tournament was in full swing and probably a dozen people went by me in each direction every half hour. I didn't know them all. I was told not to stop anyone unless they looked suspicious. That's been our instruction here at the outer gates for the last week."

"How about earlier, yesterday or in the days before that?" Michael asked.

Adam looked a little rueful. "We see so many things."

"I don't know what you mean by that," Michael said.

"Just yesterday, I witnessed a screaming match between a stable lad and one of the maids. She's pregnant, and he swears he isn't the father. That isn't going to end well." Adam took in a quick breath. "Steward Elis didn't like the taste of the first batch of ale and let his opinion be known; the baker burned half a dozen loaves of bread before he got the fire right; I saw two knights arguing intensely outside the smith's works, though about what I couldn't tell; four young noble lads were so drunk at the noon hour they were swaying; and I am aware of at least three women who have eyes for men who are not their husbands. Oh, and Cook Enith left her post in the middle of the day, to return an hour later."

Michael shifted his stance. "This was yesterday?" At Adam's nod, he added, "Do you know why?"

"Of all I just said, that is what you care about? I didn't speak to her. It wasn't any of my business, and she was hurrying in the midst of several others. She surely wasn't a threat. Now that I think on it, I knew it was she only because a sudden gust of wind blew back her hood as she entered the gatehouse. Otherwise, she had it pulled forward to shield her face."

"Thank you. You have been very helpful." Livia paused. "Do you know the identity of the two knights?"

"One was Roger de la Pole."

"You're sure?" Livia asked.

"He is well known around here because he was fostered at Manorbier Castle a few miles away. William de Barri is the castellan, a cousin to our Lord Carew and married to Roger's sister."

Roger himself was an illegitimate son of Gruffydd ap Gwenwynwyn, once the ruler of Powys, who had sided with King Edward in the wars against Llywelyn. At one point, Owain, Roger's older brother, had conspired with Dafydd, Llywelyn's younger brother, to assassinate Llywelyn. That part of the family so hated Llywelyn that they had chosen to forgo their lands west of Offa's Dyke and become English rather than bow to him when he was acknowledged King of Wales. Roger had come to the tournament with a city-sized chip on his shoulder. It was he who'd broken William de Bohun's wrist. Thankfully, Abraham had declared it only a hairline fracture.

Thus, it was no surprise to hear he was overheard having an argument. "And the other?"

"I've seen him around, but I don't know his name. All I can say is that he's very handsome."

Before Adam had answered, Michael had honestly thought their questioning was done and had been about to turn away. "Can you tell us anything more about him?"

Adam's face screwed up in thought. "He wore a badge I didn't recognize—an eagle on a red background. With a crown."

Michael frowned. "But that would be—" He glanced at Livia.

"Gela?" Livia was looking as nonplussed as Michael felt. That was the place in Sicily they had been pretending to be from in Paris. It would certainly be awkward to meet a nobleman for whom it was genuinely home. "Why did you think he was handsome?"

"Because he was." Adam spoke as if what he meant should have been obvious. "He was my height with dark hair."

"Could you tell how old he was?" Michael asked.

"Twenty-five?" Adam himself might not even be twenty, so Michael couldn't be surprised he wasn't very good at distinguishing the age of an older man. "May I ask why the questions? Does this have anything to do with the king? Did he not go to Avalon on his own volition?" It had finally occurred to Adam that the questions didn't necessarily make sense within the context of David's disappearance.

"He did," Michael said. "Not to worry."

Not to foster doubt had always been the challenge with any kind of open investigation, in that they couldn't at the same time ask intrusive questions and pretend nothing was amiss. What's more, as Adam had indicated, they still needed to allow free passage through the outer gatehouse. This wasn't just for workers. The tournament grounds were full of noblemen from, apparently, every corner of the European world. They would take offense at having their movements impeded.

For now, restricting access would hinder too many people with too many diverse jobs and needs, not to mention effectively telegraphing to everyone at the tournament that David's people were worried about something. Up until now, the world at large knew only that David couldn't die because he could travel to Avalon at will.

Unlike the man in front of him, however, Michael didn't necessarily take comfort from that fact.

22

David

As Lili disappeared inside the house with Art, she was describing Gareth's cheerful temperament. Neither David nor Deanna had moved yet, though they had bent their heads in thanks to Art for inviting them in. It was odd to think how that motion was still a cultural norm for Americans, seven centuries, a continent, and a universe away from the last time someone had bent their head to David a few hours ago.

Now David watched Deanna take in their surroundings more thoroughly, not dissimilarly to what Art had just done as he'd surveyed his domain: the cabin; the dirt yard; the long winding driveway, most of which was only faintly visible in the starlight; the half-dozen twenty-plus-year-old vehicles lined up neatly off to one side of the garage; and one new Toyota minivan that gave David a moment's pang to look at. It was white, not blue-green like Aunt Elisa's had been, but if Art offered to loan it to him, he decided right then and there he would refuse.

Deanna was still hesitating on the first step of the porch. "Sir—"

David cut her off—and not in order to quibble with her calling him *sir*. "I know you're nervous about this, but we have to eat with them."

"You're the one who almost died this afternoon," Deanna said. "You're the one who has to face the consequences of coming here being a bad idea. How are you not worried?"

"How worried should I be?"

"As an FBI agent, I am contractually obligated to reassure you about the motives of a fellow agency, but I honestly don't know what to think. Your friend Chad said your arrival produced no *flash*. Certainly nobody told me about it in the minutes before my daughter texted me that video and the phones went down. We could be on our own out here, but just because I know something about the circumstances of your time traveling doesn't mean I know everything. A lot of stuff crosses my desk, but I wouldn't know what doesn't, would I?"

David had to suppose that was true.

"The CIA knows Art is one of your contacts, so that means the Russians know it too. D.C. is a sieve under the best of circumstances. Every spy agency on the planet could be on their way here right now, just in case. The whole world saw that video. Your arrival at that Walmart is no secret. There may have been no flash, but even if you've disappeared again, nobody is going to just assume there was no flash for your departure either and you're back in Earth Two. Someone is going to guess where you might go and think it worth investigating. *And* they're going to link you to me."

"How?"

Deanna gave David a look that was truly puzzled. "Aside from the cameras in that Walmart? Or a video taken by a shopper of me crouching beside you? Or the fact that Josh the pharmacist is very talkative? The NSA has technology that picks up that stuff in real time and flags it."

"Even knowing all that, we still can't head out again. One, we aren't geared up; two, we came here in the first place because we have nowhere else to go; but more than any of that, this is Cassie's *grandfather*. It's been years since she's seen him. There is no way we can leave without sharing hospitality."

"Is that bit of politeness going to be worth it if we're caught?"

But as Deanna asked the question, Chuck returned, shotgun still held loosely in his hand. He was frowning, but not at them. "You're lucky we are here at all. Everyone else is in the teepee village in town." At David's blank expression, he added, as if it explained everything, "You know, for Round-Up."

"We hope we can keep being this lucky." David nodded, remembering from his childhood what Chuck was talking about. He'd grown up in Oregon, after all, and thus was aware that the Pendleton Round-Up was *the largest all-volunteer rodeo west of the Mississippi,* held during the second full week in September. It struck him, a little whimsically, that the rodeo here was the functional equivalent of the Arthurian tournament he'd left behind in Earth Two. "Why aren't you there?"

"Art wasn't feeling well, so me and Susanna drove him home and were going to keep an eye on him tonight. Art would say it was because we were meant to be here." Chuck appeared to accept the *karmic* element of the situation without question, for which David had to be grateful. Acceptance had taken him a lot longer, and he was pretty sure Deanna wasn't nearly as far along in the process as Chuck. Because, if Chuck and Art were *meant* to be right here, right now, so was Deanna.

At the same time, it was dangerous to assume too much about any situation. Likely, if they had arrived at Art's house and nobody had been home, but the door had been left unlocked (as Cassie reported homes often were, both in town and on the reservation), David would have called that *meant to be* too. The world, and circumstance, were often what you made them.

David came fully up onto the porch so he could stand face-to-face with Chuck. "My friend here is concerned that we are putting you in danger. It is likely we have effectively led the CIA, and who knows who else, right to you."

"We know. That's what Art sent me inside to take care of. I made a few calls."

"How could you make calls?" David said. "Deanna said there's no service out here."

"Oh, there's service, all right, if you know how to get it. Which we do."

David's heart speeded up. "I need to make a call."

At the request, Chuck's eyes narrowed. "We are a sovereign nation, and we decline to be used as a tool of any foreign government. These days, right here is where everyone who is anyone comes for privacy."

David put up both hands. "I would be calling Chad Treadman. Lili was on the phone with him in the Walmart in town when our service cut out. Chad has proved himself to be a friend. He can help get us out of here, which is what I think you really want."

Chuck's expression softened slightly. "We were getting in our vehicle and lost service too. I was talking to my cousin. It was like a whole section of town went dark."

"That shouldn't happen," Deanna said.

"Government people are behind it," Chuck said darkly. "You know they are."

David wasn't going to argue this point, since he had nothing to argue it with. Likely, Chuck was right. The question was *which* government people.

Then Chuck grinned. "We don't have to worry about that out here though. We have our own satellites." Just as quickly, the smile went away. "The company that runs it is in trouble, though. I don't know what we're going to do if they cease operations or sell to someone else. We have people counting on us." His chin hardened. "And we aren't going back to the way things were!"

Then he made a dismissive motion with his head. He was proving as talkative as Josh, once they got him going. "We'll be keeping watch for you. A minute ago, there was an accident down the road a ways in front of Bill Johnson's place. Or at least that's what it looks like. It's blocking the road. Nobody's coming to look for you just yet. And if they do, we'll have fair warning."

He turned to go back inside, indicating they should come with him. Meanwhile, Deanna said, for David's ears alone, "Real privacy went out the window a long time ago but, to their credit, the Confederated Tribes have made privacy their new money-making endeavor, moving beyond their casino to a real problem they were uniquely placed to solve. They're making a fortune charging outsiders a premium to hold meetings in their resort. It isn't the one just off the highway, but a new one, in the middle of nowhere. It's exactly where the rich and famous want to be." Deanna paused. "It's also not far from where we are currently standing."

"She's right." Chuck had apparently overheard at least the last bit of what Deanna had said. "We are *the new Sun Valley of the mountain west*." He spoke with a certain level of glee, though David wasn't entirely sure what he meant by it. It wasn't only Lili who was out of her depth with the language being used. Last time he was here, he hadn't remembered so much slang. Then again, not very many people outside his immediate circle had talked to him either, and most of them had been far more formal than Chuck.

Regardless, they had to accept Chuck's assurances. And they did need to eat. Chuck's wife, Susanna, had made enough taco fixings to feed twice as many people as were present.

Even if Deanna had been reluctant at the start, she was exuberant in her praise and thanks, proving she had been raised right. Over the course of their conversation on the porch, Chuck had become, if not friendly, at least cordial, and it seemed the two of them had achieved a certain meeting of the minds. While he and Deanna took turns eating and patrolling the perimeter of the property, David was finally able to get Chad on the phone.

"I did what we discussed, David." Chad was reassuring and, as he talked, David felt like he was hearing the first good news about Avalon in a long while. "The Bangor Institute is up and running and is open to everyone. We have a team, ready and waiting to go back with you. It can be different this time."

At long last.

Even under the current circumstances, which were (as usual) out of his control, David felt a calm settling on him. Though he would turn twenty-nine in November, and thus had now spent more of his life in Earth Two than in Avalon, he wanted things to be well here. There was still something about Avalon that was home.

23

September 19 -Avalon

Sophie

After the Walmart, they'd had no choice but to drive to Chad's compound and await events. Initially, Sophie had been talking with Chad nonstop, since the phones were working again, but even he had run out of things to say. All the while, George and Andre had been preparing their gear.

Sophie stopped by the warehouse-like basement of the house to find Andre cleaning a weapon she was quite sure he'd cleaned at least twice already. George was on the other side of the room, some thirty feet away, to all appearances preparing to assault the CIA complex at the airport. Certainly if David was thrown out of any more airplanes, they intended to be first on the scene to rescue him. The satellite system was back up. They would see a flash if David left.

Andre bumped her shoulder with his. "How are you holding up?"

"That's such an American way to phrase it."

"That isn't an answer."

"I'm fine. Trying not to worry, just like you."

"At least this Deanna person checks out," George said.

"She may have handed them right to the CIA," Sophie pointed out.

"Which is why we are getting ready." Andre snapped the magazine back into his gun and put it in its holster.

"You want to tell me what's going on with this whole satellite thing?" George asked. "I'm way behind the curve."

Sophie glanced at Andre, who shrugged. "You do it. You understand it better than I do."

"Are you aware of the intelligence gathering networks of various government agencies?" she said.

"Sure," George said, "former CIA, remember?"

"Until two years ago, the system run by the NSA relied on a web of cameras, phone networks, and satellites. It had been growing in complexity for decades, but was essentially dependent on a preponderance of available technology and people's willingness to share information about themselves."

"You talk about it as if that's all in the past."

"For a reason. Even before you shot David, a whole new system was in the works, which included the full power of GCHQ, which is the British version of the NSA. The Canadians got in on it too. And the Israelis. What's more, a significant portion of their efforts have been focused on David."

"You can't be serious. Why?" George was so intent, he hadn't even corrected her this time about how he hadn't *shot* David but *shot at* him.

"Governments are naturally conservative," Sophie said. "At the very least, they feel the need to control what they don't understand."

George laughed. "Boy do I know that."

"The network is augmented by the data the CIA collected from all the times David traveled back and forth at their instigation," Sophie continued. "It was intended to have a near-immediate response rate because it was tied to emergency services in the US and the UK. Outside either country, it would send a notice to that location's police force with a message saying, essentially, *armed and dangerous*. Once the system caught his scent, so to speak, it could track him anywhere in the world."

"It was built to track anyone, but it was *trained* to track David," Andre added.

George was looking from one to the other, a bit stunned. "So what you're saying is that it would see David and organize a response to his location in a matter of minutes."

"Exactly. It's just computers, but AI has advanced a lot since you were locked up. The data is only as good as what has been programmed into it but, as I said, the data on David is good." Then Sophie made something of a helpless motion with one hand. "What saved all of us is that the US had an election, and Chad got a bee in his bonnet. You owe your freedom to that fact." The phone in her hand buzzed again, and she flipped it over to see Chad's image on the screen. "Speaking of …"

Chad started talking the moment she connected the call. "I just talked to David."

It was as if the elephant that had been sitting on Sophie's chest had finally decided to get up and walk away. "Where is he?" She put the phone on speaker so the men could hear.

"Cassie's grandfather's house."

"Is he still with Deanna?" George asked.

"Apparently so."

"Consider us in the vehicle." Andre shrugged into a suit jacket to cover his gun. "We'll phone again once we're on the road."

George was already at the door to the tunnel that led from the basement of this mansion to a nearby house, which Chad also owned, though his name wasn't on the deed. The point was to throw anyone watching off their trail. Chad thought of everything, and tried to control everything, a natural impulse for someone with virtually unlimited resources. He couldn't fix human nature, but he could try to account for it.

The tunnel wasn't very deep nor very tall, but it was well-lit. The land upon which this part of town had been built was very rocky, which had limited the scope of the works. At least up here at the top of the hill, it was flatter, with a thick layer of soil that in many places grew wheat. It helped that Chad hadn't exactly acquired the necessary planning permission either. On the whole (and especially since he'd met David), Chad's business transactions had been by the book and above board. Ironically, when it came to David's needs, Chad became a bit less picky.

The caretakers of the neighboring house were an elderly married couple, Francine and Everett, whose job was to live in the house and join the community. And guard the tunnel. The husband, in particular, had a lovely singing voice so was a welcome addition to the local men's chorus and his church choir. They were retired, but enjoyed the free housing and salary Chad provided, along with an occasional means to keep their hand in the game they'd played very well for many years, in those days for the government rather than for Chad, as they did now.

"Did you find him?" Francine was on her feet. In her late seventies now, she had been a senior-level operative.

"Yes." Sophie said. "We are on our way to get him."

"And you!" Everett looked George up and down. "You're really out of prison! We weren't sure we'd live to see the day."

George lifted a hand. "In the flesh."

Andre tipped his head towards the garage. "We have to go."

Francine went to the window, which was open to the relatively warm night. "Clive and Jorge just left."

Once the two members of the security staff, who lived in Chad's house year round, drove out of the mansion in their big black SUV, heading east towards Portland, George, Sophie, and Andre would be leaving from Francine and Everett's house, in an anonymous white Toyota Landcruiser.

It was nighttime now, but the streetlights lit up the quiet road in front of the house. They stood listening and watching for another few seconds. Then they heard the sound of tires crunching on a bit of gravel. A dark-colored sedan slid out of its space amongst the cars parked up and down the road and headed after the big SUV.

"Only one?" Sophie asked softly.

"More will have parked down the street. They do a good job of mixing things up, but they've been watching Chad's house for as long as we've been here." Everett shrugged. "Even with the changing priorities, they're always watching."

George growled. "While I rotted in prison."

"You are out." Sophie put a hand on his arm. "I'm not going to pretend that it's ever going to be over for you, but we need to go."

"I did my evening patrol with the dog five minutes ago," Everett said. "Francine and I walked the perimeter before that. I think you're clear."

"As clear as you can be, anyway," Francine said in something of a warning tone. "The phones went out in the western part of town late this afternoon. I was at the grocery store, and even my satellite phone didn't work. Something was blocking us."

"That was the moment David arrived, which was fortunate for him." Andre had his hand on the garage door, but now he turned back. "I didn't realize the outage was so widespread, though." He and Sophie exchanged a frowning look. "We thought it was just at the Walmart. Someone's got a big suppressor."

"Someone?" Francine said. "The agency has had two years to set up a system all over town, just in case David came back here—or if one of the dozen foreign agencies who've come to town got out of hand. Flip a switch, and everyone goes dark but select, authorized phones."

"The outage didn't reach up here, but all the land down by the Walmart was dark for quite a while. Fortunately, the rodeo distracted most of 'em," Everett said.

Francine nodded at her husband. "I bet they threw that switch the second that first video was posted showing David's arrival. Flash or no flash, they knew his location. It was fortunate for David their field agents were slower off the mark."

"After it happened, I called our cell phone provider to see what they had to say," Everett said. "They implied I should be happy it was fixed."

"What about Wi-Fi?" George said.

"That's another system," Everett said. "We have fiber to our house, but it was out too."

"How could that go out?" Sophie asked.

"If the company that controls the servers is down, it would go down," Everett said. "National security would do it; nobody is going to fight that order."

"I don't believe in the boogey man," Andre said. "I want to know who gave that order."

"Paige." George was sure.

"Maybe. Maybe not." Sophie shook her head. "Shutting down the connectivity might not even have been done to hurt David, but to help him. If nobody in the store could make a call, they couldn't tell anyone he was there, could they? And nobody outside the area could call in. George is free because of that war going on within the CIA. Maybe it's time we stopped assuming we're losing it."

24

September 19 -Avalon

Chad

"**I** don't know what game you're playing, but I'm not going along with it until you tell me the truth—the *real* truth, not some half-assed story that you think will appease me." Hugh wasn't someone Chad had ever met, but he'd always admired the way he'd run his business, sharing out profits to his employees and trying to make the manufacturing of his primary product, screws, as green as possible. It was why, despite the warning from Denise about shady business people and oligarchs, he'd taken the risk and called.

Hugh was very proud of his descent from some European king a couple of hundred years ago, which was why he had made his business slogan, *King of the Screws*. Chad wouldn't have said that was the pinnacle of marketing genius, but Americans had a thing for royalty, probably because they didn't have to put up with it on a regular basis, as well as a fondness for wry humor. Chad could be glad of it, given how much regular people loved David. Hugh had taken the whole charade far enough to have built himself a faux castle as his primary residence in Arkansas.

He also had a hundred year lease on a piece of property in the Blue Mountains of Oregon, the very same mountains, in fact, where David was currently hiding out at Art's house, waiting for Chad to seal this deal so he could move them. The property could be reached directly from Art's house only via a rugged dirt road, but once there, they could link up with a better road heading east.

"I am being watched," Chad said, "every moment of every day for the last three and half years. If a single one of my planes were to file any kind of flight plan anywhere in North America, the CIA would be all over me."

"What makes you think I want them to be all over me?"

"Are you in Oregon right now?" Chad asked.

"No."

"Do you have any intention of going to Oregon anytime soon?"

"No."

"You have property there, though. More importantly, you have an RV sitting on that property that my people need."

"How do you know that?"

"One of my companies made it," Chad said gently. "I keep track."

"I suppose I knew that," Hugh was still grumbling. "Some form I signed."

Chad continued in the same calm tone. "And the reason I haven't told you who it's for is so you don't have to lie. Plausible deniability and all that." He paused. "If it makes a difference, know that I'll owe you."

That prompted a moment of silence worthy of the offer. "What exactly does that mean?"

Chad didn't want to spell it out and didn't have time to do so anyway. But Hugh was a smart guy, and he deserved some answers, given what Chad was asking. Hopefully, someday, he'd be able to give him all of them, if they survived this. "Anything you want it to mean. If you need a favor, I'm there. But I *need* this."

"You might beat around the bush, but I won't. You want me to aid a fugitive."

"He isn't a fugitive at the moment. There are no warrants out for his arrest."

"You're sure?"

"We monitor these things closely, believe me. He isn't even on the no-fly list."

"Who did you have to bribe to ensure that?"

"No bribery," Chad said mildly, telling himself not to take offense. "You do realize we're talking about the King of England? He would personally be in your debt too."

"He's king in another universe. I'm not sure what good that will do me. He's hardly ever here, and when he is here, he needs help, not the other way around."

Chad allowed himself a genuine laugh. "You wouldn't have thought it would do me any good either, splashing out millions on his behalf, much of which I'm pretty sure he doesn't even know about. But you'd be wrong. And that isn't even to mention the success of the Bangor Institute."

Chad could hear in the silence that followed how surprised Hugh was. "My daughter has just accepted a position in the political science department."

"Good for her." Political science couldn't help but be the beating heart of the Bangor Institute, given David's post-colonial approach to the medieval world. "So you believe me."

"I guess I do." He grunted. "The intelligence community hates you for what you've done."

"Not all of them. Some of them are happy to see abuses exposed." Chad waved a hand, even knowing Hugh couldn't see it. He hoped he sounded breezy. "If you need a sweetener, once this is all over, and it turns out well, I could let it be known that you helped."

"How about an endorsement from King David himself? *The King of England uses the King of the Screws.*"

Chad knew without needing to ask David that he would take a hard pass on that one. He wavered, thinking he could promise David's cooperation and ask forgiveness later, especially since David did have a tendency to disappear without warning. He was opening his mouth to say, "Sure," but instead he said, "I can't ensure that, though of course I can ask."

Hugh gave a grunt that wasn't a commitment.

Chad felt he had to add, "You'll note he hasn't endorsed any of my companies either."

"Then how has helping him helped you?"

Chad laughed outright, pleased to tell the unvarnished truth. "How has it not helped? The man drips sincerity, and to know that he is working with me has made me squeaky clean—more so than maybe I deserve, though I have been working hard on it. I divested myself of all my military contracts, thinking my net worth would take a hit, and instead it has had the opposite effect. Clean water, clean air, education, health—research! Every investment comes up roses eventually. You already know how I've profited from the sale of my planes." He paused. "I believe I use your screws in them."

And if he didn't, he would remedy that oversight immediately. "As your daughter could tell you, the Bangor Institute is the place to be for any serious scientist or researcher."

"She did call you a *rock star* the other day." While Chad tried not to preen, Hugh was still thinking hard. "I hear you just bought Ppl-link." This was a satellite communications system, which was pronounced *Peoplelink*.

"I'm impressed you know that. The finalized paperwork went through eight minutes ago. My people were cursing me up until I told them why." Chad would have rubbed his hands together in glee if he hadn't been using one to hold the phone. "I actually thought about buying it weeks ago, though the price certainly got better in the waiting."

To his credit, Hugh was less focused on the money than the circumstance. "Is that purchase related to your request of me?"

"It is." There was no sense denying it.

"I gather you intend to turn the company around, not break it up and sell it off?"

"I do. I'm not a hedge fund. I make things; I don't destroy them."

"I'm asking because they provide all the communication technology to my RV." He paused. "Which is sitting on my property in the Blue Mountains." Another pause. "I see."

"Just so."

"I want them to stay in business."

"They will."

"So yes, you can borrow my stuff, but on one condition: *I want in on the deal.*"

Chad's mouth dropped open, and he was thankful he wasn't making a video call because it wouldn't have been good for Hugh to see his shock. Bad enough that Chad had emitted a little cough of surprise.

Hugh heard it, but misinterpreted it in Chad's favor. Before Chad could get his head around giving Hugh such a fabulous gift, his new friend hastened to add, "All I want is the opportunity to buy a few shares below the open market price. I don't need anything like a controlling interest. Sell them to me at 1% more than you paid for them. You don't lose, and I win."

So now they were business partners. That wasn't where he thought this conversation was going to go, but he figured it would be okay. Hugh was a good man, and Chad certainly had no intention of screwing him over. Ha.

"Deal."

"Excellent. The RV is yours. Meanwhile, maybe first thing in the morning we'll get out of the country. My wife has been wanting me to take her on a trip. I'll bring the whole family. Grandkids too." Hugh sounded excited and happy. "Thank you!"

"A pleasure doing business."

They hung up.

As Chad held the silent phone in his hand, thinking about whom he needed to call next, he ran back over the conversation. In a matter of minutes, Hugh had gone from wary to reluctant to joyful.

As he'd told Hugh, helping David had been a net positive so far. It could be that this purchase of Ppl-link, and this new alliance with Hugh, would turn out to be one of his best investments yet.

25

September 19 -Avalon

George

George had never been so relieved to have a plan of action. He didn't even mind that he was being told what to do and working with a team rather than operating on his own. He was still on a high from coming out of prison—likely fueled by the near constant stream of caffeine he'd been consuming since that McDonald's meal—such that he almost didn't care what it was he was supposed to be doing.

Even more, he was relieved that David had been on top of things enough not only to think of finding Cassie's grandfather but to remember how to get to his house. It was impressive, especially after almost dying of anaphylaxis. Maybe it was time George stopped being surprised by him. The man could time travel, not to mention was the King of England in an alternate universe. What was a little map memorization compared to that?

The directions to Art's house conveyed by Chad had been specific, but also nonsensical until one arrived at the spot. In addition to blocking all cell and satellite signals but the ones they themselves authorized, the Confederated Tribes had removed all the road signs but those pointing towards the transcontinental highway that ran through the reservation. As it so often did, the federal government had violated the treaty they'd signed with the Tribes to build it, but since it was a done deal, not to mention useful, the Tribes had let it stay.

The invisible war amidst the airwaves, however, continued. Technology, as always, was advancing faster than human ethics or laws could keep up. Even now, George knew without question that US intelligence agencies were training satellites in this direction. Drones were illegal over tribal airspace, which was the only thing preventing the NSA from finding and targeting their vehicle. As it was, with them crouched behind tinted windows in the back, Everett had driven them out of his driveway and down the hill, making sure they didn't have a tail, before handing the keys to Andre. He said it was good exercise for him at his age to have to walk back up the hill.

The only real barrier they faced came within the last mile before Art's house, when they drove around a corner to find the road blocked by three cars and a tow truck, which was trying to pull a fourth car out of a ditch. It did not appear as if much progress was being made.

They'd been warned to expect this, however, so all three got out of the vehicle and approached one of the men standing around watching. "Are you Bill Johnson?" Andre asked.

The man turned to look at them, which was pure theatrics as far as George was concerned, since he'd had his eye on them since their headlights had appeared in the distance. "I am."

Andre made a gesture. "I'm Andre, this is George and Sophie. We are expected."

Without further ado, Bill pulled out his cell phone and snapped a picture of the three of them, which he texted to someone. They didn't bother to ask how it was that his phone worked and theirs didn't. They knew the answer by now. Twenty seconds later, Bill's phone chimed, prompting him to wave a hand at another man, who got into one of the cars. "It's them. Let 'em through."

They got back in the car and drove the last distance to Art's house. George also couldn't help but be impressed with David's thoroughness in inserting yet another layer of security into the proceedings. Or maybe that had been Deanna.

They entered the living room to find David lounging next to Lili on a sofa that was so overstuffed it might swallow them at any moment. Three more people in the room were tribal members, who looked at them with something that could be interpreted as cautious welcome.

Having greeted Art first, George walked across the room to stick out his hand to the stranger in a suit, who'd been hovering on the margins as if unsure of her welcome. "I'm George." He introduced Sophie and Andre again too.

"Deanna Hudson." She was typically FBI serious. "We need to move now. We've been here too long." She tipped her head in David's direction. "He told us about the men in the Walmart, one of whom was impersonating *me!*" Her outrage was palpable. "We need to be gone by the time they arrive." She paused. "*You* need to be gone by then."

"We were not followed," Andre said. "We took precautions."

"David still needs a hospital." Art had been listening without input up until now. Though his voice remained soft, it was impossible to ignore.

"We'll get him the best treatment possible, just as soon as we can," Sophie assured him.

George, meanwhile, had moved to stand in front of David. "Hi." He swallowed down a *my lord*, which had risen unbidden to his lips. This was Oregon, after all, not Westminster Palace. "Clywes i bo' chi wedi bod yn sal." *I heard that you have been sick*. Admittedly, he did use the formal Welsh word for "you".

David looked up at George from his slumped position and laughed. "Dach chi wedi bod yn treulio eich amser yn dda." *You have been spending your time well*. He used the formal "you" as well, something he might not have done with anyone after that first month in Wales before he found out he was Llywelyn's son.

When George had lived in Earth Two, he had heard plenty of Welsh and understood none of it. He was hoping the fact that he'd spent the last two years (which he'd thought were three) trying to learn the language counted for something. "Ges i lawer o amser i wei-thio." Then he switched to English because he wasn't sure he could manage what he wanted to say in Welsh. "If I'd known you'd just bring yourself back here and end up on the run from the CIA again, maybe I wouldn't have bothered saving your life in the first place."

"Sorry." David didn't, in fact, sound the least bit sorry. "Deanna was more concerned about Russians." He did appear exhausted, as well he might, given what their consultation with Chad had told them about the circumstances that had brought him here. "I didn't have any say in the matter."

George had heard about that too.

Lili rose to her feet to hug Sophie hard, but when she let go she glared at George. "I'm not sure why you had to come."

"Let him be, *cariad*." David waved a hand. "He did send me back to you, and here he is on the job again."

"We don't need his help," Lili said.

"If the past is anything to go by," David said, "we do."

"He betrayed us over and over again."

"He did." And then, somewhat to George's surprise, given what he'd just admitted, David held out his hand, asking to be helped to his feet.

George didn't hesitate, grasping first David's hand and then wrapping his arm around his middle, since David staggered upwards as if he were a hundred years old.

Once on his feet, David looked straight into George's eyes. "I sense he has paid for his indiscretions by now. And you have to admit, his Welsh is pretty good."

"My lady, I want to apologize for what I did." George had rehearsed that particular sentence all the way here in the car. "I can't change the past, but I hope that one day you can forgive me for it."

Though Sophie was staring at him like he'd grown two heads, Lili looked rueful. "I have to be grateful for what you did in the end. And it does seem that you paid a price for doing it."

Now George was ready to look away, from both Lili and Sophie. It was his fault their conversation had gotten so personal so quickly. But he forced himself to hold Lili's gaze for another beat before pulling his eyes away and turning back to David.

A quick assessment showed him to be much the same as when George had last seen him, other than having a puffier face, which George attributed to the lingering effects of the walnuts rather than because he'd put on weight. There shouldn't have been much change in physical appearance between twenty-seven and twenty-nine anyway.

David's eyes, however, were different, and maybe not in a good way. To be older and feel older wasn't necessarily a bad thing, but the experience George saw there carried a measure of pain as well as wisdom. And that was probably George's fault. No amount of learning Welsh could make up for being forced to die as many times as he had. Which again was George's fault, since he'd served him up to the CIA as if on a platter.

Given David's attire, he'd been at a fancy event in Earth Two, but not one that had required mail armor. It was also fairly typical of David that he'd had the wherewithal, even on the verge of death, to leave behind his sword, which in Earth Two he never went anywhere without.

"I am sorry about the consequences of helping me." David spoke this time with more feeling.

"My choice." It was the truth. George had never meant to harm David, no matter how much harm had resulted from his actions. "I was doing my job. Even when I shot at you, I was doing my job."

"It was your choice to shoot at me, not to be imprisoned."

"I did it for your own good and that of the planet. Paige could not be allowed to go back with you, and I was the only one who could stop her."

"I know that. Maybe we can leave the past in the past." David eyed him. "Not everyone who spent the last two years in a black site for doing the right thing would feel the way you do."

"They didn't hurt me." George snorted, deciding not to explain all the ways that was a lie. "It's done."

"And you're okay with that?"

"Of course not." George hoped his expression was as calm as he meant it to be. "I intend to use every resource at Chad's disposal to make sure that what happened to you and me never happens to anyone ever again. But until then, this is what we're doing, and I can't help but think that if I do this, then maybe I'll make progress towards that."

David nodded, familiar himself with accepting what one couldn't change. A man could rail against what fate sent him, or he could get on with living through it.

"You and I have a way out." Lili was looking at her husband. "They don't unless we take them with us."

"I know." David wet his lips. "Not yet."

"Do you have a plan?" Sophie asked. "You clearly have a reason to stay that you aren't sharing. Why?"

"Because I have a crazy plan."

"The last plan you had was crazy, and it went utterly awry," George said. "Maybe you ought to share a little more this time *before* you implement it."

David ran a hand through his hair, more uncertain than George had ever seen him. "Two years ago, I confronted the CIA directly. Everything went totally according to my plan until it didn't, as you know."

"Because of Paige," George said.

David nodded. "I'm thinking now that any real help needs to be from someone higher up than anyone we've dealt with so far."

"Chad can help with whatever we need," Andre said.

"Believe me, I am grateful for that. He has already helped, probably even more than he knows. But this time, I think we need more than he can give us." He looked around at everyone, including Deanna, who remained on the margins of the conversation. "It's time we shook things up. We need to stop playing the CIA's game—or any-one's game but our own. We are all sick and tired of being chased across the planet by people who want to control us. Maybe we can't stop them trying, but—"

"—but maybe we can stop thinking like we're casualties al-ready and take the fight to them." George looked at Sophie. "Is that what you meant, back at the house?"

"I guess maybe I did."

David was looking from one to the other. "I don't know what you're talking about, but I was about to point out that you were freed because of Chad's testimony before the Senate Intelligence Commit-tee. What if I testified too?"

"Is Chad powerful enough to set that up?" Art asked. "And could it be arranged soon enough? I am among those who think Da-vid should keep the length of his visits here as short as possible."

Sophie's eyes were bright, and when she spoke next she sounded both confident and excited. "I think David is on the right track, but I wouldn't put him before the SIC when there's something even better: forty-eight hours from now, on Sunday night, there's go-ing to be a joint session of Congress. The Secretary General of the United Nations will be speaking to urge them to pass the legislation package that will begin the process of dismantling the surveillance state. There may be a way to make David a part of that session. He has certainly been a victim of what that legislation is designed to fight."

"*Coincidence?*" Andre said in a sing-song voice. "I think not."

As Sophie got on the phone again with Chad, and everyone else started organizing themselves to leave, George found himself cloaked in a renewed sense of confidence. He might not know how things were going to play out, but nor did anyone else. And this time, George knew with absolute certainty he was on the right side of history.

26

Meg

"How is it you are taking all of this so well? I feel like I've been hit by a truck." Meg pulled back the covers and fell into bed beside Llywelyn, exhausted emotionally and physically. She hadn't been participating in the tournament, but she felt as if every single one of her muscles hurt. Likely that was from clenching them in fear and worry since they'd learned that David and Lili had gone to Avalon.

"Am I doing well?" Llywelyn pulled her into the circle of his arm. "Our son and daughter-in-law have been thrown into Avalon without any aid. Dafydd thought he knew what he was doing when he went with George last time. He was entirely wrong. What he described when he came home ..." His voice trailed off, causing Meg's stomach to clench again. "And yet, he was protected, as always. It will be okay."

Even as she said, "Or it won't," she loved that Llywelyn had adopted that classic Americanism, *okay*.

As it turned out, she hadn't ended up eating much for dinner, despite Llywelyn's best efforts. Her stomach had always been affected by her emotions. There was no reason to expect today to have been any different.

Llywelyn pulled her closer. "I, of all people, know full well what *won't* looks like. That December day fifteen years ago when Anna and Dafydd came to me could have been the end of everything. It wasn't. It won't be now. Avalon took them in."

That sounded good, even to her. "One more time."

Llywelyn rolled onto his side and Meg rolled with him so her back was to his chest. "Which brings me to something I have been meaning to talk to you about for a while but haven't been able to find the words."

Rather than finding her stomach clenching, Meg eased into a more relaxed position. She knew Llywelyn could feel her do it. They'd been together long enough for him to let her settle herself before he told her whatever momentous thing he had to say. "Go on."

"If what happened today with Dafydd happens to me—not that I am allergic to walnuts or anything else as far as I know—you have to let me go."

"Go ... to Avalon?" Even as she asked the question, she knew that wasn't what he meant.

"Marged."

"Llywelyn."

"I am almost seventy years old. An old man among my people. If something happens like what happened at Chepstow eight years ago, I don't want you taking me to Avalon in the hopes of fixing whatever is wrong. If I die here, so be it. Obviously, dying of old age would be my preference. Elisa and Padrig are only eight, and I want to see them grow up, but you know as well as I that the odds are against it. I don't want to die in a hospital bed in Avalon with tubes sticking out of me and none of my family by my side."

Meg settled even further into the bed—and into Llywelyn. "That is going to be hard for me."

"I know."

"Who's even to say that I could take you? I fell from that tower—"

"You went and returned so quickly you barely noticed. But if you want proof, Dafydd's absence should be good enough. God has a plan still."

Meg wasn't going to argue the point, even if she personally was peripheral to it. "If we were in Avalon, going to the hospital would be normal."

"I believe you that it would. But you yourself have said that to do so isn't always the best decision, that too many people who want to die at home die in a hospital, without family around them, enduring a continual stream of hopeless procedures to keep them alive."

"That was close to my father's experience. He should have gone into hospice months before he died rather than a matter of weeks."

"I don't know what you mean by that, but I am certain I don't want that for me." He paused. "And I don't want you to make that decision for me."

"Because that would effectively take away your choice."

"Yes. Thank you for understanding."

She let the silence lengthen. It wasn't a bad silence, and she could feel Llywelyn relaxing behind her as he prepared for sleep. "There isn't something you're not telling me, is there? This isn't the leadup to some medical issue you've been keeping from me?"

"No. I swear it."

She believed him. He might try to protect her from some things, but not this. There had been times when the truth was all they had. "I don't want you to leave me alone."

"I don't want that either, but we knew the day we married it could happen." For the first time, there was a hint of reproach in his voice. "You left me alone first."

"And we swore we wouldn't let it happen ever again. We wouldn't go alone, without each other."

He scoffed. "As if that did us any good. Some things you can't help. *This*, though, Marged; this thing I'm asking of you? *This* you can decide to do. Or not do. Will you promise me?"

Every impulse was screaming at her not to agree, but she couldn't deny him what he had every right to. "I promise."

She felt his nod, and then his arms slackened in sleep.

Meg herself lay awake for a long time afterwards, thinking of the young woman she had been the day she'd met Llywelyn. Even with the winding road her life had followed, she wouldn't change a thing, in Avalon or Earth Two. Whatever had happened and whatever might come, it was a life she and Llywelyn had made together.

27

September 20 -Avalon

George

George loved the dark. Its absence had been one of the hardest things to accustom himself to when he'd been in his cell. Yes, his captors had turned off the lights at "night"—he had to put that in quotes now—but it had never truly been as pitch black in his cell as he'd always liked. He'd learned to sleep with a piece of blanket over his eyes. Now that he was seeing his situation more clearly, it was another form of torture that they'd refused him an eye mask.

He didn't have to worry about that anymore. He was free, and he was driving a fantastical RV, speeding down the road at seventy miles an hour, all alone. The predawn hours of the morning were sometimes the best time of day to be awake. On top of all that, it had always been a mantra with George that it was safer to move than to stay in one place. Any survivor knew that.

Boy did he love his job!

The thought rose unbidden to his mind. This might well be the manic portion of the program, but he wasn't as consumed with hate right now as he had been, not with the road rolling away underneath him and his four passengers asleep. It would have been good to have Deanna with them too, if only to keep an eye on her, but they'd left her behind on a different mission.

All the better to be driving one of Chad's babies, a house on wheels that contained not only the usual kitchen, bathroom with a shower, bunk beds and a large bed in the back for David and Lili, but every upgrade he'd ever thought of and dozens he hadn't. At the very least, Chad had crammed in enough technology to run the country, modeling it on Air Force One. The only differences were that the RV was carrying the King of England instead of the president and it didn't fly.

That was just as well, since it was safer to drive than fly. They didn't have to file a flight plan, for starters. That alone meant they had been able to leave the reservation on back roads, all but undetected. There were no check points, no TSA, no passport control, or any kind of barrier between them and the open road. Even were anyone aware that David intended to speak before Congress, which seemed unlikely as yet, they didn't know how he was going to get there. At a minimum, it was a forty-hour drive to reach Washington DC.

"Could anyone have followed us, really?" David plopped himself into the passenger seat.

George's tone didn't punish him for asking something so obvious—or for disrupting his quiet communion with the road. "There are a lot of smart people in the world. Some of them work for the CIA. Some even are Russian. You need to remember that."

"Where are we now?"

"Safe. Turning towards the morning," George said, wondering as he spoke where that bit of Gordon Bok poetry had come from. His mom used to sing the song to him.

He shifted in his seat, suddenly uncomfortable. Sentiment got in the way of clear thought and action. Mile after mile, he had been eyeing every spot where he could crash the RV and send them back to Earth Two. He didn't necessarily *want* to go, but he would if the only other choice was to be caught. He wasn't going back in a cell, ever again. He certainly wasn't going to allow David to end up in one.

"Does that mean I'm allowed to sit here?"

"Why wouldn't you be?"

David raised his eyebrows. "I admit to being out of date on all things technology, but I thought when we went through a city or town, a camera could take a picture of my face. These front windows are really big."

"Not in this RV."

"I don't know what that means."

George glanced over at him and grinned. It was dark everywhere in the RV except for the lights shining from the dash. Even with every bell and whistle, the RV sported a basic clock, which said 4:03.

"You didn't think Chad would send us off in something that was going to get us caught, did you? Check this out." George pressed a button and suddenly a heads-up display appeared on the windshield in front of David as well as George. It showed how fast they were going, the speed limit, and that George had set the cruise control. It also showed a bit of the road ahead, letting them know it curved to the left beyond their headlights.

"That's cool, but it doesn't explain why I don't need to worry about cameras. I saw the front windshield from the outside before we climbed in. It's tinted a little, but anyone can see through it."

"The display surface works the other way too. To everyone outside the vehicle, we are a white couple in our sixties. I believe you have permed hair and I have a significant beer belly."

"That isn't stereotyping at all." But David had to laugh.

"You love this vehicle too. Admit it."

"I do. I will not deny it. But while the thing with the windshield is a neat trick, we are huge and obvious in every other way."

"Exactly. What better way to evade detection than by not trying? Hiding in plain sight is the oldest trick in the book, and the reason it has that status is because it still works."

"I hadn't thought about it that way."

"Yes, you have," George said. "What is this mad plan of yours other than the definition of hiding in plain sight—or not hiding at all? You clearly understand the concept of *go big or go home*."

David absorbed that idea for a mile, which at seventy miles an hour didn't take as long as it might have. "Is it a mad plan?"

George shrugged. "None of us have a better plan. And Lili is right that you can always go home."

"I admit, at this point, if I did that, I would feel like I was doing so with my tail between my legs. At the very least, we need to restock our Avalonian supplies." David looked out his side window for a moment. "And Chad's researchers from the Bangor Institute would be very disappointed if none of them got to go back with me."

"Are Callum's hands still shaking?"

"Yep."

"Sorry."

"He wouldn't let me bring him here. I've asked a dozen times."

"Just as well, considering."

David turned his head to look at him. "You mean because of this surveillance system everyone's worried about?"

"Our government has always told us we didn't need to worry about surveillance if we weren't doing anything wrong. That's so clearly not true for you, and it's time they admitted it."

"I'm still not sure I understand how it can track me."

"Every human is unique, and the way we look is the least of it. It isn't just fingerprints and DNA, but height and weight, the way we walk and talk. It knows you, David. You've been here enough and given up too much of yourself. Every aspect of you is programmed into it. That's why this RV is so necessary. We can't let you out of it until we get to where we're going."

"So ... am I to understand that this marvelous system went down for three minutes yesterday at the exact same time Lili and I traveled here?"

"Yes."

"Did it do that two years ago when my mom fell from the tower at Berkhamsted?"

"I was in prison, so I can't speak from first-hand knowledge, just what I learned from Sophie and Andre. That time, they did catch the flash. It sparked a massive manhunt that to this day has some quarters thinking one of you is still here and has been for the last two years. Nobody told you?"

"Who would have told me but you guys?"

"Right." George gave a shake of his head.

"Maybe that's why my mom was sent back so quickly two years ago. It really wasn't safe for her here."

"Maybe."

"And that means going before Congress isn't a good idea. I will be exposed like I never have been before."

"The rest of us are going to do everything in our power to ensure that isn't the case." George glanced at David again. It was rare to see him so uncertain, and this was twice since they'd reconnected at Art's house. "You're going to have to be wearing your game face from here on out, the one you put on every day as King of England. You not only have to believe in what you're doing, you have to convince everyone else you believe in it."

"I do believe in it," David said, "more than I can say. But my track record in Avalon isn't exactly stellar."

"It's about the journey, not the outcome. You can't control outcomes," George said matter-of-factly. "You know that as well as anyone."

"I don't even know what I don't know. But I am going to keep asking questions. 2025 isn't 2010 or even 2016. Avalon changes far faster than Earth Two, and my knowledge of the way things work here gets further and further behind. I accept that, but I'm going to need help processing. I'm going to keep asking stupid questions. I hope you can be patient with me."

George snorted laughter. "And that, ladies and gentlemen, is why we all do what we do." He shook his head as if in disgust, though he wasn't feeling disgusted—mostly mocking himself for who *he* had become. "You say stuff like that all the time in Earth Two, which is why your enemies think you are weak. But it means everybody else will follow you to the ends of the earth." He paused. "And beyond."

Then, just as he stopped talking, thinking better of everything he had just said, not that it wasn't true, his phone rang. He held up a hand to stop David from replying, if George's candor hadn't completely silenced him the way it had George himself. He then tapped the receiver hooked around his ear. "Deanna. What's up?"

"They came."

28

September 20 -Avalon

Deanna

Just a bit earlier …

Deanna checked the cameras again, telling herself she was far enough away—in the next house over the hill from Art's—that the intruders could have no knowledge of her presence.

"You were right." Ron, the chief of the tribal police department, looked over her shoulder at the screen, which showed the views of the multiple cameras Deanna had placed hours ago, after David had left and Art had gone to stay at Chuck and Susanna's house. "It's fortunate most of the residents of the reservation are in the teepee village in town, or we'd have an army of vigilantes on our hands."

Before today, it wouldn't have occurred to her to be grateful for the traffic and chaos of Round-Up. "Thanks for backing me up."

Ron then spoke into his radio, talking to his people posted around the exterior of Art's house. "Stay put. Nobody moves without my say-so."

Once David and the others were well away, Art had summoned the tribal police. They'd been followed by Umatilla County SWAT, at the request of both Deanna and Ron. Nobody had been happy to have to pull resources away from the hundred thousand people currently occupying the City of Pendleton, and until the intruders' vehicles had hit the reservation boundary line an hour ago, the mood had been a combination of frustrated and somber.

Naturally, Deanna had needed to read in her boss too. By now, what she had initially thought would be a solitary vigil had officially gotten out of hand. It was hard to believe that only yesterday afternoon she had innocently run into Walmart to pick up a few things and had just been happy to find a parking space.

They watched the two dark SUV's roll up to the front of the house and six figures get out. They wore armor and carried automatic weapons. A moment later, they disappeared inside the house, where she had also placed cameras. The figures moved silently through the rooms. The house wasn't large, and it didn't take them long.

"So they're not CIA," Ron said with an unexpected certainty.

Deanna leaned closer to the screen, as if that would somehow make the figures appear more clearly to her. "Why do you say that?"

"They don't move like Americans." At her glance up at him, he shrugged. "I served in Germany. These folks are European." He sounded remarkably calm about the idea of a European paramilitary force invading his reservation. "Look at the way they signal to each other, the set to their shoulders, and how they hold their weapons."

"Russians," Deanna said.

"Someone who shouldn't be here, regardless."

When Deanna had talked to David earlier about the threats against him, it hadn't been theoretical, given that they were fleeing the Walmart, but what was before her now was very, very real.

She tried to speak as matter-of-factly as Ron. "They aren't here on their own recognizance. Someone is giving them orders—"

Ron made a sharp noise, interrupting her and pointing at the screen. "Lights have come on in the house."

"They're really searching now."

"Well, they aren't leaving here in one piece, that's for sure. There's only one way in and one way out." Ron then responded to a communication via his radio, so Deanna didn't have to remind him of the back road along which Andre had driven his companions to get to Hugh's property further up the mountain. That said, Ron wasn't entirely wrong. The Landcruiser had managed it but no lesser vehicle would have.

Deanna couldn't take her eyes off the multiple camera images, flicking from one to another as she watched the intruders search Art's house. While Ron was turned away, she pulled out one of her new phones, given to her by Art and synced with Chad's new satellite system, and dialed George's number. When he answered, she said simply, "They came."

George put Deanna on speakerphone. "We knew it was only a matter of time. Where are you?"

"Set up in the next house over."

"Don't get too close," David said.

David should have been sleeping, but she wasn't going to tell that to the King of England, alternate universe or not. "I'm not close." Then she related everything that had happened since they'd left, including the idea that these intruders were European.

"Have you told anyone where we went?" David asked softly.

"I have not. They may have been led to believe you drove towards Boise."

"Thank you."

She may never have heard such sincerity in any other person's voice before.

"What was their approach?" George sounded gravelly, either because of the late hour or the stress.

"Stealth. Six guys in two dark SUVs—" She cut herself off as more vehicles drove up the road, headlights extinguished long before they neared Art's house, which was why she hadn't seen them in the cameras sooner. This was likely what had pulled Ron away.

Soon, more figures moved across the cameras' fields of vision, heading towards the entrance to Art's house. Then came the unmistakable sound of guns firing and the chugging of an automatic weapon.

Ron was shouting into his radio from where he was standing on the porch, "You were told not to engage!"

"It isn't us!" came the reply.

Since the first set of intruders had lit up the inside of the house like a Christmas tree, it was as if Deanna was watching a movie being made in real time. She couldn't drag her eyes away.

"What's happening?" George said, urgency in his voice. "Are you okay? I can hear gunfire."

"I'm fine. Two groups are duking it out inside Art's house."

"Who's the second group?" David asked.

"Who's the first? We don't know the identity of either!"

"The CIA was always going to come. They couldn't help themselves," George said.

"If they're at Art's, they could be at Hugh's place too," David said.

"They're not," George said. "His security system would have told us."

"I'm glad you're heading—" Deanna cut herself off. "Strike that. I don't know anything at all about where you're going and I don't want to."

And then Deanna's second phone rang. When she saw it was her boss, she put that phone on speaker too, so George and David could hear what was said. "What the hell is happening over there?"

"You're seeing this too, sir?"

"Of course I'm seeing it! Who are those people? You were told to let them leave, so we could follow and then arrest them at our leisure."

"I know that, sir. I don't know who they are, sir. SWAT isn't involved, nor the Tribes."

"Well we all are now!"

SWAT had closed in on the house once the firing inside ceased, in order to inform those inside that they were surrounded. They were ordered to put down their weapons and come out with their hands up.

Because of the cameras on the inside of the house, Deanna could see one of the surviving intruders hesitate, but then in accented English he shouted through the open doorway. "We surrender! We're coming out!"

For a moment, she thought he might be faking, but then he put his weapon on the floor and stuck both hands out in front of him before following them onto the porch. Four other men inside the house followed suit.

"Where are the others?" Nobody from SWAT had come out of their secure positions yet.

"They're not coming because they can't." The leader started down the steps of the porch, at which point, he was converged upon from all sides and forced to lie face down in the dirt. Only once these five men were subdued did anyone enter the house to clear it.

"Have you ever been a part of a shootout like this before?" Ron was back to looking over her shoulder at the computer screen.

"No." Deanna was so riveted she had momentarily forgotten that she was still on the phone with her boss as well as George and David.

Then their front door swung open, and the SWAT lieutenant (whose call sign was Ten David, oddly) strode towards Deanna and stuck out his hand. "I need to speak to your boss."

Silently, she turned the phone towards him. "Lieutenant Peters would like to speak to you, sir."

"We've got three dead, four seriously wounded, and five captured. Most appear to be foreign nationals. None will identify themselves. We're going to take them all in, though God knows where we're going to put them." He strode off again without waiting for an answer. Ron went with him to see to his own people.

Deanna returned to listening to her superior.

"What have you gotten us into, Hudson?"

"I saved the life of the King of England, sir, at a time when I believed he was being targeted by hostile forces. As has now been proven true."

"And where is this King of England now?"

David and George remained entirely silent, but she could feel their intensity nonetheless. "I couldn't say, sir. They didn't trust me, sir."

Her boss swore once, sharp and curt, but then an instant later reverted to a normal tone. "I wish you'd stuck with them, but then, if you had, we'd probably have a much worse situation on our hands with dead Tribal members instead of Russians. *Russians!* My God. At least it's past dawn on the east coast. The president will have had his two cups of coffee by now."

"The ... president?" Deanna said.

"You really stepped in it this time, Hudson. You are going to remember this day as the breaking of your career."

"Or the making of it, sir."

"Or that." He barked a laugh. "Knowing you."

29

September 20 -Earth Two

Michael

"This is definitely not what I hoped to be doing with my day." Michael put his shoulder to the door of Corwen's hut and shoved. "Shouldn't you be preparing for the archery contest?" Michael himself was somewhat disappointed he wasn't at the hand-to-hand fighting going on right now. Whenever he watched others who were better, he learned something.

"I am prepared," Huw said immodestly—and then added in a voice that came directly from William de Bohun, "*I was born prepared.*"

Michael laughed, as Huw meant him to, and they entered the house together. Corwen had died sometime after midnight, at which point Gwladys, Carew's healer, had confessed her surprise he'd lived that long, given that many who ingest enough yew to lose consciousness die much more quickly.

This bout of breaking and entering was the result, though now that Corwen was dead with no heirs, under the medieval system all that he owned belonged to his lord anyway. They were here as much on Carew's orders as Callum's.

"Don't take off your gloves," Michael warned as he and Huw stopped a few feet inside the door to survey what they were dealing with.

Huw spread wide the fingers of both hands, well-gloved as Michael's were. "Have no worry on that score. I have no wish to die before I win the competition."

Michael gave him a sardonic look. "You should just be happy the heats were rigged so you, Math, and Ieuan didn't have to face each other in the first round."

"It wouldn't have mattered."

Michael couldn't tell if Huw's confidence was youthful bravado or truly genuine. It wasn't the archer he needed today anyway, but the thoughtful mind and extra pair of hands. If he and Huw found something pertinent in the house, Callum wanted two sets of eyes on it and no chance that someone alone could be taken unaware by an unknown conspirator.

Corwen's house was round with a thatch roof and dirt floor like so many houses in this era. Huw crouched to the fire and put out a hand so it hovered a few inches above the coals. "It's smoldering. Someone has been here since Corwen fell ill."

Michael began circling the room with a little more urgency. Probably whoever stoked the fire was the same person supplying

Corwen with basic food items, perhaps even tidying for him. There wasn't much to see: a mattress in a wooden bedframe, a bench and table, a few dishes, and a cupboard with two eggs, half a loaf of bread, and a block of cheese.

"This does not appear to be the house of a master herbalist and poisoner." Huw picked up a carved knight from a set of figurines set out on a low table near the lone stool at the fireside. "He liked to whittle."

"He was good at it too." Michael fingered what he thought might be a baby toy, designed for little hands. Arya would like it, but he wasn't sure he would give anything to her that Corwen had touched, not until they knew more about what he'd been up to in his final days and hours.

Huw had taken to his hands and knees in order to look for irregularities in the floor that would indicate a secret hiding place. "If we don't find anything in the outbuildings, I'm going to take apart the fireplace. It is a known location for contraband."

"Where did you hear that?" Michael glanced down at the coals again. It was going to take some effort to shift the stones that formed its base. Not to mention the fact that they'd need to extinguish the fire first and let the stones cool.

"It is something our king once mentioned. He said he'd seen it in a movie." Huw's expression indicated he had heard of movies but had never seen one. "It's a clever notion."

"I have no idea if *clever* described Corwen, but by all accounts, he was an upstanding citizen. It's hard to understand why he'd be involved—" Michael broke off as he opened the rear door to the house and took in the view. Corwen's house backed up against a field, on the other side of which was Carew's church, dedicated to St. Mary. The church itself wasn't of interest to Michael, but the five yew trees in the graveyard definitely were.

Yews had been sacred to the Welsh for millennia, and several of these, going by their girth and gnarled branches, might date to pre-Roman times. In Wales, they even had a law that said you couldn't cut down *ywen sant*, or *holy yews*.

Those weren't the only yews in sight either. Corwen had piled a dozen yew branches in the back of his garden. Many of the branches had their pollen clusters still attached, indicating they must have been cut months ago, in the spring. Corwen seemed to have been trimming the branches and stacking them, as if for firewood.

Huw appeared beside Michael. "He would have been an idiot to burn yew in the fireplace. He could have poisoned himself from the smoke that way."

"Who uses yew for firewood anyway?"

"Nobody." Huw crouched to the pile and pulled out several long branches. "These would be perfect if seasoned a year or two."

"Perfect for what?"

The look of disgust at Michael's ignorance was worthy of William as well. "Bow staves." Intent now, Huw strode to a shed and pulled open the door. In an instant, his face transformed to one of delight. "Corwen knew it too."

Huw stepped back so Michael could inspect the dozen six-foot high staves that were hung inside the little hut.

"Are they all yew?"

Huw shook his head. "Several are elm."

"He's drying them?"

"It looks like it; they seem fairly unseasoned." Huw was intent as he picked through the staves. "Was he supplying the castle?"

"He supplied everyone." The voice came from behind them, and they swung around to find an elderly woman, hardly even five feet tall, looking at them with narrowed eyes. "Why are you going through Corwen's things?"

Huw took the lead, as they'd agreed in advance he would do if they encountered any villagers. The woman was speaking Welsh, and it was their thought she would accept whatever lie Huw was about to tell her better than from Michael, with his less-than-expert accent. "He has taken ill, and we were sent to discover how he might have been sickened."

"It wasn't from anything I fed him," the woman said staunchly. "You should be asking that cook up at the castle." She sniffed her derision.

"Do you mean Enith?" Huw asked.

"Of course I mean Enith. He was sweet on her. I never understood why, except maybe she would provide him with treats." She sniffed again. "You would have thought my cooking was good enough, but the way to a man's heart has always been through his stomach."

"Was Enith often here?" Michael asked.

"Aren't you a lovely one." The old woman surveyed him as if she hadn't noticed him before. "She was one of his visitors."

"He had others?"

The woman shrugged. "Do I know everything that happens here?" On the whole, Michael would have said *yes*, but then she continued, "Some don't even speak Welsh."

Huw's voice was very steady. "Who was this?"

"I don't know who he was. He brought food for Corwen, as if mine wasn't good enough."

Michael swallowed. "*When* was this?"

"Yesterday morning while Corwen was out. I would have told him off for entering a man's home without permission, but he wouldn't have understood anything I said."

"Do you know what he brought?" Huw asked.

"A little cake." For a moment she looked sheepish.

"So it was you who stoked the fire and tidied inside?" Huw said, though by now it seemed certain that she was.

"Yes." Her chin stuck out as if she was daring them to criticize. "I live on the other side of that copse of trees."

"Mistress, was there anything about the man you saw that jumped out at you or that would distinguish this one man from the hundreds at Carew today?" Huw said.

"These foreign folks are all the same, aren't they? Not like our Carew, now that he's turned Welsh."

"Was he tall with dark hair and particularly handsome?" Michael asked.

She scoffed. "Red-headed and plain as a post, that one." Then she tipped her head as she saw disappointment in their faces. "Is there some reason you're not asking all this of Corwen himself? After all, he was the one who ate the cake."

30

September 20 -Avalon

Chad

It was a rainy morning in New York, so Chad dragged on his raincoat as he went out into the foyer of his apartment where today's security detail was waiting. Being only five-foot-two, Chandra looked like a spark plug with her bullet proof vest underneath her coat, but Andre had assured Chad she was more than qualified and a gun did a great deal to level the playing field. Chad had chosen his other bodyguard just for his name: Dane, which was a warrior's name if he'd ever heard one. Fortunately, at six-foot four and blond, he looked the part, not to mention having a great tenor voice.

As Dane pressed the button for the elevator, Chad knew they looked like an odd trio, but to his mind that was half the point. The more diverse a person's entourage, the more he could be all things to all people.

"This activity wasn't on the schedule, sir." Chandra was still adjusting her raincoat, checking her gear in a fashion that looked very professional and wore sensible shoes she could run in.

"You are correct."

Dane had his hand to his earpiece. "Should I call a car?"

"No." Chad opened the bag he was carrying. "Take that off. I need all your technology in here."

That disconcerted them, late twenty-somethings that they were, but they did as he asked. They had already left their personal phones in a lockbox at the entrance to the building when they'd arrived for work. Like the rest of Chad's staff, they changed phones on an irregular schedule, with the phones going back to IT for vetting.

The pieces of the phones Chad had used to talk to Hugh, Sophie, and Denise were in his pockets. Once he was out of the building, he intended to scatter them across the city as he walked. He didn't want even his own IT department to have them. He certainly didn't want anyone but a select few to know about his upcoming call to his sister, who had a friend in the office of the Secretary-General of the United Nations. As she would.

Once in the elevator, Dane said, "Can you tell us something of what this is about?"

"Not until we're outside." Chad was making sure to keep his tone utterly level and unconcerned, even though his heart was beating hard and possibly loud enough for others to hear.

Chad glanced out of the corner of his eye at Dane, upon whom it had begun to dawn he was in the midst of an actual operation.

Learning they were on a quest to find a pay phone, of which there weren't that many in New York City anymore, might be something of a letdown.

They walked out of the building and took a left.

"Where are we going?" Chandra's head was on a swivel, as military people might say.

"To make a phone call," Chad said.

"One you can't make in your office?" Dane asked this even though it was obviously the case. He was a very literal guy and wanted everything spelled out clearly. Chad could appreciate the desire. When it came to business, it was important not to leave anything implied. "Didn't you just buy a satellite company? It's a closed system. Not even the NSA is supposed to be able to listen in."

"Better safe than sorry." On impulse, Chad stopped a teenage boy in a school uniform who was gaping at a video on his phone. "Excuse me, can I borrow your phone for a minute? I'll be right there." He pointed to the entrance to an alley, already holding out a one-hundred dollar bill in the other hand. He hoped it was enough.

The boy dragged his eyes from his phone, took in Chad and his two bodyguards with a glance, and then traded his phone for the hundred dollar bill. Insultingly, he held it up to the sky as Chad turned the screen towards him. Naturally, the young man had been watching a video of David and Lili arriving in the Walmart. This particular upload had two hundred and thirty-five million views. Chad knew for a fact there were others with more.

Denise answered on the second ring. "Hello?"

"Sis."

"*Sis* I can handle," she said. "That you're calling me again indicates you're more worried than you were yesterday, which is saying something, and you are still not calling from a number I recognize."

"I am worried. And it isn't from a number you recognize because the phone belongs to a young man who has kindly let me borrow his for a hundred bucks."

He could practically feel her blink. "So this is important."

"You could say so. I need to talk to the Secretary-General."

"*The* Secretary-General?"

"Is there more than one?" And since the question was rhetorical, Chad continued, "She is set to give a speech before a joint session of Congress tomorrow night. I need her to give way to David."

"I have to say, Chad, that's quite an ask, even for you."

"I'm not asking her to do it for me." He made a motion with his head she couldn't see. "It's for David, and for all of us."

"Do you really think I have that kind of pull?"

"Don't you?"

Her sigh was audible all the way from DC. "Maybe. I can try." Her voice turned harder. "I don't want my every move surveyed and recorded either. I don't like living this way any more than you do. You've moved heaven and earth to bring this legislation to the floor. While I won't pretend it's the whole tamale, and maybe it won't do what we want it to, I agree we have to start somewhere."

Chad let out a sharp breath. "So I'm not crazy?"

"If you are, we all are." She laughed. "How is it possible that we live in a world where kings of England appear out of nowhere in Walmarts? In the past, I might have cautioned you about putting everything on the line for a man you barely know, but here you are, calling me for this enormous favor, which may require me to cash in more chips than I would like, and I'm going along with it. Maybe I'm crazy too."

"Or maybe, darling sister, we two are among the sanest people on the planet."

31

September 20 -Earth Two

Daisy

"This is Bogo's doing," Daisy said. "It has to be. It's just the kind of thing he'd do. I know it."

"I don't disagree." William squeezed her right hand with his left (the only one available since his right arm was in a sling).

She knew he meant it kindly, which was why he didn't also remind her that Bogo's involvement was exactly what they *didn't* know. She was responding to what was in her heart, that sick feeling she'd been free of since the day William had taken her hand and introduced himself, both of them soaking wet, having escaped from Berkhamsted.

"David is well out of it. That's the important thing," William said.

The three girls (Lizzie, Elen, and Gwenllian) had arrived at their tent last night, breathless, to relate in suspiciously extensive detail what had happened to Corwen. Daisy hadn't bothered to chastise her little sister for eavesdropping. That was like blaming the sun for shining, and ever since they'd left the convent, Lizzie's sun had shone brighter with every month that had passed.

Daisy hadn't ever expected to be part of any family again, much less a royal one, but Meg and Llywelyn had opened their arms to the three sisters, and Daisy had walked right in. She hoped her own parents, as they looked down on them from heaven, could forgive her. She felt that they might, because even as she and her sisters had been raised to be tools of diplomacy, her parents had always loved them too.

"He will be seeking revenge," Daisy's fingers tightened on William's hand, "on all of us."

"Maybe especially on me for marrying you?" William laughed lightly, but there was a harder undertone to his amusement, which filled his voice a moment later when he added, "He can try."

"He *is* trying. That's the problem." Daisy tried to tamp down her worry. "You got what he wanted."

William moved his arm to put it around her waist. They were walking along a path that ran from the Bohun encampment to the tournament grounds. "You are right that I got what I wanted—which was *you*. Bogo wanted only what you represented, and that is not the same thing. Maybe he is petty enough to desire revenge on either of us, but his goal was, and always will be, his own power and pleasure, not necessarily in that order. Now that he is a cardinal, you are permanently out of his reach. A cardinal can't become a king. Nor can he become a husband. I imagine his aim now is the papacy, not a temporal throne."

"I wouldn't have said there was a higher position than that of the King of England, but Bogo has found it."

William gave her a wry glance. "I cannot be sorry that you yourself were immune to Bogo's charms."

She returned the look. "I was not immune. Resistant, maybe. He *is* beautiful. That's just a fact. And when a man is that beautiful, he draws people to him. Because he looks like an angel, people think he is one."

"We know better."

Daisy worked to calm her roiling stomach. "He also cares nothing about England's relationship with the Pope or France."

"Of course not."

"Or if he does, it's only as a means to an end." She paused. "So what *is* his end?"

"Greater minds than ours are even now working to find out."

Daisy had spent many years in convents, not doing much of anything beyond the endless round of work and prayer. That might be enough for some people. Her sister Joan appeared to excel at it. But while Daisy had resigned herself to living out her life in one place, she had never taken to it.

By contrast, William was always in motion. According to his mother, he had been from the moment he learned to roll over by himself at two months of age. At some point in their courtship, Daisy had decided she would prefer to make the attempt to keep up with him rather than always be waiting for him to return to her. She wasn't quite ready for jousting herself, but she had been on the sidelines, ready to pick up the pieces when he'd fallen. Because of his injury, he was out of the archery contest too, which she thought was just as well. He would have been frustrated to lose to those he viewed as lesser men after he'd practiced so hard. He hadn't been born to archery like Huw, however, only to the sword.

Daisy had learned to accept facts of life at an early age. Her new husband still railed at them. Anymore, she honestly wasn't sure which approach was better. "How can we help?"

William let out a laugh. "I say we walk right up to Bogo and ask him."

"He isn't going to tell us the truth."

"Are you sure about that? He told it to you before. Why not now?"

"He had to tell me in order to enlist me in his scheme."

William shook his head. "You underestimate yourself, my love. You were resistant to his charms, but I'm not so sure how resistant he was to yours."

32

September 20 -Avalon

Lili

"I don't understand how the people chasing us can be such poor listeners." Lili said. Andre laughed to hear her, but Lili wasn't being sardonic. "If they really heard what Dafydd was saying, they could never treat him so badly."

She had left her husband napping in the big bed everyone insisted they take, which she agreed made sense, since they were the only couple among their party. Lili had spent most of the journey so far staring out the window or watching Sophie walking on the treadmill built into the floor of the hallway/kitchen. Walking on it generated electricity for the vehicle, though it was mostly wasted because (according to Dafydd) the power of the RV's engine was filling the batteries too. At the moment, George and Sophie were doing an inventory of the contents of the vehicle. If, for some reason, they had to take the RV back to Earth Two, it would be nice to know what was in it.

"They listen but don't hear." Andre settled himself, taking her seriously now. "Ironically, our modern system of government is supposed to protect the individual from the kind of injustice David has been experiencing. Nobody has to bribe someone to get his mail. But then one doesn't know one's mailperson either."

"None of what you just said means anything to me. What is *mail?* We aren't talking about armor, are we? Or about ... men?"

"Definitely not the latter!" Andre grinned. "The English word is spelled the same as armor, but no, *mail* in this context is a nationwide system to deliver letters. It works something like the Templar roadside relays that David used to travel across France."

She gazed at him. "You mean, I could write a letter in London to Anna at Dinas Bran, and someone I don't know would deliver it? What would prevent such a person from reading it?"

"We do seal the letters, and if the seal is unbroken, you can trust that nobody has tampered with it, just like you do at home."

Lili knew her expression conveyed doubt. She truly couldn't get her head around allowing that kind of potential threat to her privacy.

Andre smiled gently. "It does work most of the time. Mail carriers are paid well enough to ensure they don't steal mail, and the volume of mail is such that nobody could possibly have time to open every letter, much less read them all."

As Lili continued to look skeptical, he spread his hands wide, even as he continued to hold the wheel. "Anyway, physical mail is more secure these days than any electronic correspondence. That's why we are so cautious with our mobiles."

"This is why the satellite system Chad bought is so important?"

"Yes."

It seemed simple enough to understand, once she started asking questions. "What about you, Andre? How do you feel about Dafydd being here again? Are you worried about being forced back to Earth Two with us?"

"I'm—" he cleared his throat, "not unhappy."

"Is that because you would be going with Sophie?" At his startled glance, she added, "I see how you look at her."

Andre gave a little cough that was also a laugh. "My lady, I don't think—"

"She looks at you the same way."

That cut off his laughter so quickly he almost swallowed his tongue. "I'm nearly twenty years older than she is. When I'm sixty, she'll be forty."

"How old will each of you be if you aren't together? Llywelyn and Meg have made it work."

"Oh, that's not playing fair. They're special."

"I won't deny that truth, but you are special too. Has Dafydd asked you both to come back to Earth Two with us yet?"

"He has not."

Lili had always felt comfortable in Andre's calm presence, and they were both quiet again as the miles rolled underneath the RV.

Having left the mountains behind them, this country was much flatter, but still on a scale far vaster than any Lili had ever seen or imagined.

The phone rang to interrupt their silence. It was Chad again. "Are you secure?"

"Yes, sir, making good time."

Lili had noted the way Andre generally spoke more formally than the rest of his friends and never called Chad Treadman by his given name.

"I'm using my new system, which is as airtight as technologically possible in this crazy age. I'm also calling from inside a Greek deli I have never been in before, on a burner I'll ditch as soon as we hang up. You know what? I'm going to invest in a cell phone manufacturing company because of this."

"That sounds like a good idea, sir."

"My entire life takes place on the phone. That's all I do. I live in cities, where the flora and fauna consist of stray dandelions in the pavement, and I talk on the phone. I have talked to everyone. You have a date tomorrow at nine pm eastern, during the evening session. The Secretary-General will let it be known that David is speaking for her only a few hours before. Even that is more time than I'd like, but we have to coordinate the visuals."

"And *we* have to get the timing just right, sir. I can't help feeling we are being followed."

"Even if the CIA knows about our intentions, I feel confident they will be looking for you in the wrong place."

"It's *your* movements I'm worried about, sir. They are going to be wondering why you chose to keep your appointment at FutureCon in Seattle while David is in Washington DC."

"I'm counting on them overthinking it, assuming I'm a diversion for the real event, when really David will be standing right beside me. My schedule is public knowledge and has to stay that way. At the very least, nobody has come anywhere near Hugh's property. They don't know you took the RV."

"You make a persuasive point, sir."

"Be safe. See you tomorrow evening. Seattle isn't going to know what hit it." Chad hung up abruptly.

"He always does that." Andre glanced at her. "You okay?"

Lili laughed. "Not hardly, as my husband might say."

"I'm sorry your first visit to Avalon hasn't exactly been fun."

She laughed again. "Did I say that? Amidst the confusion and fear, I'm having the time of my life."

Andre's eyes narrowed. "Are you serious?"

"Avalon is all at once beautiful, exciting, heart-breaking, and dangerous. I think this is the most danger I've ever been in. That doesn't mean I would wish away a single second of it."

"You said *second*." A smile split Andre's face. "The irony here is that for anyone from Avalon, Earth Two seems like the most dangerous, scariest place they could go. War, famine, plague. A man could die from an infected hangnail. That is very unlikely to happen here. Nor will anyone come at me with a sword."

Lili was relaxed enough by now she put one foot up on the dash as she'd seen Sophie do. It was quite comfortable. "Danger there is personal, just like the politics. You must have heard Dafydd say that many times. Here, the locus of power is—" she made a motion with her hand, "—so vague. You talk about *they* as if you don't know who opposes you."

"We don't. *Someone* is always watching, but we have no way of knowing who specifically."

"So you adapt, and learn, and prepare for all contingencies. I'm beginning to understand why everyone in Earth Two has continually underestimated Dafydd. They think because he is kind, with a heart open to strangers, and is willing to compromise, that he is soft all the way through. But he is actually much like the mattress we've been sleeping on: blessedly soft initially; a bit less squishy a few inches in; a little firmer past that; and then has a solid core at the bottom that not only doesn't move, it can't move." She turned in her seat to look at Andre. "You are the same, Andre. I think it's that solid core that is so attractive to Sophie."

"I appreciate the compliment." Andre laughed. "But I wouldn't go calling just anyone from Avalon a mattress. I assure you the usual metaphor is quite different."

33

September 20 -Earth Two

Daisy

Daisy came to a halt at the entrance to the viewing stands. "Isabel." The name was almost too painful to speak.

William frowned. "That isn't Isabelle. We just talked to her—"

Daisy cut him off. "I don't mean Christopher's Isabelle." She pronounced the word with a heavy French accent. "I mean *Isabel*."

Her husband still looked confused, but as he studied the woman Daisy indicated, understanding dawned. "I wouldn't have said that was she; she looked very different the last time we saw—"

"She did look different. It's the laughter," Daisy interrupted him, certain now, "along with the cut of her gown and the color. At Berkhamsted, she was all in gray, and the only time she smiled was when she talked of Bogo. But it's Isabel." She moved forward, almost against her will, and plastered a smile of welcome on her face. William had suggested they talk to Bogo, but talking to Isabel was the next best thing. "It is good to see you looking so well!"

Isabel turned, and her smile widened. "My lady! You are so beautiful. Marriage agrees with you."

"How is it that you are here, Isabel?" Daisy couldn't help the question. Probably they should have talked about a few more neutral subjects, like the weather, before she reached this point.

"I've come with my betrothed, Sir Roger de la Pole." She gestured to a large man who looked over at her words. "He is participating in the tournament."

Daisy gaped for a moment, stunned at how oblivious Isabel still appeared to be. It was Roger who'd broken William's wrist. She was prepared to back away, so as not to make this worse, until William himself stuck out his left arm to Roger who, after a wary moment of hesitation, took it.

"No hard feelings, Bohun?" Roger said. "I admit sometimes I want to win too much."

"You are very good, and what you did was not against the rules. It was my fault for landing wrong. I'll be rooting for you to win the whole thing."

And just like that, her husband had smoothed over the entire incident. If Daisy could have loved him more, she would have in that moment. He was a nobleman in every way, not just by birth.

Daisy turned back to Isabel. "Where did you meet?"

"Oh, don't you know? After Berkhamsted, the king was so kind as to arrange accommodation for me far away from London."

She continued to smile. "It was there I met Roger. My stay was intended to last until I could decide if I wanted to rejoin my convent or find some other path for myself. I did." Isabel's smile was so bright Daisy's own cheeks hurt to think about smiling that hard.

"Is the wedding soon?"

"Another month." Isabel gazed fondly at her betrothed, who was now talking to William about jousting techniques.

"Have you noted that Bogo is here too?" Daisy shouldn't have asked the question, but she couldn't help herself.

While Isabel had been doe-eyed over him two years ago, now she smiled a little sadly. "I am so glad to see him well. I never believed the horrible things people said about him. I'm sure all the fuss at Berkhamsted was just a big misunderstanding."

Daisy gaped at her again, prompting William to intervene *again*. "Congratulations to you."

He nodded his head at Roger, who bent his a little more respectfully back, and then William hooked his hand around Daisy's elbow, opting to take the stairs to the top of the viewing stand, which genuinely had the best view of the entire grounds. From here it was possible to follow the tournament bouts, and also see the entire region spread out before them. Carew Castle was dominant on its rock in the cleft of its dammed river and tidal pool. This fed the mill downstream, where the grain for the bread she'd had that morning was ground.

South of the river, the land was relatively flat all the way to the sea, and allowed plenty of space for the tournament and the encampments for all the lords, families, servants, and merchants who'd come.

"Not a bad fellow, when it comes down to it," William said, more charitably than Daisy felt capable.

She made a sour face. "He's marrying Isabel."

"Maybe she's the one who has made him more amenable."

From the height, Daisy could look down on the continued activities of Isabel and her fiancé. They were in the midst of a group of revelers from Ireland, who seemed to already have had plenty to drink, even in the middle of the day. She remembered how Isabel had been easy to subdue at Berkhamsted because she reliably consumed too much wine in the evening. Molly had ensured she drank from a carafe that had been dosed with poppy. After the fall of the castle to King David's forces, she had been found asleep.

"Isabel is here; Bogo is here. I don't care what she just said or how in love she is with Roger. That can't be a coincidence."

"She was never implicated in any of Bogo's machinations." William said. "Bogo used her like he used so many others. That's why she can't believe what we know to be true about him, and that's why David let her go."

"It was on my advice he did so," Daisy said softly. "If she's returned to join in whatever new mischief Bogo has planned for us, I can't help but think that would be somehow my fault."

"Your fault; Ieuan's fault; Michael's fault; probably in Avalon Lili is blaming herself for bringing walnuts into David's vicinity." William had his arm around her again. "We can blame Bogo for what he's done, but as to the rest ... sometimes stuff just happens. And that's okay."

34

September 20 -Earth Two

Lizzie

Yesterday evening, Lizzie, Elen, and Gwenllian had left the feast after they thought all the excitement was over, only to discover it had just begun. They'd ended up inside the castle around the time David and Lili had disappeared, though they hadn't known it. In the hubbub afterwards, however, they'd done what Lizzie still appeared to do best, which was to spy on her elders.

Most importantly, having seen Livia enter the inner bailey and then leave with Abraham, Callum, Michael, and Ieuan, they'd known these adults were the ones to follow. Thus, they'd listened around the back of the laundry to the whole conversation held over Corwen's body. That had given Lizzie an idea about where to go today.

"What are we really doing here?" Elen opened the door that led into the kitchen garden, located not far from the laundry in the outer bailey. The garden had been built against the northern curtain wall and was surrounded by an eight-foot-high wall on the other three sides, the better to keep the plants warm and protected from the wind. A much larger garden lay outside the castle against the south-facing curtain wall. "Corwen never made it this far."

At sixteen, Elen had just finished her training at the teachers' college in Llangollen but hadn't yet taken up a position because there was talk of sending her to the University of Cambridge. With both Gwenllian and Lizzie nearly a year younger, neither of them wanted her to go without them. Elen's parents were currently in Normandy, helping them resolve some governmental issues Lizzie quite frankly didn't care enough about to remember.

"It would have been harder for us to eavesdrop without being detected, so it's just as well," Gwenllian led the way into the healer's hut, located in the northeast corner of the garden. A small guard-house protecting the castle's postern gate was to the northwest, where the corner of the outer bailey's curtain wall met the wall of the inner bailey. "We have to start somewhere—"

She cut herself off as Lizzie put up a fist. They had all memorized the hand signals used by the royal guard, in the same way they'd learned Morse Code. One never knew when the knowledge might come in handy.

Lizzie had been standing closest to the door, which they'd left open. They hadn't been inside long enough to light any candles, and the interior was shadowed compared to the bright sunshine outside. The three of them stood silently as Enith, the castle cook, hurried from the garden door to the guardhouse and disappeared inside. She was carrying a carafe of wine.

The girls waited, but she didn't come out again.

The cook had every right to leave her post during a lull between meals. At the same time, Lizzie had no notion as to why she would come here by herself, to all appearances personally delivering a carafe of wine to the man who guarded the postern gate. Guards were not supposed to drink anything but water while on duty.

Gwenllian tossed her golden hair. "This is boring. Nothing is happening; I don't see why we're here."

"We're here," Lizzie said, patience in her voice, "for that very reason. We have to look where nobody else is."

"Nobody is looking in the latrines," Gwenllian was the very essence of logic, "and I don't see us wandering through every one of *them*."

"And yet, wasn't it in the latrines where bombs were placed at Canterbury and Caernarfon?"

Gwenllian gave her a sour look, but subsided. The Caernarfon incident had taken place in Avalon, which Elen had mentioned in passing during a conversation about something else. Lizzie had pressed hard on the question of how Avalon could have its own Caernarfon Castle, as if the whole place was a mirror to this world. Aunt Meg had finally sat her down and told her that Avalon existed in an alternate universe that was seven hundred and twenty-eight years ahead of this one. Part of Lizzie hadn't wanted to know more after that, and the rest of her had been falling all over herself with more questions. Aunt Meg had answered them all. As it turned out, Daisy had already known the truth (and kept it from Lizzie!) because William had told her, having traveled there with David a few years ago.

"If we are looking for bombs, we should look in latrines. If we are looking for poisonous substances, yew or otherwise, we should start with a healer's hut." That came from Elen, speaking absently as she poked a finger at a dish of what might be the very same yew seeds from the vial yesterday. Gwladys must have brought them from the laundry room, but given all that had been going on, she hadn't returned since to secure them. "It's hard to believe these could kill a person."

Lizzie almost snatched Elen's hand away, unable to put aside the idea that Corwen had become sick simply from handling the seeds. Before this week, the thought had never occurred to her. Then again, that David and Lili had just disappeared to Avalon was something she had never thought to see either, even if she'd wished for it—and dreamt of it—a hundred times in her life before she came to live with the very people capable of doing it. Miracles were in the air. It would be foolish to presume otherwise.

"Can you think of anything else we know about Bogo de Clare that would help us figure out if he's responsible?" Elen started walking around the small hut, at least making an effort to get into the spirit of the endeavor. "All I can think about is how he imprisoned us. Since he got away with that, I would think he'd be satisfied with being a cardinal."

"*I* don't understand how he's even here." Lizzie gave a snort of disgust. "Nobody in the Clare family is supposed to be able to set foot in England upon pain of death."

Gwenllian tipped her head. "But we aren't in England right now, are we? That law wasn't laid down by the CSB as a whole, but only by David as King of England. A sad oversight on Papa's part, I'm sorry to say."

Lizzie was feeling disappointed that her idea of investigating in the healer's hut had come to nothing, but she agreed it was time to leave, and the three girls stepped outside.

"Cook Enith never came back, did she?" Gwenllian wrinkled her nose. "Why would she exit the castle by the postern gate? I thought it wasn't allowed." The three girls knew that because they had tried to leave that way when they'd first arrived and been rebuffed.

Elen's expression turned pensive. "We should go now. We don't want her to see us."

"Why not? I'm with Gwenllian. There's nothing to see." Lizzie turned to look at her friend. "Are you saying you don't want to investigate Corwen's murder anymore?"

"I didn't say that—" Elen broke off as she looked from Lizzie to Gwenllian and back again. "There's a reason Cook Enith brought wine to the guardhouse."

When she didn't tell them immediately what that reason was, the other girls gazed at her, waiting until Lizzie finally had to ask, "So what is it?"

"She's spending time with the guard. *Privately.*" The last word came out a whisper.

"Do you think she's asking questions like we are?" Lizzie felt a moment of triumph at her conclusion, but then deflated as Elen rolled her eyes. "Of course not."

"He's her lover, Lizzie." Gwenllian's voice was gentle, as if explaining to a small child. "With the tournament in full swing, that little guardhouse is the most private place in the castle."

Lizzie could have taken offense, but instead she dismissed the idea immediately. "She's *old!* I don't believe it." She set off for the guardhouse with long strides. When she reached it, she pulled open the door—and then waited, gratified to see Gwenllian and Elen catching up.

The outer room contained racks of weapons and shelves of armor. Straight ahead was another door, which led to a room about the same size as the first. A man was seated on a stool before a table, his head on his arms and a carafe and two cups near his left elbow. Lizzie tiptoed closer, fearful they'd found another casualty, like Corwen. But before she touched him, the guard snorted in his sleep.

Elen gave a little squeak, and all three jumped back in surprise. The guard stayed asleep. Lizzie wondered how long before the shift changed and kicked herself for not memorizing the guard schedule. A real spy would have.

Gwenllian peered into the carafe. "Empty." She sniffed. "It smells like good wine."

Elen wrinkled her nose. "And where's Cook Enith?"

"Gone," Lizzie said.

Given that the postern door had been left slightly ajar, propped open by a rock, Lizzie concluded the carafe had been a bribe to allow Enith to leave the castle that way.

As the three girls looked at each other, considering their options, Elen stepped into her role as the eldest. "One of us should stay behind to find help."

"What if Enith is just taking a shortcut to the larger garden? We'll have caused a ruckus for no reason," Lizzie said reasonably.

"Besides, who can we ask?" Gwenllian said. "Everyone's at the tournament. We weren't assigned a guard because we said we weren't going to leave the castle."

"We intend to leave it now," Elen said.

"Exactly. Aunt Meg wants us to stick together." Without waiting for either of the other girls to assent, Lizzie opened the door all the way. "Come on!"

Gwenllian and Elen looked at each other, and then Elen let out a heavy sigh of capitulation. "If we hurry we might still be able to catch her."

35

Christopher

"Welcome to Carew!" Christopher entered John Primus's tent. "My apologies for not introducing myself days ago. I'm—"

"—the Hero of Westminster. And the king's cousin." John Primus advanced towards him with his hand out, his jousting armor still half on. He was slightly shorter than Christopher, with somewhat blonder hair and a more slender build, though it was hard to tell under his gear. John Secundus, who was acting as his squire, was a very young looking thirteen. That fact must have made trying to fill his father's shoes difficult, but the medieval system of inheritance required it.

Christopher had timed his approach perfectly, if he did say so himself. His goal had been to arrive during John Primus's preparations, but not so early or late that he would genuinely hinder them.

He didn't care how well John Primus did in the tournament. What he wanted was his trust.

The Johns were both very important people in Europe, so Christopher wasn't going to say out loud the names Bronwen had given them, but he found them amusing and useful nonetheless. Like Bronwen, Christopher hadn't been born into the English nobility, and it was hard enough to keep track of the various lords, earls, dukes, barons, and minor noblemen in Britain. When one started tossing in dukes from Europe, it was impossible. For him, anyway. His wife seemed to have no problem with it at all.

Isabelle, of course, had been born in Earth Two, to a noble family and had a father who was at one and the same time the Master of the Paris Temple and one of King Philippe's chief advisers. Through him they had an ear to the ground at all times as to the current situation in France. Over the years, Philippe and David had been alternately enemies and allies, and it was hard to know where exactly they were with their alliance now. As far as they knew, Philippe was still in the dark about England's role in the escape of Paris's Jewish population. He did know that England had supported Normandy's quest for independence. That had soured relations considerably. As had the attack on Aquitaine. And now Flanders.

As lords of Brabant, Holland, and Zeeland, both Johns were currently hostile to France.

Christopher's job today was to befriend them. He might have done so even if Livia hadn't suggested it as part of his role in *Y Ddraig Goch*. He had welcomed the assignment as a distraction from the fact that David and Lili hadn't yet returned. His idea of going to get them was still out there, hanging in front of his eyes. He'd promised to wait until after the tournament to push it again, however. He just prayed David and Lili would be back by then.

Meanwhile, Livia was suspicious of everyone, and she wanted to know if the Johns had anything to do with the events of yesterday, from David's disappearance on down to Corwen's death. Nobody at the tournament had ever met either John before they'd arrived a few days ago. They might not even be who they said they were.

Alternatively, since hatred of France and King Philippe was at the forefront for both, they might be willing to ally with anyone who would aid them, including Pope Boniface and Bogo de Clare. Both Johns were young enough that they might not understand that they couldn't ally with either of those two and David at the same time.

"Earl Carew asked that I check in with you to make sure you had everything you needed." Christopher grasped John Primus's forearm in what he thought of as a chivalrous fashion, while at the same time endeavoring not to turn the gripping of arms into a contest. Even after all these years of living here, it was still a tightrope to get all the social cues right.

"Earl Carew has been most accommodating, especially after our rough sea crossing. We want for nothing."

"I'm glad to hear it." Christopher was already tired of the small talk.

"I have not seen you in the jousts yourself."

"I did not enter. As you may know, I was raised in Avalon where certain skills, particularly horsemanship, were not emphasized."

"Because you ride in carriages that propel themselves." John Primus's tone was notably intent, making Christopher think all of a sudden that he should have brought Isabelle with him. He hadn't entered the jousts, but this was shaping up to be a sparring match every bit as rigorous as on the tournament field.

"Yes."

His unequivocal reply seemed to please John Primus, who nodded as if it was what he'd expected. John Secundus, however, who hadn't said a word up until now, asked eagerly. "I would love to ride in such a vehicle one day."

"If it is in my power to facilitate that, I will. Unfortunately, we have no such vehicles nearby." Then Christopher grinned. "If I could joust from within my car, that would be a very different contest!"

"Nobody would want to face you. Is that not how Clare died?" John Secundus said.

"I suppose." Christopher endeavored not to play off the *Hero of Westminster* business if he could help it. Clare's death had been an accident of his arrival and truly nothing to do with him. He had given up saying so, however, in much the same way David had given up trying to convince anyone he wasn't the return of Arthur. Christopher *had* done other deeds worthy of the knighthood since bestowed on him.

So while the story of Christopher's arrival into Westminster Castle and the death of Gilbert de Clare had been disseminated throughout Europe—maybe the whole world by now—the issue of the vehicle with which he'd done it might not be as fully understood. Thus, through this short conversation, Christopher had learned pretty much all he needed to know about how close to the ground the Johns had been keeping their ears. It was certainly something to relate to Livia.

"We had hoped to have an audience with the king as soon as possible." John Primus didn't actually say David's name, but Christopher knew he didn't mean Llywelyn. The son had surpassed the father, and Llywelyn appeared totally okay with that.

"I think you know that is not currently possible."

It was as if he'd let the air out of a balloon. Both Johns sagged a little.

"Johnny didn't think you would admit it," John Secundus said. "I was sure you would."

"You bet against me being honest?"

John Primus was a matter of three months younger than Christopher and would be twenty-two in a few days. While it seemed pretty clear that most twenty-two-year olds in Earth Two were required to be far more responsible than many in Avalon, he still had the same twenty-two years of life experience as Christopher, and now he suddenly looked worried and started to stutter. "I mean ... I just ..."

Christopher cut him off with a wave of his hand. "You will learn soon enough that things are done differently in David's court. Yes, he has gone to Avalon. No, we don't know when he'll be back. Is there someone you would like to talk to instead?"

"Who has the power to speak for him when the queen is gone too?"

"Alexander Callum or Nicholas de Carew."

John Primus bowed his head. "I would be honored to have an audience with either man."

"May I ask about the topic of discussion?" Christopher had to inquire, even if he thought he already knew.

"The predations of the King of France, of course."

Christopher bent his own head now. The *of course* was deserved. It had been obvious.

John Primus nodded, more to himself than to Christopher. "Others tried to tell me I would find how things were done in England a bit unusual. I did not entirely believe them."

"Well, this is Wales, so I would advise against making that mistake again," Christopher said. "I don't know what exactly you have heard, but take whatever that is and multiply it by ten."

John Primus's brow furrowed. "I never was very good at maths."

"No worries. David makes all the calculations easy."

36

September 20 -Earth Two

Michael

"There! See! She has it in her hand." Ieuan had been looking over Michael's shoulder as he went through the footage from the camera they'd put in the kitchen the previous night.

Six different people had entered and exited multiple times over the intervening hours, surprisingly late into the night. One of them had been Nicholas de Carew himself, who had acquired a late evening snack of bread and cheese. He was the only one who acted in any way strangely, gazing around the room before commenting to the world at large. "We're hungry."

That had been approximately two in the morning, after which the pantry had stayed quiet until around four, when work started up again. The kitchen staff had to get a jump start on the day, if only to feed those already awake. The tournament events themselves didn't start until mid-morning, but even if too many people had stayed up far too late the night before, plenty were out and about at the crack of dawn.

Finally, hardly five minutes earlier, Sara-the-vegetable-girl had entered, rummaged amongst the shelves looking for who knew what, and latched upon the vial of seeds. She'd studied it hard, held it up to the light, even pulling out the stopper, before heading back into the kitchen with the vial still in her hand.

And then, though they couldn't see her on camera anymore, they could hear her ask, "What are these seeds doing in the pantry?"

As soon as she'd picked up the vial, the two men had risen to their feet and headed towards the kitchen. Michael poked his head in first to take in the scene, which was calm, no different than the usual organized chaos of a castle kitchen in the middle of the day.

Cook Enith wasn't present, but her second-in-command, Gronw, hurried closer at the sight of them. "May I help you, my lord?" Then he did a double-take as he saw Ieuan standing behind him. "My lords, I mean."

"I was just checking in for my wife." Michael made up a story on the spot, which wasn't his forte. He stepped through the doorway in what he hoped was a casual fashion, encouraging Gronw to step back to give him room. "She was thinking that Arya might be getting a rash from something she ate, and I was hoping I could talk to Cook Enith about what that might be."

It wasn't a very good story, but it allowed Ieuan to slip into the kitchen behind Michael without eliciting comment.

The corners of Gronw's mouth turned down. "I'm afraid Enith has stepped out."

"Do you know when she will return?"

"Not-not exactly." Gronw appeared flustered. "Perhaps Healer Gwladys could be of service in this regard?"

"That does sound like a good idea," Michael said easily, pretending he thought it was. If he'd actually had the problem he'd suggested, it would have been.

Ieuan, meanwhile, had drifted near to where the vial of apple seeds had been set on a sideboard, out of the way. "What's this?" He picked it up and turned to show Gronw.

"I found those in the pantry." Sara smiled sweetly, making Michael very glad Ieuan had her attention instead of him, since Sara's hundred watt smile made him uncomfortable. Fortunately, Ieuan was as in love with Bronwen as Michael was with Livia.

Ieuan handled the situation with aplomb. "What are they?"

"Apple seeds, I think," Sara said. "Nobody could tell me what they were doing in the pantry. I set them there for Cook Enith to look at when she gets back."

This was all delivered in an ordinary tone, imparting the facts without emotion. Michael had been watching Gronw's face as Sara was speaking, and he appeared equally unconcerned, as if the vial was of so little interest he'd forgotten about it within moments of Sara finding it. Apple seeds were not nearly as poisonous as yew seeds, and apple trees produced food, whereas yew trees did not.

"Is there anything else?" Gronw was looking to get back to work.

"No. Thank you for your time." Even as Michael crossed the threshold after Ieuan, heading back into the bailey, he was pulling out his phone.

Ieuan stuck out a hand to shield the device from general view. "What are you looking at that for? The trap has been sprung. We can't put the seeds back now."

Michael nudged Ieuan up the stairs to the battlement. They had no hope of time traveling if something went awry with either of them, but that didn't mean it still wasn't a great place to talk privately. David had been right about that. They settled halfway along one wall, in a turret that overlooked the exterior kitchen garden to the south of the castle.

"For a moment I almost felt like I was back in Avalon." Michael looked at the phone with something akin to longing. Most of the time, he accepted the lack of technology in Earth Two—welcomed it, even. He hadn't realized how much he missed what it brought him until he spent a few hours carrying his mobile around in his pocket. "But I have to ask, why isn't Enith in the kitchen?"

"I don't know what you're getting at," Ieuan said. "She was there. She came into the pantry not long ago."

"Exactly my point. This is literally the biggest cooking day of the year and the head cook is nowhere to be seen. As Gronw was talking, I realized she hadn't been in the pantry for some time. Where did she go?"

"Maybe she was unwell."

"Then why didn't Gronw just say so?"

While Michael had been talking, he'd been swiping through all the visits to the pantry today. Enith had been in and out half a dozen times. The final time, she'd gone to the cheeses, counting them and moving them around. He turned the screen so Ieuan could see the clip, and he watched in silence until the end. "I think I see."

Michael paused the video, rewound it, and ran it forward at half speed. "You agree that she hesitates?"

"Her hand moves in the direction of the vial and then she draws it back."

Michael fast forwarded to the moment when Sara arrived to do essentially the same thing. She hadn't hesitated, however, but simply reached out and picked it up.

"Enith is loyal," Ieuan said. "She's worked here for years, her whole life, in fact."

"She *was* loyal," Michael said. "Given the right lever, anyone can be moved."

37

September 20 -Avalon

Lizzie

Exiting the castle put Lizzie, Elen, and Gwenllian right on the edge of the mill pool. The River Carew was tidal, meaning that when the tide was in, sea water mingled with river water flowing down from the hills, and the water level was much higher than when the tide was out. At high tide, water was collected in the mill pool and slowly let out through the dam in order to run the mill until the next high tide when the water in the pool could be replenished.

At the moment, the tidal pool was almost completely drained. If they had been standing a few feet farther down the bank, they would have been walking in mud.

After a quick argument the three girls decided to allow the postern gate to close behind them. If Enith was doing something innocuous, then they could apologize for the inconvenience to her of reentering the castle through the main gate. If Enith's plan was to open the castle to attack—or to a lone visitor so he could poison someone—they weren't going to facilitate that. They might be in trouble for following Enith before they got help, but so far they hadn't done anything truly catastrophic.

A trail cut through tufts of grass clinging to the rock upon which the castle was built. The girls followed it around the back of the castle, directly below the giant walls and towers on the western side. The substantial kitchen garden lay on the south side of the castle, and they walked through it, seeing no signs of Cook Enith, before reaching a road that led from the castle to the mill.

That Enith could have been going to the garden was one reason Lizzie hadn't wanted to raise the alarm. Yes, the guard had been asleep, but who was to say why that was? The carafe could have been a gift between friends. Lizzie certainly didn't want to get anyone in trouble without cause. She got herself in enough trouble as it was.

Once past the garden, the road either turned south to the village of Carew or headed the other way towards the tournament grounds. As they arrived at the crossroads, Cook Enith was just disappearing into the market fair. Lizzie breathed a sigh of relief to see her shape in the distance. If they'd waited any longer to follow her, she would have been lost in the crowd and all their sneaking about would have been for nothing.

They'd seen Enith hustle across the garden, but she must have slowed her pace as soon as she'd left the castle, perhaps not wanting to call attention to herself. Now, she was surrounded by so many people that she couldn't move fast, giving the three of them a chance to catch up. The girls were very good at following, if Lizzie did say so herself, having had a great deal of practice. Even Elen, who more than Gwenllian or Lizzie disliked bending the rules, had been torn at one point between being a spy and being a teacher.

Lizzie herself still wanted to join *Y Ddraig Goch*, and she saw no better way to hone her skills for her eventual employment than to spy on actual people. She kept their secrets too; that was part of her self-imposed code, not even regaling her friends with what she learned if she hadn't been with them when she'd learned it. Last night's relating of events to Daisy and William had been an exception.

By the time she was allowed a real job, she hoped to have collected many secrets about the royal court and have a head start on the skills required for spying.

So while Gwenllian and Elen walked together openly, keeping well back from Enith, Lizzie bounded through the tents and pavilions, hoping to get ahead of wherever she was going.

Enith didn't go to any of the market stalls that sold herbs and spices, nor even to one where she might purchase a hair ribbon or household item. Instead, she wended her way through the whole market and out the back, ending up where the various lords had set up their encampments. It was a little more awkward to be following here, since Lizzie felt like she was trespassing. She was also more likely to be recognized, as were Gwenllian and Elen. All three were members of the Welsh court, and Gwenllian, in particular, was notably beautiful. At the same time, the further they came from the castle, the more excited Lizzie became that this was a real endeavor.

Lizzie had turned down a narrow corridor between the Bohun encampment and that of the Percy family, when Christopher and another young man his age, who was dressed in tournament regalia, came around the side of a pavilion and almost ran into her.

Christopher caught her arms as she tried to look past him to where Enith had gone. "You okay?"

"I'm fine." Lizzie was more concerned about losing her quarry than about her awkwardness. She had more to prove than Christopher, who already worked for *Y Ddraig Goch*. "Did you see Cook Enith? She's the head cook at the castle."

Christopher's eyes narrowed. "We've seen a lot of people."

Lizzie rattled off the description. "My height, Aunt Meg's age, but not as pretty and a bit rounder and grayer."

"May I ask to whom I am speaking? I am John, Duke of Brabant." The man with Christopher was looking at Lizzie with an expression that was a cross between amusement and interest. She'd seen it before, and it made her impatient.

"Sorry, John." Christopher waggled a hand back and forth. "This is Princess Elizabeth."

"Lizzie," she corrected. "And I'm not a princess anymore."

"It is my pleasure to meet you, my lady. I do believe I saw the woman you mentioned. She was ducking between those two tents over there." He pointed behind him.

By now, Elen and Gwenllian had caught up to them, and Christopher fixed his sister with a beady eye. "What have you three gotten yourselves into?"

"Why would you assume we've gotten ourselves into anything?" Elen replied tartly.

"Because Lizzie practically ran me over, looking for Cook Enith."

Before Lizzie could protest that it was *he* who'd run over *her,* Elen said, "We were following her."

Christopher raised his eyebrows. "Why?"

Lizzie suddenly felt uncomfortable about answering and looked at the others. Then Gwenllian lifted one shoulder. "Probably we should tell him. He's part of DG, after all."

"Fine," Elen said, ungracefully. "We followed her because she left the castle by the postern gate, which she left propped open. What's more, the man who is supposed to be guarding it was asleep with his head on the table when we went by."

Christopher straightened, gratifyingly interested. "While I hate to even ask how it is you came to know all that, for now, I don't need to. Elen, you and Gwenllian go find someone to tell all that too—whether Aunt Meg, Ieuan, Livia—I don't care. Lizzie, come with me. If John saw her just now, she can't have gone far."

"I better come too," John said. "That's my encampment she was heading towards."

"You have a bout to prepare for," Christopher said.

"I have time."

Christopher looked as if he wanted to argue, but Lizzie was already taking quick steps in the direction John had indicated. It may be that Christopher hadn't sent her to find Aunt Meg because he didn't trust her to follow through, but if so, Lizzie wasn't sorry. This was where the action was.

"Any idea what Enith is doing all the way over here?" Christopher caught up to Lizzie with long strides.

Lizzie took a couple more quick steps to stay ahead of him. "I don't know. We were in the healer's hut and saw her go by. We thought she was behaving oddly, so we followed her."

"As you do." He shot her an amused glance.

"You're not angry?"

"Why would I be angry?" he asked with what appeared to be genuine puzzlement.

"My sister thinks I seek out trouble."

He laughed. "Well, you do, but I'm all for trouble if it brings some answers with it."

38

September 20 -Avalon

George

"We're getting gas?" David peered over George's shoulder towards the small station with its adjacent convenience store.

"For all that Chad has done amazing things with energy efficiency, this is a slightly older model of RV so it isn't either a hybrid or hydrogen fueled. We have solar panels and a treadmill, but we still need gas for it to run. We're out. Nothing to be done but stop."

"What about these cameras we've been talking about?"

"We don't have a choice." George glanced back. Clearly his lecture about the danger of being tracked had impacted David. Even when they'd stopped at a rest area or a roadside pull-out, killing time since they didn't have that far to go, he hadn't asked to leave the RV.

They'd started out in the Blue Mountains of Oregon, driven east and then north, looping through the countryside on small roads. They'd crossed into Washington State east of Walla Walla and ultimately ended up back on reservation land again, in this case belonging to the Spokane Tribe. While this tribe hadn't taken the extreme privacy measures of the Umatilla, George was counting on less surveillance here nonetheless.

As George exited the vehicle, he felt his shoulders hunching at the very obvious cameras he saw at the entrance to the store. He wore a baseball cap he'd found in one of the RV's cupboards, pulled down low over his eyes, and could hope that his two years in prison had (ironically) kept him out of the system enough for his general shape not to send up any red flags.

As to the actual purchase of the fuel, they had debated with Chad the merits of various means of payment. They had cash, thanks to the stash kept at Chad's house. Unfortunately, paying in cash required one of them to enter the little store. But it was better than an electronic payment of any kind, which would instantly flag them and their location.

George poked his head back into the RV. "Anyone want anything while I'm at it?" He was personally looking forward to another fountain diet Coke and took their orders for various high-calorie snack foods, laughing at Andre's request for chocolate mini-donuts. That was George's fault, since he'd introduced him to them years ago, back before their sojourn in Earth Two.

Shortening his gait in what was probably a feeble attempt to thwart recognition, he entered the store and made a beeline for the soda machine. Having picked up the snacks as well, he was just checking out when Sophie appeared at his left shoulder and said in a low voice, "We have to go."

George didn't look at her as he peeled off a raft of twenties and then accepted the change the checker offered, dropping four pennies into the little tray for spare change. He was trying to walk the fine line between being friendly and unmemorable.

Then two state patrolmen pushed through the door.

"I see the problem." He smiled down at Sophie and handed her the donuts. "Just act natural."

"There are two other patrol cars outside. It's like a convention out there."

"They can't have caught on to us that fast."

"Can't they?" She said this with a too wide smile, as if they were talking about something pleasant instead of imminent incarceration.

The two state troopers were looking intently at the caffeinated beverage section as George and Sophie exited ... only to find two tribal police officers standing outside the RV speaking to Andre.

Sophie wet her lips. "There's nothing we can do. There's nowhere we can go that they can't find us now."

"Uh huh." His reply was noncommittal because George wasn't giving up yet. As they arrived at the passenger side door, a whole host of opening lines fought for supremacy at his lips.

But Andre spoke first, gesturing to both of them. "This is my wife, Sophie, and her cousin, George."

The officer's eyes were alight as he looked at George. "You're driving a Treadman! I've always wanted to see one."

"That's right." George endeavored not to shoot Andre a dark look at not giving them pseudonyms. Still, not everyone was capable of instant deception, and truly, if they were asked for ID, they'd have to show what they had, which was their own, with their real names. "Honestly, I'd love to show you around inside, but my wife's in there asleep. She's pregnant."

This was crazy improvisation, and he was laying it on thick, but he wasn't coming up with anything else. He hadn't planned to be stopped by cops excited about the RV rather than who was inside—namely, the King of England in an alternate universe.

"Sorry about that," Andre said.

The officer put up his hands, ironically in something of a *hands up* gesture. "Totally get it. Have a nice day, now."

The three of them couldn't pile back into the RV fast enough, and George made sure not to turn on the visuals in the giant windscreen that disguised him as one-half of an elderly couple. With a wave, he pulled the RV out of the gas station and back onto the road, heading south. They didn't want to go that way, since the route they intended to take from here went north along similarly small roads as much as possible all the way to Seattle. But it was best not to telegraph that to the watching cops. George would find a way to turn around in another mile or two.

"The arena in Seattle where Chad is speaking is less than four hundred miles away," Sophie settled herself into the passenger seat. "We won't have to get gas again."

George flipped on the visuals, a sigh of relief escaping his lips to have suddenly become anonymous again. "Ready or not, FutureCon, here we come."

39

September 20 -Earth Two

Christopher

They reached the far edge of the encampment without seeing Enith again, at which point Christopher looked a bit darkly at Lizzie. He would have accused her of making the whole thing up if not for the involvement of Elen and Gwenllian and the fact that John had seen Enith too.

"Where could she have gone?" He asked the question of John Primus, rather than Lizzie.

John stood with his hands on his hips, looking across the sea of tents and pavilions. Every entourage had brought a minimum of a dozen tents and his was no exception. He and John Secundus each had their own personal space, and both also traveled with a company of ten guards, plus their servants, stable hands, and other retainers. All told, each entourage numbered close to fifty people. All great lords traveled that way, David among them. If nothing else, there was safety in numbers, and a limited range of people a lord could truly trust.

Lizzie started to lift a hand to point before dropping it so as not to call attention to herself. "Over there. Do you see?"

Enith had just come out of a tent distinguishable from the dozen others nearby because of its banner, picturing an eagle with a crown on a red background.

John Primus frowned. "What business could the castle cook have had with Baron Walter?"

The three of them moved as one in that direction, coming at the tent from the side so Enith wouldn't see them. While Christopher kept his eyes on Enith, John Primus ducked his head inside and almost immediately came out again. It was too bad John Secundus had gone ahead to prepare John Primus's horse for the jousts because they could have used his eyes too.

"Just for a moment, I feared I might find the baron dead in his bed, but the tent is empty," John said.

Lizzie was already following after Enith, and the two men settled into a fast walk to exactly match Enith's hurried pace.

They trailed the cook at that distance all the way back to the castle, which Lizzie said exactly retraced their steps. They had just reached the garden outside the castle walls when Michael arrived from the opposite direction, having come around the southwest tower.

Enith hesitated, made to turn back, and then saw Lizzie, Christopher, and John Primus right behind her.

She looked back to Michael, still hesitating, and when it became clear he was coming directly for her, she threw her apron over her face and burst into tears.

Christopher took her arm, trying to shush her, while at the same time directing her closer to Michael. Together, they walked around the wall of the castle to the little postern gate the girls had discovered, Enith all the while babbling in Welsh so fast Christopher could barely keep up with what she was saying.

Instead of a sleeping guard, it was Ieuan waiting for them. "Sit down, Enith." He was solicitous. "Take a breath."

Enith managed to stop her sobs long enough to drink from a cup of water Ieuan had ready for her, allowing Christopher to ask into the momentary silence, "Why did you go to the tent belonging to Baron Walter of Gela?"

"He has abducted my grandson! Ifan is only eight, and he's deaf, you see. Even if I had called for him, he couldn't have heard."

That was very much what Christopher had thought she'd said in their mutual walk through the garden, but he had hoped he'd misunderstood her Welsh.

"What is she saying?" John Primus asked, and when Michael translated Enith's accusation, his expression turned disbelieving. "This is a fantasy, my lord."

Enith understood enough French to argue with him. "It isn't! He took him!" She turned eagerly to Ieuan. "He was the man in the kitchen Sara mentioned."

"The man you said you spoke to only briefly?" Ieuan asked.

"I lied!"

"This is absurd." John Primus continued to scoff. "He's a no-blem—"

He stopped talking as Michael said to Enith, "I believe you." Then, to John, he added, "I can tell you right now that your Baron Walter isn't who he says he is. The Baron Walter of Gela doesn't exist."

John Primus was really gaping now. "How can you say that? Of course he exists. He has a tent in my encampment!"

Michael shook his head. "How do you know that's his real name and identity? Had you ever met him before the tournament?"

It was the same thought some in *Yr Ddraig Goch* had had about John Primus himself. "No. But he rode a horse; he bore a sword; he was dressed well." He stopped, comprehension finally entering his eyes.

Michael tipped his head, no longer having to openly state the obvious: that when a man who was dressed as a lord traveled in a foreign country, he could be anyone he wanted to be. In the same way, there was no better disguise for a knight—or a king—than to journey through the world as someone of a lower station. David had transformed himself in exactly that way a time or two. He just couldn't do it in England anymore because everyone knew what he looked like. "Two years ago in Paris, *I* was impersonating a baron from Gela, a place I chose because it barely exists on any map, has changed hands many times, and most recently has been under the authority of the widow of the King of Aragon, who has never visited it."

Christopher had been fascinated by this deception at the time and remembered that in Avalon, that widow should have been Eleanor, a daughter of King Edward of England. Here in Earth Two she had died before she could marry, and the King of Aragon had subsequently married someone else. He himself had died in 1291. None of that was something any of them were going to explain to Enith or John Primus.

Christopher spoke now to Enith, who'd been listening to this exchange with an open mouth. "We'll take it instead that *someone* has your grandson. Were you at Walter's tent because you believed your grandson might be in there?"

"I had to look!" She wailed her reply that was a plea as well, and Christopher was glad they were in the guardhouse rather than any place more public where her cries could have been overheard. "I tried to get into the encampment two days ago, but I lost my nerve."

Michael met Christopher's eyes with a knowing look. That's where she'd been in such a hurry to go when the guard at the outer gatehouse had observed her.

"Start at the beginning," Ieuan said. "When did this man first approach you?"

"It was a few days before the tournament started. He told me he had stolen my grandson, and if I wanted him back, I would do exactly as I was told."

"And you are sure it was this false Walter of Gela?" Ieuan said.

"As sure as I can be. It was dark, and he wore a hood, so I didn't see his face, but his voice was the same as when he came to me later in the kitchen."

"What did he want you to do?"

Enith threw her apron back over her face so she wouldn't have to look at anyone while she spoke. "Poison a dish with yew seeds."

"A dish intended for whom?" This was also from Ieuan. Enith seemed to be responding better to him than to any of the rest of them, even if she didn't want to answer.

"The cardinal."

"Cardinal Bogo?"

"No!" Enith seemed shocked by this. "The other one. There is a dish he likes, from Italy. *Panforte*, it's called. It was to be a present for him specially."

Ieuan looked at Michael, who nodded, indicating he knew it. "It's like fruitcake but better, as you might expect from the Italians. It would have hidden the crushed yew seeds well."

Enith pulled down her apron. "I wasn't going to *do* it! I really wasn't. But he had Ifan, so I had no choice but to play along. I made the small cake he asked for, as a trial." She put her face in her hands. "That is what I gave to Baron Walter the other day when he came to the kitchen."

"Where did the yew seeds come from?" Ieuan said.

"He had given a small number to me, that first day, and then the whole vial when he came to the kitchen later. They were in a box with other herbs and spices for the *panforte*. I kept the spices together, but I feared to keep the yew seeds with them. What if someone had asked about the box or looked inside? I hid the vial behind the cheeses."

"That was days ago. What prompted you to try again today to look into his tent?" Michael said.

"The vial had been moved." Her eyes took in each one of them, and when they landed on Ieuan, she bit her lip. "When I saw how they were, I remembered you had been in the kitchen asking all those questions. It suddenly came to me that you must have seen the vial, maybe even opened it. I felt watched. Even if Ifan wasn't in the tent, I had decided to tell Walter I couldn't do what he wanted, no matter what happened to my grandson."

"We knew something was going on," Ieuan said, without giving away the bit about the camera. "It sounds more and more like this is the link we needed between the yew seeds and Corwen's death."

"Cor-Corwen's *what*?" Enith gaped at him.

"You didn't know?" Ieuan said.

Enith shook her head, her tears renewed in genuine grief.

Christopher was honestly surprised she hadn't heard. While they'd brought Corwen's body out of the castle without fanfare in the early hours of the morning, it was currently lying in the village church, awaiting burial with the setting sun. They hadn't advertised his death, but they hadn't tried to keep it a secret either. It would have been too disrespectful.

"We don't know for certain that he ate the cake you made," Michael said, "but it seemed likely even before we talked to you."

Unfortunately, they had not come across the red-headed young man whom Corwen's neighbor had seen delivering the cake to his empty house.

Enith slumped forward in her seat, her head in her hands, weeping through her fingers. "I quite liked Corwen. I would never have wished him harm."

Lizzie had been unusually silent throughout Enith's confession, but now she suddenly blurted out, "How could you do it? Why didn't you simply *tell* someone what was happening?"

Enith turned to look at Lizzie, her face screwed up to weep again. "That very first day, he gave me another box, which he told me not to open until after he left. It held the finger bones of a child! I knew if I didn't do exactly as he said, the next fingers in the box would be Ifan's."

40

September 20 -Earth Two

Daisy

While Daisy hadn't exactly lied to her husband about where she was going, she hadn't sought him out to tell him either. She didn't think he would have objected to her destination, but he definitely would have wanted to come too, and she thought she would do better alone.

Isabel's tent was pitched close to the papal encampment, for reasons that were obvious to Daisy, even if Isabel and Bogo would deny any kind of relationship. Isabel had *loved* Bogo to the point of obsession. Daisy herself had an outsized hatred for the man, but that didn't mean she was imagining things. Back at Berkhamsted, Daisy had felt that Bogo had been using Isabel in the same way he used everyone else with whom he came into contact. Now, she wasn't so sure. That they were both here indicated to Daisy that Isabel had been complicit in his machinations last time and made it all the more likely they were working together again.

"Hello, Isabel. I'm glad to find you here."

"It is a pleasure to see you again so soon, my lady." It was late in the day, so naturally Isabel had a cup of wine in her hand. She had been seated in a small pavilion that served to keep the sun off her face as well as the rain if it came. When they'd first met, Daisy had been the daughter of a king, even if that king was dead. Now, she was married to the future Earl of Hereford. Either way, her station was far above Isabel's, which required Isabel to rise to her feet in greeting. "May I ask what brings you all the way out here?"

Daisy couldn't tell if the question was innocent or a not-so-subtle dig at the way her new father-in-law, who loved being in the center of everything, had set up his encampment closest to the castle and the tournament grounds. The papal entourage, as well as Isabel's from Powys, was camped on the outskirts.

"I didn't feel we had sufficient time to talk earlier." Daisy hoped Isabel couldn't see through that lie. "I wanted to hear more about what you've been doing these last two years."

"As I told you, everything has been wonderful, and isn't it marvelous how Bogo has landed on his feet?" She shook her head admiringly. "I always did hope for the best for him."

Daisy hoped Isabel couldn't tell how fixed her smile had become. As usual, Isabel had turned the conversation immediately to Bogo. It had been her habit two years ago too, and she had again glossed over the fact that he'd tried to overthrow the King of England.

"Do you know how it is that Bogo ended up in Rome?"

"Since he couldn't return to England, where else could he go?" Isabel seemed surprised that Daisy had to ask.

"Where else could who go?" All of a sudden, the man himself was there, greeting them both with a smile. Daisy had a horrible feeling he had been lurking behind Isabel's pavilion, listening to their conversation. She quickly ran through the little she'd said so far, hoping it was innocuous. If she was going to learn anything of note, she couldn't make them suspicious of her motives. At the same time, she didn't see how Bogo could be unaware of her opinion of him.

And maybe that was the reason he went first to Isabel (rather than to Daisy), holding out a hand for her to take.

Isabel kissed his ring.

Daisy tried not to vomit.

"None of that, my dear." Bogo raised her up. "We are related." He kissed her cheeks and then moved to Daisy to do the same.

Daisy was suddenly incredibly thankful her husband hadn't come with her. In the past, when Bogo had turned to her, she had adopted a polite demeanor and done what he wanted, which in this case would be to accept his attentions. It was still her first instinct after a lifetime of pleasing everyone around her.

This time, however, at the last moment she took a step back, avoiding the kiss on the cheek and forcing Bogo to settle for one to the back of her hand.

"I see you have landed on your feet." Her words were straightforward and very unlike the Daisy she had been. It probably wasn't going to get her the answers she wanted either, but she found herself so *angry* at his manner. She shouldn't ever have had to see him again.

Bogo, in that disgustingly gracious way of his, renewed his smile, as if he was determined to smooth over her rudeness.

"My dear, you are looking as beautiful as ever."

"I'm not your *dear*, and since it's only the three of us here, you can stop pretending to like me."

"But I do like you."

It was too much. "You tried to kill the king, and you tried to get me to help you do it."

"I was a pawn in Almain's game, just as you were."

She noted the way he didn't demur at her characterization, and the words he did say only made her angrier. *Of course*, Bogo would say that. To his mind, he was no more responsible for his actions than Isabel.

Bogo then had the temerity to wave his hand dismissively. "The pope has pardoned me. Why can't you?"

For a moment, Daisy's façade of self-control slipped entirely, and she said the most unguarded thing yet: "The only reason the pope pardoned you and made you a cardinal is because he wants something from you. I don't."

Bogo laughed. "My dear, I can't imagine what I did to deserve such hostility." He made the sign of the cross in front of her. "May you find peace in your new life." Then he tipped his head. "Allowances must be made for a woman with child."

Daisy's surprise overcame her fury. How he had known she was pregnant was beyond her. She barely knew it and had said nothing about it to anyone, even her husband. Reining in her temper, she coated herself at long last in that polite veneer she'd worn for so many years. "I would ask you not to please mention it to anyone. It's very early days yet."

He bowed his head. "Of course."

The fact that he had guessed correctly meant the moment she left Bogo's presence she would have to tell William. In retrospect, that Bogo had forced her into asking for a favor made him look on her with beneficence. She thought her anger gave her strength when dealing with him personally, but it hadn't aided her investigation—and that should have been her first priority, rather than scoring points like in a joust.

"Have you fully recovered from your own illness now? How long were you abed?" This was the question she should have asked at the start, before he put her hackles up.

"A full week." Bogo appeared to think nothing of the question. "I feel I'm lucky to be alive."

"Others were sick too, I understand."

"Most of our company, in fact."

"Was it just seasickness or something more?"

"More?" Isabel asked. "What more could it have been?"

"Usually seasickness abates shortly after one leaves the boat." Daisy couldn't believe Isabel could be that ignorant, but the look on the other woman's face was of such innocence, Daisy felt forced to elaborate. "Men of importance such as Cardinal Francesco and Cardinal Bogo can sometimes be a target of a certain animosity."

"Surely not. Who would do such a thing?" Now Isabel was looking at her with such surprise, Daisy struggled not to apologize.

Instead she asked, "What about you, Isabel? What made you decide to come to the tournament?"

"To tell the truth, we weren't going to come at all." Isabel had already refilled her cup with wine twice while they'd been talking, so she was well on her way to being oblivious to anyone else's intentions. "But once it became clear how many men of standing would be here—" she shot Bogo that familiar beatific smile, "—not to mention the king himself, my betrothed determined that we should make the journey. Everyone is here! It was too important an event to miss, especially as Earl Carew has made it clear that all are welcome. And how fortunate are we now to be graced by the presence of two cardinals!"

"I'm interested to know how that came about." Daisy turned to Bogo, hoping he didn't notice that she couldn't bring herself to call him *your grace*. "Were they speaking of this tournament as far away as Italy?"

"If they were, it wouldn't have surprised me, given the magnificence of the occasion—but no. After we arrived in Lamphey, the Archbishop told us of it. Since we hoped to speak to both King Llywelyn and King David, and would have traveled as far as necessary for the honor, we took the closeness of their presence as heaven-sent."

As well he might. It was even a reasonable thought, given that Francesco was the representative of the Holy See to all of Britain and its Guardian. Given how ill he had been too, it must have been a relief to discover they had such a short distance to travel.

That Bogo and Isabel remained friendly was no surprise either, and if something nefarious was going on between them, or at Bogo's behest, Daisy couldn't see how further conversation would uncover it. Despite his past malfeasance and how odious she found him, his illness would be so easy to confirm, there was no point in doing it.

Then again, maybe that was exactly what he was counting on.

41

September 20 -Earth Two

Callum

Callum ducked through the entrance to Cardinal Francesco's tent to find the man eating. This appeared to be a usual state for him since he was quite rotund. Bogo de Clare was at his side, along with several other noblemen Callum recognized, among them Roger de la Pole, who was well on his way to winning the jousts. Callum had been chosen as the one to speak to the cardinals because he hadn't personally been involved in any of the dealings at Berkhamsted two years ago, and thus was the most neutral of the members of David's court. If someone had to deal with Bogo de Clare, it might as well be him. He also would have preferred not to see a member of the Pole family cozying up to either Francesco or Bogo.

Not for the first time, Callum was glad David wasn't here. And that Callum himself hadn't gone with him, not that he'd had the chance today. His conversation with Cassie on the topic still played in his head:

"Why wouldn't you let David take you?"

"I didn't feel right saying yes."

"What's that supposed to mean?" Cassie's eyes had been very narrowed.

"I can't explain it. It was a feeling, as if something or some-one was telling me, This is a mistake. Don't do it. *David had to ask, but I had to say no. I told him so at the time. It wasn't the right time to be going to Avalon, even for me."*

Cassie had subsided because she'd had to admit half the reason Callum even listened to his feelings, not to say admitted he had them, was because of her. They'd been together for eight years now, and her own ability to trust how she felt had rubbed off on him. For that reason, she could hardly complain when he followed his instincts, even if it went against his own interests. Her grandfather would have been proud of him.

It made sense to Callum—and, in fact, to Cassie by now—that the reason he had told David *no* was so he could be here, right now, today, standing in this tent with these pernicious cardinals. Callum didn't actually have anything against Francesco himself, but given the persistent opposition towards David's policies from Rome, he was not predisposed to like him.

Nonetheless, he felt duty bound to save his life.

"We have become aware of a credible threat against you, Cardinal Francesco. While we believe we have intervened sufficiently at this time, the primary culprit is still at large; we have no notion of his whereabouts, but we are looking."

"Who is this person who dares threaten me?"

"We do not know his true identity. He has been passing himself off as a nobleman from Gela."

Callum had the full attention of everyone in the pavilion, and he was sorry it would have been rude to look into anyone else's face but Francesco's. In particular, he would have liked to see how Bogo or Roger was taking this news.

"Isn't your Earl of Lancaster originally from Sicily?" Francesco said.

"Indeed." Callum bent his head slightly. "He is not our quarry."

Francesco looked dubious, as well he might, since Callum had just told him of an unspecified man threatening an unspecified attack but reassured him that it couldn't *possibly* be one of their own.

Bogo leaned forward, having set down his cup of wine. "Perhaps I can help, as I have been out and about among the tournament goers more than my colleague. Do you have a description of the man?"

Callum didn't say, *he looks something like you but younger,* and instead brought out a charcoal sketch drawn by one of his people, who might find herself promoted from clerk to artist if she wanted. At the direction of Enith and John Primus, she'd drawn a very handsome man, but not Bogo.

Bogo studied the drawing, shaking his head all the while, and then shared it with Roger. He too gave it a long look. Then he glanced once at Bogo, before indicating he didn't recognize him either.

All of a sudden, Callum couldn't have been happier to find Roger in this company. He'd already shown this sketch to the castle guard who'd witnessed the argument between Walter and Roger. And now Roger denied knowing him.

Callum returned his gaze to Francesco. "During the course of his attempt to murder you, your holiness, he abducted an eight-year-old boy and threatened bodily harm to him if his grandmother didn't prepare a cake to poison you to death."

"Sacre Dieu!" Francesco's shock seemed genuine, and even Bogo looked disconcerted, his expression indicating that he could get what he wanted without resorting to threatening the lives of little boys. It seemed to Callum that, while their culprit appeared to be an attractive man, Bogo had something *more* going for him than just his appearance. When he focused on any one person, whether a maid, a grown woman, or Callum himself, his whole being vibrated with interest. He had charisma in such quantity he'd even overcome the pope.

That said, Bogo hadn't relied on it exclusively nor been above abducting female members of the royal family, past and present.

Bogo took back the sketch and frowned over it. "Now that I have given this face some thought, I may have seen this man on the road as we were traveling here. He was riding by himself and heading away from the tournament rather than towards it."

"When and where would this have been?" Callum couldn't help the way his voice went up a notch in intensity. According to John Primus, as confirmed by the members of his entourage, Walter had joined *his* party for the last leg of their journey to Carew, coming from the east. John had even started to wonder if the way Walter had come upon them as they were just starting out implied he'd been waiting for them.

"A matter of a quarter-mile from the castle. I'm afraid I didn't look at him closely at the time, since I was thinking of our imminent arrival, but the man was handsome and that caught my attention."

"Thank you very much." Callum casually showed the sketch to Roger again. "Are you sure you have never seen him?"

"Never." His answer was definitive.

And continued to be a total lie.

42

September 21 -Earth Two

Elen

"When you and Enith went back through the postern gate into the guardroom, Lizzie, Gwenllian and I were standing on the battlement, pretty much in the exact spot we are now," Elen said.

"I wanted to wave, but Elen wouldn't let me," Gwenllian added. "She was afraid if Michael saw us, he would remember you were with him and make you leave too."

"It doesn't matter now which of us saw what," Lizzie said magnanimously. "We have a murderer to catch."

"Do you really think we can do what everyone else cannot?" Gwenllian asked glumly, her elbow on the crenel and her chin in her hand.

"Of course!" Lizzie was as irrepressible as always.

Since Enith's revelation yesterday, the three girls had put considerable effort into learning everything their elders were doing.

Various people had seen this false nobleman from Gela over the course of the day, but eventually he must have realized something was amiss because he never returned to his tent. Though Callum had started out wanting to keep the entire investigation a secret, they'd eventually decided that, with Walter's plot foiled and the situation with Enith's grandson potentially desperate, they needed to go public. Callum had begun last night by speaking to Cardinal Francesco directly about the plot against his life, and word had spread from there.

By that morning, every person at the tournament knew at least part of the story, from the poisoning of Corwen on. The entire countryside had risen for the hunt, with many of the festivities put on hold until the boy was found. Today was Sunday, so no tournament events had been scheduled anyway.

"I'd settle for finding the boy," Elen said. "The fact that everyone else is focused on the murderer instead of the boy means they're looking at this all wrong."

"That's because Ifan could be anywhere." Lizzie checked the location of the sun. It was afternoon already. Elen could appreciate her frustration with their lack of results. "Besides, it isn't as if nobody has looked for him. They just can't find him. The fact that he's deaf means he would never hear anyone calling, nor be able to call out to them."

"Or he's already dead," Gwenllian said in a small voice.

She wasn't wrong. Another day of this and the boy might be dead from dehydration or starvation if Walter had left him without supplies. He wouldn't have to kill him.

"That's what's worrying Aunt Meg. I heard her say that if Walter could threaten to dismember him, he wouldn't think twice about abandoning him in some old cellar where nobody would ever find him, just to save himself. That's essentially what Bogo did to Almain." Since Elen had been imprisoned at Berkhamsted along with Lizzie and Gwenllian, she well remembered that fear. The boy's must be worse. "I think he has to be somewhere close by and also some place so obvious that nobody would think to look there."

"How do you figure?" Lizzie said, using a twenty-firster phrase as if born to it.

"Because Walter isn't from around here. Enith didn't know him to look at. She genuinely thought he was a nobleman from Gela. He might even be, though I think Michael is right that Walter looked for the farthest spot a Norman could be from and chose to be from there, just like Michael and Livia did in Paris."

The three girls gazed out from the battlement. Much of the area around Carew was very flat, and they could see for miles. If she was right, and the more Elen thought about it the more she hoped she really might be, stashing the boy miles away from Carew would have increased the chance of exposure. Hauling a struggling eight-year-old boy even a short distance without being noticed couldn't have been easy.

Maybe Walter had dosed him with poppy. Maybe he had already murdered him, in which case the whole thing was hopeless anyway. They would lose nothing but time by searching. The fact that nobody had found him yet—alive or dead—meant only that they were still looking in the wrong place.

Elen turned to her friends, "Has anyone asked yet about where Walter got a boy's finger bones?"

Lizzie wrinkled her nose. "From a grave?"

Gwenllian pursed her lips. "He wouldn't have had to dig up a body. He would just need access to a charnel house."

"Is there one nearby?" Elen's twenty-first century persona had been horrified when she'd first discovered the existence of charnel houses, where the bones of the dead were kept to prevent church graveyards from getting too full. In her experience, charnel houses were something out of an Indiana Jones movie, not a part of life people dealt with every day. But once she started looking, she realized that the sheds she'd seen in churchyards, which she'd assumed were for storage, were actually small chapels over crypts in the ground where bones were deposited.

Since then, she'd looked for them at every place they stayed. Most churches were hundreds of years old, with full graveyards because it was so important to be buried in sacred ground. Rather than dedicating an endless number of new cemeteries, the sexton simply dug up the bones of people who'd been dead for years and placed those bones in the charnel house built within the graveyard. Then he had room for people who'd died more recently.

Gwenllian pointed across the fields towards the town of Carew. The steeple of the church was visible above the trees. "Has anyone looked there?"

"I don't know." Even Lizzie, who was always up for most any adventure, couldn't help but feel horror at the sacrilege.

"Then we should." Elen threw the words over her shoulder, having already set off at a run for the stairs down from the battlement.

Gwenllian and Lizzie followed her, as Elen knew they would, through the inner gatehouse, across the outer bailey, and then out of the castle, all at a run. She heard someone call her name after she was already past them, but she merely waved a hand and said, "We're fine!"

"Maybe we should be riding?" Gwenllian said as she caught up to Elen.

"Riding would take time and explanation, and I think most of the horses are out with the search parties." Elen settled into a jog, which was a much more manageable pace. "We don't have far to go anyway, just to the village."

They jogged the mile from the castle to St. Mary's Church in the village of Carew. The church itself was larger than many churches found in villages, thanks to the patronage of the Carews for so many years. Having reached the little gate in the northwest corner of the wall, Elen led them into the churchyard, which stretched nearly four hundred feet to the opposite corner to the southeast. They had overheard Michael talking about the way the church lay across a field from Corwen's house. Honestly, churches were the center of any community, so while Carew Castle had its own chapel, it was no surprise to find a real church in close proximity here.

Elen stopped at the first building she came to along the path. Though a quarter of the size of the church, it was a great deal larger than a shed, with two sets of stairs: one down to a basement door and one up to the entrance on the main floor.

Gwenllian gazed at it. "I don't want to go in there. All those bones." She shivered.

"You and everybody else." Elen had spent the last mile bracing herself for what they had to do. "It's just bones."

"Bones and ghosts." Lizzie appeared to have recovered from her earlier horror, and unlike Gwenllian's voice, hers held morbid interest. She didn't even seem to be resenting the fact that this had been Elen's idea. Normally Lizzie was their ringleader, despite the fact she was the youngest of the three.

But maybe because of it, Lizzie was the one to pull on the handle of the basement door. It didn't budge, not surprising since it sported a big lock for which they didn't have a key. Then she banged on the wood with her fist, calling, "Ifan!"

"He's deaf, so he can't hear you." Elen pressed her ear to the door. "I can't hear anything inside."

"We'll have to try the other way." Gwenllian took the steps up to the chapel two at a time. After a hasty genuflection, she ran to the trap door located in the floor in front of the altar. Grabbing the iron ring, she tried to lift it up, but it was too heavy by herself. With Elen's help, and with Lizzie prying at the opposite edge with her fingers, they pulled it up with a sudden thrust, causing Lizzie to fall onto her rear and Elen and Gwenllian to stumble backwards.

Elen wasn't feeling as casual about entering a charnel house as she'd conveyed to her friends, but she was first down the steps nonetheless. As expected, the crypt was full of bones, sorted by type: long bones on that shelf, pelvises over there, and an entire wall of skulls.

And in one corner, just sitting up as if he'd been sleeping, eyes widening at the sight of them, was a little boy. To her relief, his bound hands still had all ten fingers.

43

September 21 -Avalon

Lili

"I can't be sorry everyone seems to be taking their own sweet time about finding us," Dafydd said from his position behind Andre, who was driving the RV. Lili had heard Meg use that turn of phrase. It had never seemed quite right coming out of Lili's own mouth, but it was nice to hear a bit of home from her husband.

"We're not going in the direction they expected," Sophie said from the front passenger seat. "We aren't going where anyone thinks we're going. Everyone expects us to be cruising into Washington DC about now, heading for the capitol building. Instead, we are all of three hundred miles from where we started."

Lili was seated next to her husband, both ensconced in unbelievably comfortable chairs. Lili's swiveled and rocked, but still held her safe with a seatbelt, one she was dutifully wearing. They had driven all day again, doing what George called "killing" time rather than fleeing pursuit, and had reached the city of Seattle. A body of water was to Lili's right, and they were heading south to the large arena where Chad was the scheduled speaker. His speech was to take place at six o'clock in the evening, which was somehow nine o'clock in Washington DC. Time zones were something Lili was still getting used to. They had never been relevant to her before.

Dafydd would be simultaneously replacing Chad here in Seattle and the Secretary-General of the United Nations in Washington DC, his words broadcast across the planet.

Had his enemies really expected him to speak in person before the Congress? Even Lili could have told them that wasn't going to happen, not even taking into account the difficulty of driving across the entire country, some three thousand miles, in three days. It was possible, George had assured Lili. It would have been *a piece of cake,* to use George's phrase, to fly. But that surely would have meant capture.

"I can't believe I'm going to FutureCon." Dafydd laughed as he gazed out his side window. "I begged my mom to let me go when it came to Portland that September before Anna and I came to Earth Two."

"Did she let you?" Sophie asked.

"She did."

"What a good mom."

"So you know what to expect," Andre put in.

"I doubt it." Dafydd laughed again. "As I am continually reminded, that was a long time ago."

"The audience is going to go wild to see you," Sophie said.

"Do you really think many people will show up?" Dafydd asked. "It's a Sunday evening."

Andre and Sophie exchanged an amused look. "Of course it will be packed. We already know it's sold out. They're coming to see Chad Treadman talk about you."

"And instead, they're going to get *you*." George came up from the back of the RV, his hand to his earpiece. "Chad's already there, meeting and greeting."

"Good," Andre said. "Tell him we're a mile and a half out. Forty minutes to spare."

Sophie, who had been at such events with Chad before, assured them that being a little late would be okay and give Chad a chance to get started. Dafydd was back in his medieval attire, as was Lili, which they had decided would be appropriate for this venue as a reminder of who he was.

"I don't like this route now. It feels like a mistake." Andre gripped the wheel a little tighter. The RV had just bounced through a hole in the road, against which even the luxurious vehicle couldn't completely compensate. "With this greenbelt on the left and the water on our right, we're boxed in. I should have scouted this better."

"You couldn't have scouted it without leaving the RV," Sophie said. "All of us are targets now, not just David."

"We are in a massive vehicle in too small a space," George said. "We can't just drive through neighborhoods."

"I submit we should have tried," Andre said.

Everyone was sitting up straight, alert. George was too restless to sit and had moved into the space between the two front seats, bent slightly to look through the front windscreen. For most of the day, he had been monitoring police frequencies, which didn't appear to have lessened his concern about what they might be facing.

Sophie motioned to her right. "That's the Royal Caribbean port." And then she let out a terrified screech that curdled Lili's blood even before she screamed, "Watch out—"

Between one heartbeat and the next, a giant vehicle had sped through the intersection on the right side of the RV and hit it full on. Lili watched it happen, unable to get out a single sound before the world blew apart with shrieking metal and exploding glass.

The oncoming vehicle had looked very much like the front of the train that had passed through Pendleton. It was so large and powerful, in fact, that it threw the RV onto its side. George was tossed around, slamming first into the ceiling, and then the wall, and then the other wall, which became the new floor. When the world finally stopped moving, Lili and Dafydd found themselves strapped into chairs suspended from the right-hand wall.

Dafydd's chair was closest to the ground, and with a click he detached his seatbelt and fell onto what had been a window. Through the broken glass, Lili could see the surface of the road.

Lili's chest hurt where the belt had held her to the chair. Dafydd found the lock on her seatbelt, detached it, and then caught her as she fell into his arms. "Are you okay?"

His solid presence amidst the chaos was calming. "I think so."

Even as she answered, Dafydd set her on her feet and was moving to where George lay across what had once been their couch. He felt for a pulse. "He's alive."

Stunned and still not thinking straight, Lili watched her husband pat George down, looking for obvious wounds. And then she got herself together enough to make her way to where Sophie and Andre were suspended from the side wall in a similar fashion to how she and Dafydd had come to rest. They were unconscious but alive. Andre had a bleeding cut on his forehead.

"This was no accident." Surprisingly, George was the first to open his eyes. "You have to get to that speech, David! You and Lili. If you miss it, nobody will ever take you seriously again. Even more, if you stay, you give whoever did this the chance to capture you, right here, right now. Take Lili and run."

"We can't leave you like this." Dafydd was still crouched beside him.

"We are in less danger with you gone." George sketched a motion towards a hatch in what had been the roof but was now a wall. "You can get out there. They won't expect it."

"What about surveillance? We haven't left the RV out of fear of it."

"Everyone was going to know where you are soon enough anyway. Go!"

Dafydd went to the hatch, pressed the release, and the little door popped open.

"See anyone?" George asked.

"Nobody." David held out his hand to Lili who took it, and a moment later they were out of the vehicle and running east along a road, the entrance to which was entirely blocked by the overturned RV behind them.

"Can you hear the sirens?" Dafydd said.

The caterwauling Lili hadn't been able to identify had been faint at first but now was coming closer and closer.

"We passed a fire station half a mile back. They'll be okay." It sounded like David was reassuring himself as much as Lili.

"They're alive," she consoled him in return. "As awful as it feels, George is right that running away may be the best way for us to stay that way too."

44

September 21 -Earth Two

Michael

On the surface, the particular tip they were following wasn't a very good one, not to mention the fact that it had drawn them miles away from Carew. But by this point, they were willing to grasp at any straw. Going home meant abandoning the search and admitting defeat.

Michael put his finger to his lips while at the same time motioning Christopher and his little band forward towards the barn. They'd already checked the associated house. It showed signs of occupation, particularly the remains of food and rumpled bedclothes. The fire was still warm. Someone had been there very recently.

As well as two usual comrades—Huw and Robbie—the band now included John Primus in the place of William with his broken wrist. He'd tried to insist he could still be of use. Nobody denied it in principle, just not in this particular capacity.

John was involved because Walter had traveled with his party for the last day of their journey to Carew, which was understood now to have been a ploy to disguise the fact that he'd come earlier in order to threaten Enith. For their purposes, that meant all of John's people would recognize him on sight.

Thus, various members of his entourage had been distributed amongst the search parties. John Primus was now a follower and fast friend of Christopher—no surprise there—and there had never been any question as to with which group he was going.

Thanks to the intrepid trio of girls, the most important work was done with the recovery of Ifan. Nobody was getting poisoned at the tournament, unless self-inflicted from consuming too much alcohol.

The problem with not catching this Walter character was the same problem they'd faced in allowing Bogo to flee Berkhamsted. They hadn't "allowed" it deliberately, of course, but by not capturing him, he had been free to rear his very pretty head again two years later as a cardinal, of all things. Meg had commented tartly that she could see *this whole France ploy* (her words) as a back-handed attempt to undermine David's throne. Either all hell would break loose when David left the country, or he would die in battle and then Pope Boniface could throw his weight behind a hand-picked successor.

What must be frustrating the Pope immensely was that David would do as he thought best, as always.

"You realize we are about to scare the hell out of some poor, unsuspecting farmer." Christopher slid into place behind the crumbling wall next to Michael, his attention on the bit of light coming through the slits in the planks that made up the wall of the barn.

If Michael had to guess, he would have said the light was coming from a lantern held low to the ground. "If so, we will apologize."

A moment later, the others were lined up behind Christopher. Michael motioned that Robbie should circle around the barn to the left, Christopher and John to the right, and he and Huw would take the front. If the man inside was a farmer, so be it, but if this was their quarry, they were going to do everything in their power to prevent his escape.

As the others moved away, Michael had one last thought: "Alive, remember."

Christopher waved a hand. They knew what to do, and Michael was mother-henning unnecessarily to tell them their business. He should have known better by now.

Instead of asking *where do you want me,* Huw did exactly what Michael would have suggested, moving to a position on the other side of the dirt road. If Walter was to escape by the front door of the barn, he'd have to come this way.

An owl hooted, answered by the call of another. That was Robbie and Christopher respectively, both of whom had developed a credible imitation of a real owl. It was just as well William wasn't here because he had no ability in that regard, which he claimed was beneath him anyway. His forte was a turtle dove, but it was the wrong time of day and year for it. Michael honestly agreed that he could put on a virtuoso performance, but it was pretty useless if he could use it only in spring and summer. Fortunately, owls were never out of place or time.

The calls were the sign for which Michael had been waiting, telling him his companions were in position. He rose to his feet and stepped into the yard. He would have been in plain sight if anyone was looking. It was probably too late to be worrying that Walter had a crossbow.

"Walter! This is the Earl of Lancaster, who has been known as Michael of Gela. We know you're in there! It's time to give yourself up."

The light stopped moving, and then it went out entirely. The silence was almost as loud as his movements had been earlier.

"Walter!" This came from John Primus, despite Michael's stated desire to do all the talking. The man was a duke, for all that he was young, so he was not accustomed to taking orders and would see them rather as guidelines. "You betrayed my trust, but I'm willing to forgive you if you come out!"

Michael would have rolled his eyes if it wasn't a good line. Walter would now be afraid he was surrounded, since John's voice had come from the other side of the barn.

Then it was Robbie's turn, at which point Michael felt like throwing up his hands and saying, *why do I bother to make a plan?* "We know who you are! Come out, and we will spare your life."

By this point, if the man inside had been a farmer, he would have been quite confused, if only because they'd all been speaking

French. But since he didn't protest his innocence, Michael was pretty sure they had their man. The question was whether they were going to have to go in and get him.

Then Christopher struck flint and lit his torch. A moment later, the rest of them did the same, since this *was* part of the plan. There were only five of them standing in a circle around the barn, but Walter would never believe so many men of such high standing were here alone.

"Do we have to burn the barn down around you?" Christopher asked.

"All right! All right! I'm coming out!"

Slowly, the door swung wide.

One moment the figure of a man was shadowed in the doorway, and the next he was surging through it on a charger, one bred for jousting. For that reason, the horse was accustomed to driving at other men and didn't balk as it bore down on Michael where he stood in the yard.

"Move, Michael!" Christopher literally threw his torch at the galloping horse.

It was a good attempt, considering, and didn't miss by much. The torch landed at the horse's feet, causing him to swerve dramatically. Walter managed to hang on and keep the horse headed in the right direction. At the last moment, Michael dove out of the way.

If they'd been in England, Walter might have made his escape, but one of the men opposing him was Welsh, born and bred. Huw dropped his torch to the dirt of the yard and, in a smooth movement born of thousands of hours of practice, had his bow in one hand and an arrow in the other. *Nock, pull, loose.*

The arrow flew through the air, followed in rapid succession by two more, all perfectly aimed. The first hit Walter in the left calf; the second drove into Walter's thigh on the same side, while the third clipped the horse's ear—at which point it finally reared. Walter, already in pain and unable to control the beast, fell to the ground. Huw had been told to stop him, not kill him, and that was what he had done.

While Christopher ran to calm the horse, Michael picked up his torch from where it had fallen and made his way to their culprit, who lay groaning in the dirt of the road. Holding up the torch, he illuminated the man's face. If it hadn't been so contorted in pain, he might have been as handsome as everyone said. "Who are you? And don't say Walter of Gela. We know that's a lie."

"I claim sanctuary!" He scrabbled under his clothing and came up with an amulet. "It's a papal bulla! You can't touch me!"

John Primus immediately crossed himself. The other men, especially Michael and Christopher, as twenty-firsters, were much less impressed.

"What are you babbling about?" Christopher said.

"My sins are forgiven!" Walter was desperate now, showing the amulet to each of them in turn.

The papal bulla was a formal seal of office used by the Pope. Only a person enormously trusted would bear it.

"Where did you get it?" Michael asked.

"It was blessed by the hand of the pope himself!" Walter clutched it now in his fist, as if he was afraid one of them would take it from him. Michael might have done so if he were alone, but he couldn't do it in front of other believers, whether or not they shared his disdain for Walter.

"The pope ordered you to murder a cardinal?" John Primus moved to a crouch in front of the fallen man.

"Murder a cardinal? How could you think that?"

Michael felt a headache coming on. "Do you deny that the pope ordered you to murder his nephew, the Cardinal Francesco?"

"Of course I deny it!" Walter's mouth was gaping wide. "Who told you such a thing? It isn't true!"

"You abducted the grandson of Enith, the head cook at Carew Castle, to blackmail her into poisoning the cardinal. You poisoned Corwen, the castle woodsman, as a trial run."

Walter's head was moving back and forth repeatedly. "I didn't abduct anyone. I don't know what you're talking about! Who do you take me for?"

"A murderer." They had been so sure they knew what they knew. Walter had abducted Ifan, threatened Enith, and fled, all in the service of murdering Cardinal Francesco.

"No! No! I didn't kill anybody!"

"Why were you in this barn?"

"I was hiding!"

Michael's patience was running thin. "Why would you hide if you didn't do anything wrong?"

By now Walter was weeping with fear and pain. "I had to! I learned I was being hunted, though I didn't know why. It was better to leave than risk being hanged for crimes I didn't commit."

It sounded like the truth as he saw it. It was certainly becoming clear that nobody this wide-eyed could be the criminal mastermind they had thought they were hunting. As when Michael had questioned Enith, it was time to start over. "Do you deny speaking to Cook Enith in the castle kitchen a few days ago?"

"Why would I deny it?"

He'd answered Michael's question with a question, which Michael didn't like, but it had also been a question that implied *yes.* "What did you say to her?"

"I gave her a box containing special ingredients so she could make a treat for the cardinal. She had made a small sample already from stores she had, which she gave to me in return." Walter was rocking back and forth in a way that might be jarring his wounds. In his desperation to be believed, he appeared to have forgotten about them.

"Was this treat your idea?"

"N-n-no."

Michael went back further. "Who gave you the spices, and what did you do with the cake she gave you?"

"M-m-my father gave them to me to give to her, and I brought the cake to him. I had to ride all the way to Lamphey to do it! Please, you have me all wrong. If you just bring me to him, I'm sure he will be able to explain everything."

"Who is your father?" Even as Christopher asked the question, Michael knew the inevitable reply, and his stomach sank into his boots.

"Cardinal Bogo de Clare, of course."

45

September 21 -Avalon

David

Fleeing the scene while his friends were in trouble was so against David's nature, he could hardly believe he was doing it. But he also knew that if George was right and the accident hadn't been an accident, then his friends were safer without him. In retrospect, he had to think that fateful encounter at the gas station yesterday had led to discovery—perhaps inevitably. But by whom, he couldn't say, and maybe at this point almost didn't want to know.

Once through the hatch, they'd stumbled past a very large billboard advertising a cruise to Alaska, and then down a neglected street fronting a series of derelict buildings of unknown identity. Andre had expressed concern about the rundown nature of this part of Seattle, and this little corner was worse, as evidenced by potholes, trash, overturned shopping carts, and cracked sidewalks with a plethora of weeds growing out of them. Ideally, it would not have been a place David would have ended up with Lili on this or any other trip to Avalon.

He wasn't entirely sure how to get to the arena from here, but he had seen the map, same as everyone else, and knew the address and the general direction they needed to go: east and south.

All David could think was that the drivers of the semi-truck had crushed the RV with the hope of forcing him to time travel. With the two vehicles connected, David would have taken them with him. He was betting there were a ton of supplies in the back of the truck that would have meant all sorts of things to Earth Two.

Two years ago, the CIA had put David in deadly situations over and over again in an attempt to force him to shift universes. Which he had done, though never in the way they'd expected. That he hadn't actually died all those times didn't mean he wasn't scarred by the experience. Even now, he could feel the force of the seatbelt on his chest. The pressure from it had prevented him from breathing long enough that he was flashing back to two days ago when he and Lili had arrived in Avalon. Anaphylaxis, as it turned out, was a more terrifying experience than being thrown out of an airplane or nearly beheaded.

Hand-in-hand, they made it past the first block without thinking, their medieval cloaks streaming behind them. Above them was an overpass, which they crossed under, to find a man rising up in front of them, having appeared suddenly out of a mass of foliage. Lili gave a little squeak, and David might have barreled into him, or fled in another direction, if it wasn't immediately obvious he wasn't a threat. He reeked of alcohol and might have been relieving himself in the bushes.

He also might have been the one person who could help them in this moment. "Where can we hide?"

The man gaped blearily at them, and then pointed east. "That way."

It seemed as good an option as any, and within a dozen steps, they came upon a genuine woodland trail through the green space Andre had been grumbling about.

A last glance back showed the twirling lights of the fire truck and ambulance just coming to a stop near the giant semi-truck blocking the intersection. Cars were backed up both north and south. If other people were driving that route to the arena, thinking they had forty minutes to spare, they would soon find going on foot like David and Lili were accidentally doing would be faster.

"We can cross the park," he said to Lili. "As far as I can tell, nobody is following us."

"We need to be careful not to end up on that main street again," she said. "It's just off to our right."

The park wasn't the lovely flat forest he'd imagined but involved a steep incline on the eastern side. It looked to him as if the city stewards had made a virtue out of a necessity. Because the cliff was so steep, nobody could build a house on it anyway. "I hear it, even if I can't see it. I'm going to head straight up instead." He took a left-hand path.

It was human nature for a right-handed person to go to the right when in danger, but it was also instinct to look for higher ground. In this instance, the latter impulse seemed more productive than the former. He just had to hope they wouldn't end up against a giant chain-link fence with hurricane wire, separating the neighborhoods at the top from the riffraff below.

The trail was narrow enough and so enclosed left and right by overgrown vegetation that he had to let go of Lili's hand. Still within the park, they came to an old road that continued the way they'd been climbing. But then, at the very top, an eight-foot-high, black metal gate blocked their way.

David pulled up, cursing under his breath, but then Lili tugged at his hand. The streetlights in the neighborhood on the other side of the path were bright enough to illuminate another path through the vegetation to the right. Following it for ten yards took them around the gate and directly onto a residential street.

As he'd honestly hoped, the street was tree-lined and upscale. Committing to a fast walk, as if they were regular pedestrians instead of fleeing for their lives, he and Lili set off due east.

However they'd managed it, they'd left any pursuers behind.

Admittedly, their opponents didn't have to follow them. Chad Treadman's schedule wasn't a secret, nor was his flight to Seattle. This talk he was supposed to be giving had been on the books for a while. That knowledge, plus those pesky satellites which by now should be well occupied tracing his every move, would tell anyone who cared to look where he was and what he was about to do.

Besides, if one agency or group had come up with the idea that David would be in Seattle far enough in advance to smash into their RV with a semi-truck, so could another. And another.

This was a hilly part of Seattle, and the street they were on appeared to end a few blocks ahead at a row of bushes. They kept following it anyway, and in the end were saved by a stairway that took them to the next road over. David's medieval boots were not designed for lengthy walking on pavement, and he was also cursing himself for not being in quite the shape he should be. Twenty-nine wasn't old, but it was definitely old-*er*.

"Are we going to talk about what just happened?" Lili said, speaking for the first time since they'd left the woods.

Most of David's attention was on the neighborhoods to the south. He was sure they needed to take a right eventually. Still, he managed to say, "You want to talk about it *now*?"

"We didn't *travel*, Dafydd."

"I know." He urged her across the road, all the while hating every moment they were exposed. "My life wasn't in danger."

"That's what you think?"

"What else can I think?" They hurried along, finally taking that right. In the distance, he could see the lights of downtown Seattle.

And the arena.

He didn't dare breathe a sigh of relief, even as he was relieved. The closer they came to it, the more he wanted to run, and the more he made himself act normally.

Finally, when they were within a few blocks, their pace really had to slow, in part because they were both out of breath, but also because they had joined a crowd of people heading in the same direction. Many were in costume. Seeing it, David pulled his hood over his head and helped Lili do the same.

"I think George, Sophie, and Andre are hurt, and they might not have survived if they'd been taken to Earth Two," Lili finally said. "We are still here because *they* need to be here. And maybe you do too."

Seattle had a lot of trees, he'd give the city that. He felt much more comfortable under cover. "Maybe." David wasn't ready to commit.

They had been told to enter the arena at the "Club" entrance, which sounded like a place for VIPs, but the moment they distinguished themselves from the crowd by going a different way would also be the moment they were most exposed. This side of the arena was also exclusively for pedestrians, so even if they'd still been with the RV, they would have had to get out and walk. Of course, they would also have had Andre, Sophie, and George with them.

A big clock above the entrance was lit up in fluorescent green, counting down the minutes and seconds until the session was due to start. It said 5:59:05. It was now or never.

David stepped into the open, Lili's hand in his, and headed across the plaza towards the doors. A cluster of people near a rack of bikes turned to look at them. He lengthened his strides. "Hopefully nobody is going to think it's a good idea to shoot me right here where anyone can see."

"If they did, we'd time travel home, and we wouldn't have to worry about any of this anymore," Lili said reasonably.

Her surety settled him for the last ten yards.

And then Chad's people surged out of the doors, engulfing David and Lili on every side.

They were safe at last.

For now.

46

September 21 -Earth Two

Callum

With the castle's other residents settling in to sleep, only Livia and Cassie remained with Callum to wait for the return of the search parties, warming themselves in Carew Castle's receiving room, since it was turning into a colder-than-normal evening.

"I still think we need to look harder at Bogo." Cassie took up a spot near the fireplace. "Do we even know what he told the pope? I would like to have all this cleaned up before David gets back."

"If he gets back." Callum didn't mean to be the dark cloud in the room, but he wasn't feeling particularly positive in this moment. "According to everyone in Bogo's party, he sailed from France with the cardinal, became ill on the journey, as they all did, and remained bedridden up until the day they departed for Carew. He can't be involved."

"Even if he didn't do anything himself," Livia said, her voice as full of frustration as the rest of them, "he could know who did. He could have sent us looking for Walter in the wrong direction. It would be just like him, in fact, to let someone else take all the risks for him."

They'd generated Bogo's guilt out of whole cloth, but Callum couldn't blame them for doing it.

"He genuinely did go to Berkhamsted," Cassie said, a little musingly. "He could have come to Carew earlier, even if ill. The Bishop's palace at Lamphey is all of five miles away."

"More like four." Livia looked at her friend. "A matter of an hour's ride."

"Bogo, Roger, and Walter. There's not much to choose between them," Cassie said. "But I can't see how they could genuinely be working together. How would they even know each other? It isn't as if there's an underground message board for people who hate David."

"Like is drawn to like," Callum said.

"Maybe that's something for which we should be grateful," Livia said. "At least we know whom to watch—" She broke off, as her attention was caught by the opening of the receiving room door.

Callum turned with her to see Isabel and Roger de la Pole standing on the threshold of the receiving room. Although the sight was unexpected, Callum didn't glare nor ask *what are you doing here?* He could tell from the expression of distaste on Roger's face that he didn't want to be here any more than Callum wanted him here.

But he *was* here. With a gesture, Callum invited him into the room. He had been a lord long enough, and a manager of people before that, to give Roger the benefit of the doubt, at least for the length of time it took to hear what he had to say. A rumble in his gut even had him thinking Roger might not even be the enemy Callum had thought. "Welcome."

Roger glanced down at Isabel, who looked up at him, nodded encouragingly, and said, "Go ahead. We agreed this was important."

Roger squared his shoulders. "I couldn't help overhearing what you just said. I don't care to be lumped in with Cardinal Bogo. Walter, on the other hand, has been my friend for many years. I think this situation is not quite as it seems or you have made it out to be. There are truths here that are hidden." Now he took a more resolute step into the room. "Isabel and I would very much like to help you uncover them if we can."

47

September 21 -Avalon

George

"Where are they?"

After David and Lili had fled, George had been drifting around in his mind, trying not to think about the fact that he was bleeding from several new orifices, and his ankle might be broken. Now he opened his eyes to see a bearded man with dark eyes and dark hair speaking English to him with a thick Spanish accent. These Russians were turning out not to be Russian after all.

"Who do you mean?" George replied in Spanish, to match the man's accent. He was thankful he wasn't having to use his Welsh, since at the moment he couldn't remember any of it. "I don't know what you're talking about."

At the change of language, the man's expression grew furious, and he made to backhand George across the face with his gun. He would have done it too, if his companion hadn't caught his arm and said, back to Spanish-accented English, "We don't have time for your temper. He isn't going to tell you, and we are running out of time. This RV could even have been a diversion, which is why we didn't travel to Earth Two. David is long gone, if he was ever here."

It wasn't an outrageous theory. Splitting up, even sending David and Lili to Seattle by other means, might have been smarter than driving their giant vehicle through the middle of Seattle. Too late to second-guess themselves now. George's brain was fuzzed by pain, but he wanted to keep the attention of the men in the RV on him as long as possible. The longer they stayed with him, the more likely they were to be caught and the farther away David and Lili might be able to run. "What was your plan? What do you want?"

"You know what we want." The second man gestured the first man away.

He went, his lip curling in disgust, to look through the open portal through which David and Lili had exited.

If George hadn't been so fuzzy, he would have reminded David to close it before he ran. "I don't, actually."

"We want King David." The man enunciated each word clearly, all the while studying George in a manner that made him fear he was actually dying. Then he placed the ball of his foot on George's ankle, not pressing down at all, just waiting. Even that little bit of pressure hurt enough to make George feel like he was going to vomit. "I'll ask only once more. Where is he?"

"He isn't hiding in the RV, if that's what you're asking. He's gone."

"To the arena?"

For a moment George weighed the pros and cons of telling the truth. The *pro* was very clear. He just wasn't sure about the *con*.

The man didn't wait for George to reply but pressed down with the toe of his boot. George immediately bent to retch onto the floor. Nobody likes vomit, and it caused the man to step back so as not to get spatter on his shoes. George hadn't meant to throw up, but it did result in another bit of delay for the intruders. If he could stall them for thirty seconds more, the authorities would be all over them. "*Why* do you want him?"

"Why?" The first man had been crouched in the entrance to the portal, but now he swung around. "To right a grave wrong."

"I still don't understand."

The man sneered. "Of course you don't. You Americans with your money and your *freedom,* which you deny the rest of the world. Tell *that* to your CIA." He pronounced each letter distinctly.

Then he was through the portal, followed by the man who'd stepped on George's ankle. George fell back, exhausted and sick, cursing himself for his inability to follow. Almost immediately, an EMT poked his nose through a broken window in what was now the roof of the RV. He didn't have to ask how injured George was, in that it appeared to be obvious. "How many are you?"

"Three." George drew his attention to where Sophie and Andre were still strapped into the front seats. They had both moaned while the intruders had been harassing George, but not woken—or at least not shown that they were awake. If that was the case, and

George himself hadn't been feeling so terrible, he would have applauded their tradecraft.

"We're alive," Andre said. "Can't say much else for certain."

More sirens sounded in the distance. George prayed it truly was the cavalry coming, not the CIA or whomever else was chasing them. It would not be out of the realm of possibility that his former colleagues would pretend to be emergency services.

In the brief moment the EMT was gone to consult with his fellows about how to get them out, George managed to pull his phone from his pocket with two fingers. He felt a swell of relief that the screen wasn't broken. Although he'd lost his earpiece somewhere in the RV during the wrecking of it, his phone worked without it. The time on the phone said 5:40.

He dialed Chad's number, and the man himself picked up. "I've been calling and calling. What happened?"

"A semi-truck t-boned us in the middle of an intersection near the port. David and Lili are on their way to you on foot. The three of us are going to be tied up in a hospital for a time." He paused. "Hopefully, not literally."

Chad absorbed this news without exclamation, allowing George to tell him in quick sentences his condition and that of Andre and Sophie. He was fearing now that he had broken ribs too. At least the fact that he could speak meant he hadn't actually punctured a lung.

"My people are on their way to you; more will meet you at the hospital."

"You need to protect Dav—"

"I brought enough to spare." Chad paused. "I want to know how they found you."

"I'm sure there were a hundred ways."

The unfortunate truth was that they were surrounded by people with interests and agendas that didn't match their own. There was immense irony in the fact that the same organizations that had put together an edifice of continual surveillance seemed incapable of scrutinizing their own people.

"I'll leave the line open so you can hear everything that happens," George added. "I'd get your people working on whoever attacked us. I don't know where they're from, but they sure weren't Russian."

48

September 21 -Earth Two

Bogo

"Are you sure you won't stay, my lord? Why couldn't your own people provide you with a horse and provisions?" Isabel smiled at Bogo as she approached, holding the reins of the horse she'd brought him.

"Cardinals don't have their own horses, my dear Isabel. We ride in carriages." How convenient for him that she was marrying his new ally! He would be able to use her for years to come. "You know what sticklers servants can be for tradition. I have some business of my own to attend to. I'll be back before you know it."

"Is there anything else I can do for you?" Isabel smiled again.

He knew in that moment that she was still in love with him, despite her betrothal. He had known he could call upon her again, and she would believe everything he told her.

Bogo had determined as evening approached that it was too much of a risk to remain at Carew Castle. The plan to poison Francesco aside, he'd been taken aback by the animosity shown to him by Princess Margaret, absurdly nicknamed Daisy. He had come to realize that she herself had poisoned the entirety of the English and Welsh courts against him. He had also begun to wonder if Llywelyn's acceptance of his presence at the tournament hadn't been a ploy to lull him into a false sense of security. They had admitted him to the tournament, but that didn't mean they'd let him leave.

With no alarm yet raised, however, he'd determined that if he were stopped on his way out, he'd simply say he'd mistakenly left behind an important document at Lamphey and was riding to retrieve it. It was a cold night, but a beautiful one.

Bogo was quite sure the situation was still salvageable for him in principle, if only he could get to the coast and on a ship to France. At the very least, if all else failed, his sister would know what to do, as she always did. For a while, he had doubted Maggie's loyalty. She had failed to poison David two years ago, despite her assurances to Almain that Bronwen was a close friend and that infiltrating the English court in Normandy would be easy. In the aftermath of that failure, it was she who'd sent him to the Pope, and he could admit it had changed his life. It might even be that he owed her.

He could have been sorry about leaving Walter behind, but since the boy knew nothing about Bogo's actual plans, he couldn't reveal any secrets. Besides, he was not that bright and thus a little bit of an embarrassment. From the very beginning, ever since Bogo had discovered Walter's existence when he was ten years old, his son had understood that Bogo could never openly acknowledge him. It wasn't as if their family was Welsh!

Walter had lived under a false identity his whole life, so coming to the tournament as a knight of Gela had been a promotion of sorts. He had just been happy to be in his father's presence and didn't mind running a few errands for him.

The only parts of the entire scheme Bogo had been required to accomplish himself were the initial capture of Ifan and a single conversation with Cook Enith, during which time his cloak had hidden his face, leaving his voice to do all the work, since it sounded just like Walter's. Cook Enith shouldn't have been able to tell the difference.

Buying those fake papal bullas on the streets of Rome had been the best investment he'd ever made. He'd given one to the maid at Lamphey, who told everyone he was still sick when he wasn't. He had given one to his son. He would have given one to Walter's childhood friend, Roger de la Pole, if it hadn't been evident he couldn't be bought with trinkets. It was Roger's friendship with Walter, in fact, and the information about Carew Castle thus elicited, that had given Bogo the idea to abduct Enith's deaf grandson in the first place. Bogo himself had been to Carew Castle many times as a youth and knew the area well. He'd just needed guidance to find weaknesses in its current occupants. The world of Norman nobility was very small, and thus easy for a man with the proper knowledge to exploit.

Admittedly, it had been touch and go for a few hours after Roger had discovered his good friend Walter masquerading as a knight of Gela. They'd had a far-too-public fight about it. Truly, it was unfortunate Roger had come to Carew at all. Walter had assured him he wouldn't, given his family's animosity to Llywelyn.

Regardless, Bogo didn't regret bringing Roger into his confidence with the admission that Walter was his son. Roger appreciated being one of the few people trusted by a newly elevated cardinal, and since then had attributed any irregularities in Bogo's and Walter's behavior to the uncertainty of their relationship. Roger had even followed his lead by denying knowledge of Walter to Earl Callum last night.

By doing so, Roger had given Bogo leverage over him.

Ironically, David himself hadn't been Bogo's target this week at all. In fact, if he'd stuck around long enough for Bogo to talk to him, he would have seen Bogo's value. Once Francesco was eliminated, Bogo would have been first in line for his position in the Holy See as Guardian of Britain. David would have eventually understood that Bogo would make a better ally than enemy. And becoming the representative of the curia to Britain would have meant Bogo could come home.

Truly, the very idea of having an Italian cardinal responsible for the spiritual welfare of Britain was absurd. It should always have been someone born and bred here. But the Italians, just like the French, thought they were superior to everyone else, which had made the last two years of exile an appalling experience from beginning to end.

Bogo had hoped Francesco would have just died from the illness on the boat. That the entire company had fallen ill hadn't even been Bogo's doing! But it had given him the impetus to enact a plan that had been brewing in his mind for most of the journey from Rome. The problem, as always, now that he considered the matter fully, was working through other people. He couldn't elevate himself to the station he deserved on his own. He'd spent much of his life trying, so he knew how impossible a task it truly was. Even his own brother hadn't seen his potential, and, of course, Gilbert himself had died trying to overthrow King David.

Bogo was perfectly capable of admitting mistakes on the rare occasion he made them. Usually his error was in trusting the wrong people. This time, he'd trusted nobody, and his plan had *worked*.

Right up until it hadn't.

What he realized now was that he'd been *too* clever. He should have been more patient and not complicated matters so profoundly. For example, he had thought having one of the sailors he'd befriended on board their ship deliver the poisoned *panforte* to the castle woodsman *before* Bogo had officially arrived at Carew had been a genius idea. Corwen worked with yew and had an attachment to Enith, from whom he naturally had thought the food had been gifted. If by chance anyone had been able to trace Francesco's death to yew seeds, to the cake, and thus to Enith, Corwen was the perfect villain. All the better for being dead.

But no. The fact that David's people had decided early on that Corwen himself had been poisoned was still astonishing. The man was a peasant. It shouldn't have mattered how he died. Somehow, Bogo's trial run and clever scheme to divert attention had ended up doing the exact opposite. It had honestly never occurred to him that the plodding minds around David could have reached all the way to him simply by following where the evidence led.

Fortunately, Bogo had had the foresight to send Walter away yesterday before the search for him really got underway. Walter had come to him, terrified that people were looking for him for a crime he hadn't committed! He had thrown himself at Bogo's feet, begging to be aided. Bogo had found him a place to hide and sent a buxom woman with him to keep him company.

The final straw for Bogo himself was when one of the maids at the castle had reported that a new tip had come in, which seemed to point to Walter's current location. With the cook's grandson recovered, there'd been a renewed intensity in the search for Walter himself. Bogo feared he was dimwitted enough to trade his father's safety for his own.

Bogo held out his hand to Isabel, asking for the reins, which for some reason she was still holding. "This is all I need from you for now." As soon as he was mounted, he would give her one of the bullas too.

Then a voice came from behind him. "Is it, though?" Daisy stepped onto the road.

"Margaret! My dear, it is very late. What are you doing here?"

Rather than answering, she looked past him to Isabel and said, "Thank you, Isabel."

Bogo wanted to sneer, but he had a persona to maintain. "How wonderful to see you again, though, I'm sorry to say, I am pressed for time. I was hoping to reach Lamphey within the hour."

"I thought you were here to speak to the Kings of England and Wales about France?" Daisy said.

"Has David returned?" Bogo made his eyes wide.

"No."

"Thus, there is no need to concern yourself. I intend to return by the start of the tournament events tomorrow afternoon." Bogo kept his expression as innocent as possible, not wanting her to look past it to the way he was fingering the hilt of his knife under his cloak. Her manner was not accommodating, and he wasn't sure what to make of it. If Isabel had given him the horse already, he could have mounted and been on his way.

He reminded himself that nobody knew he was involved in any of the events of the last few days. Daisy was hostile to him because of the misunderstandings in Berkhamsted, none of which were his fault. Some people couldn't let go of the past.

"I think you should stay." Daisy's husband, William de Bohun, arrived, his arm in a sling.

Bogo didn't have to be as polite to him. He felt a rage rising within himself to be spoken to in such a fashion by this upstart youth. "What do you want, Bohun?"

"I think it's what *I* want that we should be discussing." Cardinal Francesco's voice rose out of the dark. "Did you really think you could get away with murdering me?"

Bogo swung around. "Your grace, I simply ride to Lamph—" He broke off at the sight not only of Francesco but of Roger de la Pole beside him.

This wasn't a time for anger but rather quick calculation. That had been one of his strengths in the past, and it could be again now. Between one moment and the next, he decided the time was ripe for a new truth. He fell to his knees before Francesco and threw himself on his mercy, as Walter had done before Bogo himself yesterday. "I would never want to harm you, your grace! This was all your uncle's doing. He said he would see me dead and my son with me if I didn't ensure you never came home. I couldn't disobey the pope! I didn't have a choice!"

"Haven't you heard, Cardinal Bogo? You always have a choice." Roger waved forward several more men, some in Bohun colors and some in his own. "I made the right one just now. You could have too."

Bogo started to protest further, to explain the parameters Pope Boniface had set for him, including that he would disown any knowledge of the plot if Bogo was caught.

Cardinal Francesco cut him off with a hand under Bogo's chin, which he tipped up so he could look into Bogo's face. "You lie."

And yet, even with this assertion, Bogo saw a flicker of doubt in his eyes. By the time Francesco returned to Rome, that doubt might have grown to full-fledged distrust, and Pope Boniface's right-hand man might have become his worst enemy.

Really, David's people should be thanking Bogo instead of arresting him. He would say exactly that to David when he returned.

49

September 21 -Avalon

Lili

The noise inside the arena was louder than an airplane engine. It was louder than that train by the Walmart. In fact, it was louder than any sound Lili had ever heard. It came at her like she'd run headfirst into a stone wall, and it might have overwhelmed her if she hadn't been holding tightly to Dafydd's hand.

Then a woman approached and fitted both her and Dafydd with ear devices that suddenly reduced the sound to a manageable level. The woman also attached a box to Lili's belt and showed her how she might turn various switches to talk just to Dafydd, and then to talk to the entire audience.

As if she would.

Chad took the stage, holding up his hands for quiet, which was given him in a matter of a few heartbeats. "Thank you for coming! I must apologize to you, however, for the fact that I won't actually be speaking to you tonight—"

The crowd roared its disapproval. Chad took the abuse for a count of ten and then raised his hands again. Grudgingly, the crowd quieted once more.

"You thought you were coming to hear me speak about my work with King David and the Bangor Institute, but in fact—"

As he paused, Lili and Dafydd were urged down an aisle, between what seemed like endless rows of seating, to the stage upon which Chad was standing, his arms now spread wide in greeting. Behind him was a screen bigger than the curtain wall at Carew castle and projected onto it was *her* face—hers and Dafydd's.

"—you're here to listen to King David himself!"

If she had thought the roar from the crowd had been loud before, now it was heart-stopping. The people in every row were rising to their feet, applauding, smiling, laughing, and shouting. And then videoing. Once again, every single person had his or her arm raised in the air, a bright light shining off the front of their phone. She knew without being told that, within thirty seconds, her face was going to be uploaded to the internet and broadcast for eight billion people to see. Not that it wasn't already, since Chad was broadcasting this event live.

It was unreasonable, but also entirely predictable.

They reached the stage, and Chad hugged them both. If anything, the roar increased, not the least because now streaming all around the middle deck between one level of seats and another were the words, *Dafydd ap Llywelyn, the Return of King Arthur*. Brightly colored banners decorating the levels of the arena were adorned with red dragons on various backgrounds; crowns; swords; and shields, all very kingly in their presentation. A second screen was showing images of Dafydd. The initial shots were of a sandy-haired, round-faced little boy, pictures she presumed were taken during his childhood but ones Lili herself had never seen.

"Now he's done it," Dafydd said, for her ears alone.

"He told you he was going to." Lili put a hand on Dafydd's arm. "We're here. In this moment, nothing else matters."

Now Chad flipped a switch at the box at his waist so he could speak into only their ears. "George, Sophie, and Andre are at a nearby hospital. They're going to be okay. My people are with them, and the hospital is under tight security. They're safe. Nobody is going to arrest you either." Chad made a gesture to indicate the crowded arena. "They wouldn't let them."

Lili took in the endless sea of faces, mostly anonymous and shadowed because of the stage's bright lights, preventing her from seeing very much beyond them. Perhaps that was a good thing.

"Congress is coming on now." Chad turned to look up at the screens. Now one showed a similar auditorium full of people, though not as tightly packed; the second showed a woman in a suit.

"We're ready, Mr. Treadman," the woman said.

Chad put up a hand to the screen, indicating he'd heard her, while at the same time saying to Dafydd, "I'll introduce you, and then—"

"No." Lili swung around to face her husband and Chad, terrified and at the same time sure of what she was saying. "Let me do it."

Both men looked at her blankly, and then Dafydd said, "You're sure?"

"I am beginning to understand the power the people of your world give events like this one. There is no better way in this day and age to reach every corner of the earth. I'm sorry if there was ever a moment where I questioned it." She lifted a hand and smiled to the crowd, which responded with another roar. "I am from Earth Two. I am Dafydd's wife and the Queen of England. Other than Dafydd himself, nobody has more stake in the outcome of tonight than I."

By way of reply, Chad made a gesture like a courtier. "The floor is yours, my lady." Then he flicked a finger to turn on her microphone so she was speaking to everyone, not just to Dafydd and him.

"Thank you for coming." Her voice boomed out, as large as the arena. As she moved to the central position on the stage, a single light shone down on her. The crowd responded by settling into their seats. They were as much a part of this drama as Lili, though she had been an understudy for a walk-on part, and now had a chance at the main stage.

She began: "All these years, I have heard about David's life before he came to me. In Earth Two, we don't try to keep his traveling a secret anymore. There, we call his home its true name: Avalon, the land of wonder and the place King Arthur resides." She said his name the American way, so there would be no misunderstanding.

Her gaze took in as many eyes as she could meet. "*This* land. *Your* home."

She had their attention. In the past, she'd never sought the limelight; never needed to step out from Dafydd's shadow. As she gazed at the thousands of people before her, she still didn't. As when she'd spoken on the radio during Gilbert de Clare's insurrection, sometimes it was necessary. That time, nobody but Rupert had been able to see her face. "Even with the stories, there was no way I could have ever understood what your life was like. I am here to tell you that it is so very different. And yet it is very much the same.

"When we first arrived two days ago, David was dying. Most of you have probably seen the videos. The people in the store, total strangers, showed kindness to us, having no idea who we were at first, only that we were in need. For all your amazing technology, you are no less human than I. I have seen, in the few days I've been here, the way you use your technology and depend on it. I think many of you, maybe even most of you, think you *need* it.

"But you don't. What you need is connection. What you need is *hope*."

She paused so her next words would truly penetrate. "I see so much in this world to be proud of, so much to look forward to and believe in. Maybe with these words I have lost some of you, or most of you. But I think you are here because you do believe in something greater than yourselves. Or at least you *want* to.

"I think that's why my husband came here this week. The people of Avalon have assumed he traveled that first time to Earth

Two to make our world a better place. We are certainly grateful that he has chosen to make our world his home.

"But I think now he came to us so he could return to you, and we could all be transformed. He saved us from a life without hope. He's here, this week, to do the same for you. I give you, David ap Llywelyn."

50

September 21 -Avalon

David

"Lili was amazing!" David settled against the door by the wall in George's hospital room, still on a high from the event.

"I did hardly anything, just introduced you." Lili had found a chair near George's head. Everyone was staying well away from his left side and his broken ankle. He had two cracked ribs as well, something David himself had experienced, and extensive bruising and contusions down the left side of his body where he'd hit the wall of the RV.

David rolled his eyes. "She stole the show. After you talked, I could have said anything, and they would have loved me." And before Lili could protest again, he put out a hand. "Believe me, I am grateful. You made it easy for me. You meant what you said, and it showed."

After Lili had stepped aside, he'd stood before all those people, the spotlight on him now, and began: *"Fifteen years ago, my sis-*

ter and I were driving my aunt's minivan to pick up my cousin Christopher, when we slid through a snowbank into medieval Wales and inadvertently saved my father's life ..."

He'd spoken in front of large audiences hundreds of times before, but somehow it had never felt as momentous as this. After he'd given his speech, he'd followed up for nearly two hours with a question-and-answer session, first from members of Congress and even the Secretary-General herself, and then from the arena audience. It had been exhilarating and exhausting at the same time.

"She's trending more than you are," Sophie said, her eyes on her phone. She and Andre were bruised in places and suffering from whiplash. Even with excellent airbags, the RV had literally been hit by a semi-truck. They'd been released from the hospital officially but hadn't left George's side—nor each other's for that matter. Lili and David had also been given a good looking over by the hospital staff and were here on their own recognizance.

David grinned at his wife, who fortunately had no idea what Sophie meant by *trending*. David barely did. "That is good news."

"Unfortunately, that's about all that's good." Chad entered the room. "You did great, you guys, but it looks like it isn't going to be enough."

The others frowned, and when Chad didn't elaborate, David felt forced to ask, "What does that mean?"

"Word is, we still don't have the necessary votes to pass the legislation."

"How can that be?" David felt both outraged and let-down.

Chad made an apologetic motion with one hand. "There's too much money at stake. So much has been invested in surveillance that nobody involved wants to change course now."

"You'd think they'd at least care that their oh-so-secure system isn't." George's words dripped with disgust. "Those terrorists that crashed our RV had to have had inside information."

"I would agree," Chad said. "Unfortunately, everyone's a cynic. And before you ask, David, the Senate Intelligence Committee makes recommendations, not laws. They are one small-and-getting-smaller part of our government. In the end, it seems we barely moved the needle."

"Worse, the failure of the bill means many will be emboldened." After a perfunctory tap on the door, Deanna entered the room too. Despite her news, David found himself happy to see her. "I wish an apology could be enough. The other security services also deserve to be censured for chasing you across the planet. I regret now they might never be. I can say that I have personally checked your security here. We are doing what we can to protect you."

"Thank you." David looked at Chad. "The bill is really dead in the water?"

"So it appears."

Deanna gave another shake of her head. "You guys should have won tonight. I'm sorry that it looks like everything you've gone through has been for nothing."

"Not nothing." Chad looked hard at David. "I don't want you to think this means we are giving up, that you should view your time here as a failure or think you haven't made a difference. Because of you, no field of study is what it was ten years ago. The impossible is now possible, even if we don't know how that is, and every effort is being directed towards finding out. You *have* changed the world, David. You've changed *me*. To *pull a David* is heard on the streets of even so jaded a city as New York."

"Does that mean to disappear?" David was genuinely confused.

"No." Chad looked at him pityingly. "It means to do the honorable thing, even when you don't think it's going to be of benefit to yourself."

"I don't—I don't think I'm comfortable with that," David said. "Bad enough to be confused with King Arthur."

"We are not going over that again," Lili warned him. "Enough already."

"Yes, ma'am. Since that's how we got here in the first place, I'll shut up." He paused. "I do think it's time we went home."

"I would fly you if I could be cleared for it," Andre said.

"I would too." George appeared surprised at what had just come out of his mouth. "I feel like I owe you a do-over."

"You're *persona non grata* in Earth Two still," David said. "Maybe you should heal up a bit first. Let me pave the way."

Lili patted George's hand. "We appreciate the offer. Thank you for everything. You've been amazing."

Chad cleared his throat. "May I once again accept the offer you made two years ago? With modifications, of course! A helicopter, my people, and all their gear are ready and waiting. Just say the word."

"Word." David glanced at Deanna. "I won't involve the CIA, but I'd like to save a space for you if you'd take it." He had heard about Chad's existing relationship with the FBI. It was to Deanna's credit that she hadn't leaned on it when she'd first introduced herself in the Walmart, knowing she'd have to earn his trust on her own merits.

Deanna immediately shook her head. "I wouldn't want to bump someone else who deserves to go."

"You wouldn't," Chad said. "We can make room, and you wouldn't be alone either. One of your colleagues has already been tapped as the pilot."

Deanna bit her lip with what looked like genuine regret. "I can't. And I'd appreciate it if you didn't tell my boss you asked me. He would not be happy that I turned you down."

"I kind of figured. You have children. Obligations." David made a motion with his head. "You can't go any more than Lili and I can stay."

51

September 22 -Avalon

David

David had left the preparations to Chad, who, naturally, had latched upon the splashiest solution to their problem of how best to kill themselves. What's more, he intended to broadcast it live and in color for all the world to see. They hadn't convinced Congress to do the right thing, but Chad wasn't ready to give up on convincing the rest of the world.

"I'm impressed, Chad." David said into his earpiece. "I am also terrified."

"You have nothing to be afraid of!" Chad was beyond enthusiastic about his new state-of-the-art helicopter. His manufacturing plant was adjacent to a small, municipal airport in South Seattle, one which had gladly augmented its physical plant with his money. "We're pre-production, so we would have been flying today anyway, with or without you." He paused. "Well, I knew I was giving this talk at FutureCon, so it made sense for me to make a trip out here to see how things were going."

"We don't believe in coincidences, remember," Lili said from where she was strapped in beside David.

They were connected by a rope around their ankles, tying them together to ensure that if he time traveled without the helicopter, however that might happen, he would take her with him. The rope also snaked from them to the three other participants in the endeavor—the pilot, the co-pilot, and the co-co-pilot.

"Sorry we're going to take this one away from you." David eyed the multitudinous built-in instruments and gadgets. There were many more in the cargo hold. He hadn't cared very much about his method of travel, but he and Lili had definitely wanted a say in some of what they were bringing back with them. That cargo included a stack of EpiPens, a whole suite of possible medications for Callum, and a portable CT scanner. "I assure you it will be well-used."

The rotors started to spin, amazingly quietly. The engine was hydrogen fueled, sleek and efficient as one might expect from something Chad had built. Truthfully, David's first choice of vehicle would have been a ship, for the sheer volume of cargo it could carry, but the helicopter would definitely be more flexible in Earth Two—and this one seemed bigger on the inside than it looked on the outside, like the *Tardis* from Dr. Who, as Sophie had said when Chad had given them the tour.

It also had onboard solar panels for converting water to hydrogen, so if they did make it back to Earth Two, it would never run out of fuel as long as there continued to be such a thing as rain. That meant it could also run or charge their existing electronics. Chad had worked hard to think of everything, and David had thanked him profusely. Despite Chad's protestations to the contrary, David still felt that the benefits of their relationship went mostly one way.

"Just a few more checks." As agreed, although the helicopter was built by Chad, the pilot was FBI, one of several who had been training on them since the FBI had commissioned a fleet. Her name was Marie. The co-pilot, Samantha, was one of Chad's scientists from the Bangor Institute, adept in the use of the instruments they were bringing. Brunette where Marie was blonde, she was still Marie's twin in their helmets, flight uniforms, and grave expressions.

But as they readied themselves for takeoff, all of a sudden there seemed to be something wrong with the rotors. They were making a rhythmic rat-a-tat-tat sound that didn't bode well for getting off the ground.

David leaned forward. "Do you hear that?"

"That isn't the blades." This was from Birdy, the third member of their party, a linguist and historian from the Bangor Institute, as well as the acting representative of the British government. Tall and slender, with auburn hair and freckles, she was sitting kitty-corner to David and Lili in the cabin area. "Let's go! What are we waiting for?"

"This is an aircraft like any other," Marie said, patience in her voice. "I can't just take off without authorization."

Honestly, that did sound very FBI, but maybe less like the thoughts of someone who was coming to Earth Two where authorization might be hard to come by at times. Meanwhile, calls and exclamations were flowing hard and fast through their earpieces, along with more rat-a-tat-tatting.

Chad was shouting, "Go! Go! Go!"

"Give me a minute!" Marie kept pressing buttons and speaking urgently into her microphone, words David wasn't receiving.

Then the sliding door to the helicopter was flung open and five men in riot gear and machine guns climbed in. The last man inside turned to face outward and laid down a field of fire from his weapon. The two helicopters that should have been taking off with them had become disabled, and David hoped those pilots weren't dead. The last thing David had ever intended was to put anyone else's life in danger. Bad enough to be taking these three women with them, never mind that they'd volunteered.

It wouldn't be the first time someone had died for him. Every time it happened, whether in Avalon or Earth Two, he prayed it might be the last.

While the first man to enter pointed his gun at Marie and ordered her to take off, a second said to David in a heavy accent he couldn't place, "At long last, you will do as you are told."

David gripped Lili's hand, prepared to be shot. He was going with her or he wasn't going at all. But all that happened was Marie finally took to the air, heading across the city of Seattle towards

Mount Rainier. As it was a beautiful September day, *the mountain was out*, as they said in the western part of the state.

The hijackers were simply following the same flight path David and Chad had worked out. All of a sudden, David wished for Lili's sake they were riding inside a cargo plane like when the CIA had tried to kill him rather than in Chad's spiffy helicopter. The windows on the sides and front were large, so she could see where they were going—and how they would be dying.

As would the entire planet, via their various cameras, including one on his helmet, broadcasting these events. While David and Lili looked on silently, one of the other hijackers started patting down each of the women accompanying them, looking for weapons. Birdy gave up two pistols and a knife.

"Are you okay?" Chad spoke softly in his ear.

"For now. Are you?"

Chad didn't answer the question and instead said, "They came in force in two armored personnel carriers, right through the airport fence. I'm sorry; I let you down."

"You didn't. We'll be okay."

The leader of the hijackers finally noticed him talking and shoved his gun towards David's chest. "Who is that? What are you saying?"

A distraction seemed in order. "Why are you doing this?"

"You know why."

"I genuinely don't."

"You have abandoned our people to their fate."

This was starting to sound familiar, though this man's accent wasn't Spanish-like, as George had reported from the men who crashed the RV, or Russian, but rather more northern European. "I don't know who your people are."

"We are Zeelanders."

David gaped at him. As a splinter group, they came from so far out of left field they weren't even on the field. "I'm the King of England, not the Duke of Flanders."

The man put his face right into David's. "You abandoned us! Why do your people get to be free, and we don't?" He spoke like John Primus and John Secundus might have, as if the war against France had just happened instead of occurring seven hundred and twenty-eight years ago.

"If the people of Zeeland petitioned for help, I would always listen. But they did not."

"The men of Zeeland do not beg!"

David wanted to spread his hands wide but he feared to anger the man further.

Birdy leaned forward to draw the man's attention. As a historian, she should also know exactly what the men were talking about. She also was displaying an impressive coolness under extreme pressure. "He isn't really the return of Arthur, you know. He's a man, just like you, though seemingly a far better one."

The man swung his gun towards her, making David hope he understood enough of physics to see the problem with firing a weapon inside this flying metal can. "I don't have to listen to—"

"Coming up on the mountain, sir," Marie said.

All five hijackers turned to look out the front window. Mount Rainier loomed larger and larger, with more snow than usual for this time of year. Perhaps this would have been the optimal time to over-power them, but David was still tied to Lili, and it was exactly the wrong time to leave her side. Instead he put his arm around her shoulders and gripped her tight. Lili, in turn, stuck out her hand to Birdy, who took it.

"Don't look at the mountain, *cariad*," David said. "Look at me."

"I want to see it."

What they could see was rock and snow. And more snow.

And then an impenetrable darkness.

One ... two ... three ...

52

September 21 -Earth Two

David

Christopher was more nervous than he'd expected to be about the events of the day, and he wasn't even participating. From the few times he'd been to a tournament in England, he'd seen that archery, if it was included at all, was considered a minor contest. Since this was Wales, it was pre-eminent. For that reason, it was taking place on the last day, in the early afternoon. Prime time, for medieval people. There would be a feast afterwards, as of course there had to be.

Huw settled his shoulders. "Whatever happens, by tonight, it will all be over."

"You can do it." William had said the same thing every time they'd sent Huw off to the butts. The competition had begun with two hundred archers. Now they were down to the last five, and Huw was among them. Math and Ieuan had had to duke it out in the previous round, resulting in Ieuan's ascension. In the next hour, those five would be winnowed to two, and then finally to one.

"If you lose," Christopher said, trying to be supportive, "we'll still—"

"—mock you forever," Robbie finished.

Christopher's wife, Isabelle, shot the Scotsman a quelling look and put a hand on Huw's shoulder. "Don't listen to them. The women will still love you, win or lose."

That prompted a flicker of a smile from Huw, which grew broader as William added, "According to Daisy, you are the most eligible bachelor at court. Just getting this far will increase your cachet, no matter what happens."

"Hey! What about me?" Robbie was eldest of the four of them at twenty-five, and had long grown out of Bronwen's moniker for him, Baby Bruce.

"If you were the King of Scots, maybe," William said.

Robbie punched his uninjured arm, and their dispute might have degenerated into actual wrestling if William hadn't hidden behind Isabelle. "I'm wounded, remember!"

Robbie subsided, at which point Huw bumped fists with him and the two headed off towards the competition ground, since Robbie would be acting as his squire for the event.

Isabelle took Christopher's left arm while William strolled at his right, bereft of his own wife, who had been mothering Lizzie, much to her dismay, and insisting she turn herself out as appropriate for a princess. They intended to catch up with them by the time the shooting started.

"I invented that bit about Daisy, but I'm not wrong," William said.

"You were very kind to tell him that. I've never seen Huw so nervous. I'm also not sure we should leave finding a wife up to him or Robbie." Isabelle had started to look thoughtful. "Daisy and I should see what we can do about the both of them."

Christopher was going to stay far, far away from that issue. By now, they'd reached the sidelines anyway, all of them too nervous to sit. The archery ground was turned ninety degrees from the stands so the contestants faced away from where Christopher's Uncle Llywelyn and Aunt Meg sat in the central seats. As the archers shot, the spectators would be looking at their backs, but they would have a good view of the flight of the arrows and the targets away in the distance.

Nicholas de Carew was MC, as was appropriate. He placed himself at the very front of the stands, a few feet into the field, and held up one hand to silence the crowd. Cassie stood beside him, a bow in her hand and a quiver on her back. Though she had declined to participate in the competition directly, she had been persuaded to shoot an honorary arrow to start the final round.

Carew welcomed everyone to the event with enthusiastic language and then dropped his hand. "Let the competition begin!"

Between one heartbeat and the next, Cassie spun and shot at the central target in the first row. Christopher was pleased for her that the arrow hit the bull's eye. She hadn't lost her touch.

Callum had come out of the stands to give her a hug of congratulations, and they were both about to give way to the contestants when Callum's head jerked up at a very modern sound: the hum of helicopter blades.

Christopher himself practically leapt into the field, spinning all the way around to catch sight of the helicopter as it flew over the stands. The sound had been faint at first, so he'd thought it still far away, but then it swooped over the castle, heading for the grassy expanse between the archers and their targets.

"Stay here with William, Isabelle!" Christopher threw the command he knew in advance his wife would hate over his shoulder, already racing towards where the helicopter was settling down to land on the grass just this side of the row of targets. He was a hundred feet away when the door slid open and four men surged out, wearing riot gear and bearing machine guns that were up and ready to fire.

As the lead soldier swung his weapon towards Christopher, Callum shouted over the crowd, "Christopher! Get down!"

He obeyed the order as if they'd practiced it, throwing himself to the grass—an instant before an arrow flew right through the spot where he'd been and embedded itself in the soldier's throat.

* * * * *

Lili and David had held onto each other as the darkness closed in around them, dimming the lights inside the helicopter and finally cutting off Chad's voice in David's ears. Lili seemed frozen to her seat, unable to keep her eyes off the leader's weapon.

They burst into the splendor of a sunny afternoon in Wales, soaring over Carew Castle and the tournament grounds. If David hadn't been full enough already with fear and anger, he might have felt satisfaction that they were back at Carew because that was precisely where they needed to be.

In Welsh, David said, "If they wanted to kill us, they would have done it already."

Lili spoke around clenched teeth. "That doesn't mean they can't murder half the people in the stands if they oppose them."

"Their guns aren't the advantage they think they are."

The lead hijacker ordered Marie to aim for the grassy space in front of the archery targets, saying, "Many people are here. Good. You may land us now. They must see our power and that we have their king."

"You don't need your guns," David said softly. "Please put them away."

The lead hijacker looked at him with disdain. "Do you think me a fool?"

"If you come out with guns, my people will shoot you." He was only being honest, as he always tried to be.

The man sneered. "Arrows and swords are no match for our weapons."

"They have spears too. And eventually you are going to run out of bullets."

"We have enough for this."

David hadn't been arguing so much as stating the same fact he'd said to Lili in Welsh, as part of his general policy of full disclosure. Now he stopped. *Far be it from me to stop a man so determined to dig his own grave.* Instead, David occupied himself with loosening the rope that tied him to the others. If anyone was going to draw the hijackers' fire, he wanted it to be him and, if need be, he would let them send him back to Avalon alone.

The helicopter landed in the grass, and the leader motioned for the hijacker nearest the door to open it. Once he'd done so, that man pressed in close to David to allow the leader and the three other hijackers to exit the helicopter in front of him.

Christopher was already racing towards them, and David wanted to scream at him to stop. But a split second later, he didn't have to because Christopher dropped to the ground—just as Cassie released an arrow, which found its target just as David had said it would.

Cassie's lone arrow was followed by a flurry of others from all directions, pummeling the men like a rainstorm and just as unstoppable.

"Or not." The sardonic comment came from the last hijacker, replying to the leader's last words to David. Then he pointed his gun at the back of Marie's head. "You too."

"Me? I don't know what—"

The hijacker cut her off with a bark. "You're one of them, a Zeelander. I have no qualms about shooting a woman, so cooperate, or we're going to be cleaning your brains off the controls."

Marie's hands flew into the air. Samantha had her hands up too, her eyes wide. Birdy was like a statue in her seat.

To David, the man said, "I have been embedded with the Zeelanders for nearly two years, ever since we first got wind of their plan to abduct you and force you to bring them here. We couldn't allow it, of course, not with what you have done for our people." Then he pulled one of the confiscated guns he'd secreted in his gear and handed it hilt-first to Birdy. "Shoot her if she moves. She may look pretty, but she's as bad as the rest of them."

Birdy took the weapon confidently, since it had been one of hers to begin with.

Then, having removed his helmet, the hijacker-turned-ally bowed to David, who had observed this scene as it unfolded without finding his voice. "My apologies for any inconvenience this operation has caused you or your wife." He put a hand to his chest. "If I may introduce myself, I am Ari Cohen, Mossad."

* * * * * *

Under normal circumstances, arrows were no match for automatic weapons, nor could they penetrate the armor these men wore. The men in the archery contest, plus dozens of others on the periphery, had released barrage after barrage anyway. And they were the best of the best or they wouldn't have been in the tournament in the first place. So even if none of these arrows had been as well-placed as Cassie's initial shot, the surviving three men ended up cowering on the ground anyway, each punctured at least once. Their armor had protected their chests, but arrows stuck out of their appendages.

From the front of the stands, Callum bellowed a new command: "Hold!"

The moment the arrows ceased to fly, upwards of forty heavily-armed tournament goers descended on the men on the ground. They were completely subdued by the time Christopher reached the entrance to the helicopter, and David was standing in the doorway, his own hands in the air. "We're clear! It's just us!"

Christopher pulled him into a bear hug. "You sure know how to make an entrance!"

"I learned from the best."

By then, Callum had arrived too, and even before he greeted David, he bent to pick up the automatic weapon fallen near the dead man's hand. Then he and Michael proceeded to retrieve all the modern weapons from the rest of his companions.

"Give the word, sire, and I'll end this right here." A modern soldier, dark-haired and dark-eyed, had followed David out of the helicopter, and now he pointed his weapon at one of the men on the ground. This one had an arrow sticking out of his thigh, and his hands were raised too. He didn't look to be going anywhere.

"I appreciate the offer, Ari, but that isn't the way we do things here. I may have a better idea anyway." He looked down at the man, whose face showed equal parts anger, fear, and pain. "I hear you want to free Zeeland from the French?"

Before coming to Earth Two, Christopher would have found the question nonsensical. After a few days with John Primus and John Secundus, he knew exactly what David was talking about.

The man on the ground did too, and although the question was obviously rhetorical, he answered anyway. "Yes. If I can."

David nodded. "It may be we can find a use for you in that regard, after all."

53

September 21 -Avalon

George

"I don't care what the doctor says. You still shouldn't be here." Deanna glanced at George. "Your ankle is broken. So are your ribs. At the very least, you should be sitting down."

"I will in a minute." George found his old organization's prejudice against the FBI rising before he could properly tamp it down. Deanna was extremely competent. He could work with her, and he didn't work for the CIA anymore anyway. So he gestured to the medical boot he wore. "It doesn't even hurt much. The crutches under my arms are actually worse because of the pressure they put on my ribs."

"I hear your boss is working on better ones."

"Be nice if he hurried." He turned back to the one-way glass, looking in on one of the men they'd captured during the assault on the airstrip where David's helicopter had taken off.

Deanna's boss had just entered the room. Up until now, the interrogation had focused on who had paid for and organized the two dozen Zeelanders into a paramilitary unit with the goal of getting into the same vehicle as David and forcing him to take them to Earth Two. Though they hadn't elicited much of anything from their prisoner, on the whole they hadn't needed to. The surveillance state, as it turned out, had been good for something, in that it had enabled the FBI to track the terrorists to their origin in a warehouse in an industrial district, and from there to their homes.

That didn't mean they'd arrested anyone else yet. The FBI was supreme at biding their time, and with David gone, they could take as much time as they needed.

"At least everything that happened yesterday wasn't entirely for nothing," Deanna said with a smile that implied *I know something you don't.*

George glanced at her, startled. "Are you saying the new legislation passed? Already?" He glanced at his watch. It was so late at night it was early. "It was brought to the floor, like, twelve hours ago."

"Twelve hours was all it took. It's headed to the president's desk."

Chad was right. Once again the world had changed because of David.

Ironically, this new legislation was far more ambitious than the previous one had been, in that it took Chad's Bangor Initiative and made it global. Between yesterday and today, the United States had agreed to fund, through the UN, a non-governmental, time-travel focused, research and development initiative in which every country could participate. Even the Russians would be allowed to join. They had only to ask. It was like the International Space Station, except for time travel.

And they'd done it because everyone had seen, in living color and in real time, the consequences of the US government's continual harassment of David. Chad had livestreamed the events of the day, which meant the entire world had been shocked at the hijacking of the helicopter, overheard David's conversation with the Zeelanders, and witnessed their subsequent departure from this universe. In addition, it had become clear that the Zeelanders had been the fourth of four separate entities that had targeted David over the course of the time he was in Avalon. And that number didn't even include the CIA, which had shut down the connectivity at the Walmart and whose agents George had met at the pharmacy.

It had been the Russians and the Chinese fighting it out in Art's house, and an outfit called the *Basque-Navarre alliance* that had crashed their semi-truck into the RV to force David to time travel, in the hope that he would take them with him. At the airport, the Zeelanders had achieved what the rest of them couldn't.

As one senator had put it, "This guy has done nothing wrong, and he's been hounded across the planet. First by us. And then, because of us, by everyone else."

Privately, George still thought the surveillance state needed to be dealt with too. After all, the CIA was still the CIA. They kept secrets for a living, as he well knew. But if the whole world could benefit from David's time traveling, rather than seeing him as an asset to be contained or exploited, then maybe they really were looking at the fruition of everything David had been working towards, both in Earth Two and Avalon, since he was fourteen years old.

Meanwhile, they still had what remained of the Zeelander organization to deal with.

Deanna's boss opened the file in front of him and began looking through the pictures therein. "You didn't know about the Walmart, but you caught up quick."

The prisoner on the other side of the table didn't reply, which was pretty much par for the course.

"You knew where David and Lili were going to be. Who's your mole?"

At long last, the man blinked. He had to be exhausted, and that had let down his guard.

George blinked too. As far as he knew, the existence of a mole wasn't an official line of inquiry. A contact of Chad's sister, Denise, had given up a CIA mole in Chad's organization, but nobody had yet talked about another one anywhere else. They'd speculated that the RV had been tracked from its single stop at the gas station, but they hadn't been able to connect the dots as to who might have inquired about them and how the Basque-Navarre group or the Zeelanders had found them once they'd left.

George rocked back and forth on the ball of his good foot. He honestly hadn't expected Deanna's boss to get anything new from the man. A dozen other people had questioned him already, but for the first time, the Zeelander looked disconcerted.

Beside him, he sensed Deanna's renewed intensity.

"This was your idea?" George asked her.

She lifted one shoulder. "It was time to look into something different."

The photos her boss had brought were mostly of the airfield, where three of the prisoner's comrades had died. They had come with overwhelming force, and had, in fact, overwhelmed the agents and officers present to protect David. Chad himself was lucky to be alive, having been spirited into a nearby hangar as the Zeelanders' armored personnel carriers had arrived. These had been homemade, not military grade, but had been effective nonetheless. They'd come with intent, driving right through the gate and straight up to the helicopter.

Subsequently, they'd had to fend off a counterattack by a combined force of FBI agents, Seattle police officers, and Chad's people, but the two carriers had worked in tandem, and they'd presented a powerful enough force that they'd managed to drive out of the airport again once they'd achieved their objective—which was to put five of their men on the helicopter with David and disable the other two helicopters meant to fly with them as witness and protection until they reached the mountain.

"You should be in there," George said. "If you get something from him, it could make your career."

"I am not highly ranked enough." Deanna glanced at him. "Yet. Between this and Art's house, I might soon be."

"How certain are you that we have a mole?"

Deanna stayed silent through a count of ten, by which point he knew she hadn't mistaken his meaning. "You think it's me?" She laughed. "Why wouldn't I have warned my people that David wasn't at Art's house?" And then her eyes narrowed, this time at him. "It could be you."

He laughed too. "How could I be the betrayer, given where I spent the last two years? *I* was the one with David's best interests at heart."

Deanna nodded, as if this answer was what she'd expected him to say. "So we can trust each other."

It wasn't a question, but George treated it like one. "I guess we can."

Deanna's boss spread the pictures across the table.

At the sight of them, George took a step closer to the window. These he hadn't seen and didn't know where they'd come from. They could be very recent or it was possible the FBI wasn't sharing everything. That would have been irksome if George hadn't been standing with Deanna right now, a newly proclaimed ally, and one picture in particular caught the prisoner's eye. His subsequent refusal to acknowledge that fact spoke as loudly as if he'd reached out a finger and poked at it.

The picture he'd overtly not chosen was of Marie, the FBI pilot of the helicopter, sitting at an outdoor café and looking up at someone just out of the image.

Deanna had moved to stand right beside George, and when she spoke next, it was in a whisper, as if she couldn't bear to hear her own words. "We sent a double-agent to Earth Two."

She was right, but even without the picture, they should have guessed the pilot was a traitor, since she had inexplicably delayed takeoff until the hijackers were on board.

"I read her file. She entered the FBI right around the time I left for Earth Two. Worked her way up." George had his forehead pressed against the glass. "I knew I should have gone with them."

54

September 21 -Earth Two

Lili

"I feel as if we're right back where we started." Dafydd had started to pace a bit, as was his wont. "It's like what happened after the arrival of the Cardiff bus, and this time we *really* don't trust the strangers we brought with us. I'm honestly not sure we can trust any of them, even the ones that appear to be on our side."

Without talking about it in advance, they'd all woken early and gathered in Math and Anna's pavilion, their respective children still asleep. The night before, Lili had cried in Bronwen's arms, overwhelmed with gratitude at knowing her sister-in-law had been a second mother to her sons while she was gone, and that they'd been fine without her. Nannies were wonderful, but there were some things only family could do. All the while Lili had been in Avalon, she had known they would be just as happy as if she herself were with them, but it was a relief to discover how true that was. Always in the past, it had been others who'd left their children with Lili.

"Whatever your initial impulse, you can't send Avalonian mercenaries, no matter their political allegiances, off with the two Johns to fight the King of France," Math had probably been holding back that thought since the previous day but hadn't felt he could barrage Dafydd with his opinion first thing.

"You're right, of course," Dafydd said. "It was an impulse to suggest it, and one that would foist the problem off onto someone else. It doesn't mean something can't be worked out, though. Already, the hijackers' superior attitude is fading. They had assumed, from their modern vantage point, that they would be able to impose their will on our world. But the medieval world is not the backwater they thought, and they aren't the all-knowing superhumans they expected to be."

Dafydd also needed to think about how to incorporate Birdy and Samantha, not to mention Ari, into society, and how to fulfill his pledge to facilitate their multitudinous research projects.

"And then there's Bogo," Lili said. "What's the phrase I've heard you use? *Hoisted on his own petard?*"

"The central irony being," Bronwen said, "that the only reason the investigation into Bogo began at all was because David ate a walnut. Corwen's sickness would have been viewed as just that, and we would never have followed all the clues Bogo inadvertently left. He was undone by coincidence!"

Anna laughed. "We don't believe in those, remember?"

"That will teach him to abandon his own son," Math added.

Dafydd flung out a hand. "But why use *yew seeds*, of all things, and how is it that I have Roger de la Pole to thank for any of this?"

"Not to mention Isabel," Bronwen said. "Hard to imagine a clearer instance of love turning to hate. Thank goodness she appears to love Roger."

"Never mind all that. We have Bogo now, David and Lili are home, and all these problems will resolve themselves eventually." Anna waved a hand airily. "What did *you* think about Avalon, Lili? We are dying to know!"

"Poor choice of words, sis," Dafydd said.

Anna wrinkled her nose at him. "You know what I mean."

"I do," Lili said, "and it's hard to put into words. Maybe I need more time to process it all."

"Did you *like* it?" Bronwen asked.

"*Like* is a strange word too. I liked the ice cream. The hot showers were amazing. I could have stood under one for hours."

"She did stand under one for a long time in the RV, since it had continuously circulating hot water." Dafydd shook his head, still as amazed by that as Lili. "She got another one that last night in the hotel after the meeting in the arena."

"Avalon does material things very well," Bronwen said gently.

Lili put out a hand to her. "It's more than that. The people weren't so different, you know. That's basically what I said to the crowd in the arena. Those in the Walmart were more immediately kind to two total strangers than I had any right to expect. They *cared.* It was heartening." She paused. "The truth is, *everyone* cared. Fourteen thousand people had packed into that arena to hear Chad speak about Dafydd. That's more than half the population of London in one place! What's more, they not only cared, they wanted to *believe.*"

For a moment her eyes met her husband's, and he said, "You don't have to say it again. I can see it too."

Bronwen was looking from one to the other. "What are we talking about?"

"King Arthur." Dafydd made a noise low in his throat. "Where this began is also where it can end."

Lili explained: "The reason Dafydd ate that bit of walnut in the first place was to distract me from the argument we were having about him playing the role of Arthur at the tournament."

Anna frowned at her brother. "You were still complaining about that?"

"Still," Dafydd said. "To pretend to be what I am not has always felt like lying. Even more, I have hated the whole concept of the modern world as the magical abode of Arthur when it's really an alternate universe that is further along the historical timeline than we are here."

Anna tipped her head. "You speak in the past tense. *Always felt? Have hated?* Not anymore?"

"Lili is right, dare I say, as always." Dafydd finally settled in a chair and kicked it back on its rear legs. "In the end, it doesn't matter whether or not I'm the physical return of Arthur. What matters is that, through me, people see a possible future where the principles he stood for—and that I stand for—

"—and embody," Lili put in.

"—can be made manifest."

Anna looked close to tearing up. "I'm so happy to hear that."

"That isn't to say I'm still not disturbed by some things." Dafydd eyed his sister. "I don't want to be worshipped."

"I would hope not!" Bronwen said.

Anna, however, grinned. "I don't care what anyone else says. You're *not* Superman."

"Definitely not." David made a motion with his head. "That said, can I complain that Chad is willing to put his company and his very life on the line because he believes in me and what we're doing here? No, I cannot. I have to honor his perspective. It would be petty of me to do otherwise. I certainly can't argue with change for the good. If people make better decisions because of me, and Avalon becomes a better place, how can I complain?"

"George was transformed," Lili said. "He became a different person because of you."

"Paige didn't," Dafydd said.

Lili wrinkled her nose. "You can't win them all, but if some people can change, maybe that means anyone can."

She hadn't meant anything particularly momentous with her comment, but all of a sudden Dafydd's head came up, and when he spoke next, his voice had a resonance to it she hadn't heard in a long time.

"Before we left, George pulled me aside to say something along the lines of: *Congress can do what it likes, but I want to know how you are going to use this power you have? In six years you will be old enough to run for President. As it stands now, congressional vote or no congressional vote, you would win.*"

Dafydd hadn't told her about that. It must have been sitting on his heart for the last day. By way of response, his family simply looked at him.

And then Anna asked, "How did you reply?"

"I told him to think that way was wrongheaded and that I was already using my power, such as it is, in the best way possible. Really, in the only way possible. Anything else would be thinking too small."

"I don't understand." Bronwen was frowning at him. "The Presidency of the United States is thinking too small?"

"Most people misunderstand the nature of power," Dafydd said. "I admit for me to say such a thing is easy here in Earth Two. I am the King of England and will remain so for the foreseeable future, even as you all know how hard I have worked to divest myself of as much power as I can. It isn't about how much power *I* wield. It's about facilitating ways for everyone else to be powerful themselves."

Bronwen gave a tsk. "I might be annoyed at all this high-mindedness if you weren't so right. A president is the most powerful man on earth for four to eight years, and then what happens? Some other bozo comes in and changes all his policies and all the wonderful things he was doing for the planet go out the window in favor of someone else's theory about the way the world works."

"Putting aside how much *bozo* sounds like *Bogo*," Anna chimed in, "what *you* are doing—" she emphasized the *you* with a poke of a finger in Dafydd's direction, "—is creating a system where you lead and inspire and in doing so get everyone else to do the right thing."

"Like King Arthur did," Lili said softly, "because the people truly feel that what you are asking of them *is* the right thing, and they not only believe it should be done but *choose* to do it."

Dafydd nodded. "Like King Arthur did."

Lili had honestly never thought she'd see the day when Dafydd would take on the mantle of Arthur as he had just done. What's more, who would have thought to do so would serve to lighten the load he carried every day of his life instead of making it heavier?

He had thought that in order to make the world a better place, he needed to set down his burden ... when in fact, the solution was to lift it higher.

Author's Note

I often say when asked about the historical accuracy of my books, especially those in the *After Cilmeri* series, that they are as accurate as I can make them … except when they're not.

That's both a joke and not a joke, in that I confess to being obsessive about historical accuracy in my own books. If a battle occurred in real history on a certain date, I won't move the battle to another day or year for the purpose of my plot. This is fiction, and I'm happy to make up characters and events when called for, but only to fill a space left open by the historical record.

The *After Cilmeri* series is fantasy, of course, as much as we might wish it were real. We don't currently know anyone capable of time traveling (or rather, *world shifting*) to an alternate universe that has only reached the Middle Ages.

For that reason, Bogo de Clare, while a real, historical figure, gets new life in Earth Two when in our world he died in 1294 at the age of forty-six. He genuinely was Gilbert de Clare's younger brother, however, a failed priest, and an all-around ne'er-do-well with delusions of grandeur.

Carew Castle can be visited to this day and, in particular, the charnel house in the village churchyard is still standing. Elen gives an accurate description of their use in the Middle Ages. Like her, these days I survey every "shed" at every church I visit, wondering if it was repurposed after the Reformation, when charnel houses were abandoned because the practice of making room in a graveyard by moving the bones of the dead was deemed too "popish". Protestant practice also put less emphasis on being buried in sacred ground, so when churchyards couldn't be expanded any further, independent cemeteries came into being. The existence of charnel houses may also be why it is rare to find a graveyard with grave markers that date to a time earlier than the 1600s.

As to the threat to individual liberties created by the current surveillance systems in the modern world, I'll leave it up to you to decide how seriously to take it.

As always, I am grateful every day to every one of you for reading my books. It's you who make this job the best in the world. And just as a side note, I'll keep writing the *After Cilmeri* series as long as I have stories to tell and you keep reading them ☺

Happy reading!

--Sarah

Thank you continuing this journey into the Middle Ages with me!
There will be another book in the *After Cilmeri* series.

Acknowledgments

First and foremost, I'd like to thank my lovely readers for encouraging me to continue the *After Cilmeri* series. I have always been passionate about these books, and it's wonderful to be able to share my stories with readers who love them too. Thank you also to all my editors, proof-readers, and beta readers. I am grateful for all the ways each and every one of you make the book better.

Thank you to my husband, without whose love and support I would never have tried to make a living as a writer, and thank to my family who has been nothing but encouraging of my writing, despite the fact that I spend half my life in medieval Wales. I couldn't do this without you.

About the Author

With over two million books sold, Sarah Woodbury is the author of more than fifty novels, all set in medieval Wales. Although an anthropologist by training, and then a full-time homeschooling mom for twenty years, she began writing fiction when the stories in her head overflowed and demanded that she let them out. While her ancestry is Welsh, she only visited Wales for the first time at university. She has been in love with the country, language, and people ever since. She even convinced her husband to give all four of their children Welsh names. She makes her home in Oregon.

www.sarahwoodbury.com